EASY GOLD

"It can be done." He grinned. "We stake a claim, or jump one already staked. We don't lift a pick or rattle a pan. We don't work, we don't sweat, we don't starve. Yet come clean-up time next fall we take out more dust than any ten-claim-filers in Montana. You want in or out?"

"Talk," I said boldly. "Your method of operation?"

"Oh." He nodded unblinkingly. "The best way there is. One that's worked sure and simple ever since Cain used it to salt Abel away."

WILL HENRY

RECKONING AT YANKEE FLAT

AVON BOOKS ⬢ NEW YORK

For Will Cook

AVON BOOKS
A division of
The Hearst Corporation
105 Madison Avenue
New York, New York 10016

Copyright © 1958 by Will Henry
Published by arrangement with the author
Library of Congress Catalog Card Number: 88-92125
ISBN: 0-380-70603-2

First Avon Books Printing: March 1989

AVON TRADEMARK REG. U.S. PAT. OFF. AND IN OTHER COUNTRIES, MARCA REGISTRADA, HECHO EN U.S.A.

Printed in the U.S.A.

K-R   10 9 8 7 6 5 4 3 2 1

"Which is the villain? Let me see his eyes,
That when I note another man like him
I may avoid him."

MUCH ADO ABOUT NOTHING
Act V, Scene 1

This is an account of the coming of mountain law and mining-camp order to Montana Territory during the grim days when the witness chair was a wagon seat, the judge a masked man on horseback, the jury a thirty-foot rope flung over the nearest rafter.

It is taken from the handwritten records and unpublished press notes of William C. McCandles, sometime California newspaperman turned wilderness wanderer and Executive Committee member of Montana vigilantes.

Although not as yet authenticated, the McCandles notes would appear to offer a new and substantially accurate eyewitness report of the riotous beginnings of Alder Gulch, the richest "single-pocket" gold strike of them all.

In any context, these memoirs constitute a first-hand casebook of the secret oaths and sudden justices administered in that stormy time.

W. H.

I first met him in April of 1852. I can remember the day and details as though it were but the past week. We were fellow passengers aboard a mining-camp freight wagon inward bound from California's Sacramento Valley to Nevada City in the granite heart of the Mother Lode. He rode with our grizzled driver upon the seat box, I jolted along among the bean and onion sacks in the rear of the bed. It was the fourth spring of the great rush set off by the discovery cry at Sutter's sawmill, and I assumed correctly that my young companion, like all the rest of us in those days, had been drawn into the Sierras by the siren call of the precious yellow metal. My sole mistake lay in imagining he meant to dig for his gold in the usual manner. The error was understandable.

A tall, dark and slender fifteen-year-old, the lad was remarkably courteous and well spoken. His voice was peculiarly soft, his smile, if somewhat too swift, was still bright enough to warm one's hands by. He showed a quick mind and ready wit, was sociable as a lost dog, made it appealingly plain that he wanted people to like him and to be his friends.

To suspect that the morals of such a fine youngster might assay less than sixteen dollars to the ounce never occurred to me. This despite the fact that as a journeyman newspaper reporter I should have been alert to the possibility. Our old driver, however, was not to be so easily gotten around. He had not quit eyeing his seat companion since leaving Auburn, where the youth and I had joined him. Now he dappled the rumps of his wheel team with Burley juice, wiped his dribbled beard with the back of his hand and said, "Name's Henry, eh? Henry what?"

The ragged youth sat quiet for a considerable spell before replying. He was thinking. He seemed, in fact, never to quit thinking. You could tell that by the way his light gray eyes watched everything in sight while at the same time they were centered down and deep-pupiled with inner looking. Eventually he nodded cheerfully. "Plummer, sir. Henry Clay Plummer. From Kentucky."

But he had waited too long with his answer. The old man merely bobbed his head, spat again, looked out across the shadowed foothills.

"Well, Henry," he said at last, "you'll go a long ways, but will get a short drop. You got a double-hung tongue and an honest eye. That's a hard combination to bet into. Sort of like two black aces dealt natural, back to back. But you cain't win with it."

"Shucks, mister, what you mean?" grinned his innocent-faced listener, but it was a shallow grin and the old man saw the hard gravel of its bottom below the false ripple of its surface sunshine.

"Jest fergit it, young un," he advised him tersely. "A man gits old he ain't fitten company fer young folks. He sees everything wrinkled and dismal. Fergit it, like I say. You'll make out fust rate in the mountains."

The old man was right. Within the second year following his arrival in the gold camps along the Yuba's brawling North and South Forks, young Henry Plummer had acquired half-ownership in Nevada City's prosperous Empire Bakery. He was not yet seventeen.

By 1856, four short springs after our mutual passage of the Auburn-Grass Valley Road, he had wiled and smiled his way into the confidence of the rough California miners and, via that direct route, into the town marshalship of Nevada City. He was that week of the election turned eighteen.

In 1857 he was reëlected marshal, ran for and received the nomination of the Democratic party for state assemblyman. He was widely regarded as a shoo-in for that office but before the polls could open he had made his first serious misstep, and the voters turned him out with ballots marked considerably stronger than "young scoundrel."

This was the sordid affair in which he was caught making a cuckold of Josef Vedder, an immigrant German assayer of solid reputation, whose handsome young wife Plummer unwisely coveted.

He rashly chose high noon for the hour of his visit to the Vedder house. Finding the master absent and the mistress malleable, he was drawn into the fatal move. It was ten minutes past twelve when Vedder tiptoed into the rear bedroom of his home. He had not found his youthful bride busy in the kitchen preparing his noon dinner and sought, apparently, to surprise her lazing in bed. He did, indeed, surprise her and in bed. But not lazing. The resultant situation, from Henry Plummer's viewpoint, admitted of but one practical solution. He did not hesitate to apply it. It was precisely 12:13 when his revolver went off and boorish Josef Vedder became a vital statistic.

The County of Nevada charged Henry with the crime, denied his plea of self-defense and sentenced him to ten years in state's prison. He at once put his famous smile and patent-leather charms to work, managing thereby a change of venue to Yuba County. But it was too late. The case had by then become something of a local cause and the Yuba Court, denying the appeal of his fine white teeth and influential friends, confirmed the findings of her sister county. Justice had been done, barring delays, and Henry Plummer went to jail.

His stay there was short. His health, always somewhere between that of a logger's boot and a braided bull whip for delicacy, gave way beneath the rigors of confinement. He fell victim to what was then called the "black" or "galloping" consumption. He was released to die in dignity.

His subsequent complete recovery was rumored to have taken place within fifteen minutes after grieving friends had borne him out from beneath the high gray walls on a makeshift stretcher and, thus, directly, to the nearest saloon. Here, the story went, the arisen prisoner called for drinks for all present and a permanent toast to the value of true friends; particularly those in an official position to corrupt or cripple the public weal.

Although his brilliant shamming of a fatal case of tuberculosis was not immediately discovered—I myself wrote the report of his "waxen face, debilitated form and labored breathing," which appeared in the Nevada City press—his genius as an actor, so evident in his later history, was here revealed for the first time.

Also demonstrated in this coup, so that even the dullest of us could see and understand it, was the value of Henry's lifelong practice of making friends.

It was never brought to light who his supporters were but the legal fact of his release was a regulation full pardon signed, not by any subordinate, but by Governor P. Weller himself. Whoever Henry's friends were, there were enough of them to reach from Yuba City to Sacramento, a rather respectable distance. And their unquestioned loyalty represented a sobering tribute to the beguiling ways and dangerous attractions of a young man not yet twenty-one years old. Unfortunately for him, Henry did not improve with age.

I had been a reporter on various California newspapers, so my observation of young Henry Plummer was more or less professional. Therefore, under an autumn of '58 entry in the "casebook" I had by that time begun to compile on him, the following forecast appears:

> ". . . P. is back in town. In my opinion he had far better have stayed where he was, for his reception here, where all have long since gotten onto his sweet talk and 'salted' smile, will be a mighty poor one. . . ."

Despite my prediction the rascal remained in Nevada City

3

and for an unpleasant while it looked as though I would have to alter the above notation. He went back into the bakery business with Henry Hyer, his former partner, and for a considerable spell there was no faulting him.

He took to church and charitable work. He tipped his hat to the proper ladies, no longer patronized the improper ones. He bought candy for the little children. He consorted no more with loose companions, spoke out at every opportunity in favor of home and community. But in the end he could no more stick to the strict terms of his second start than he could fly by flapping his arms.

In swift succession he conspired with a local ruffian named Oral Thompson for the latter to run for town marshal and, if elected, to resign in his, Plummer's, favor; fatally pistol whipped a drunken miner from San Juan in a brothel dispute; went across the state line to Washoe, Nevada and bungled the first daylight highway robbery of a Wells Fargo bullion shipment; returned to Nevada City and in a second house-of-ill-fame argument gunned down one Charley Ryder, a popular and harmless rowdy-about-town.

For this last crime he was promptly brought into custody, charged with second-degree murder and lodged for trial in Nevada County's recently completed, solid stone jail. But where physically sound, the new prison proved morally vulnerable. Within twenty-four hours Henry Plummer was a free man. This time his deliverance was arranged neither by personal acting ability nor the intercession of powerful friends, but by good old-fashioned bribery. He walked out of the Nevada County jail in broad daylight, borrowed the first good horse at the next-door hardware store hitching rack, and was seen no more in Nevada City, California.

But his kind do not long remain unsighted. A coarse brute named William Mayfield was shortly apprehended in neighboring Sierra County for the senseless knife slaying of the popular County Sheriff John Blackburn. The rope, the rafter and the packing box were a foregone sequence for the killer. Then, shockingly, he was set free, delivered by an unmasked gunman whose description by a dozen eyewitnesses was a perfect word chromo of Henry Clay Plummer.

His unexplained part in this second jailbreak closed California forever to the erstwhile Nevada City baker's boy. What Mayfield could have meant to Plummer was never established, but what John Blackburn meant to the miners of the Mother Lode was a matter of affectionate record. No abler, more courageous officer ever wore the star. Plummer's warped act in saving his murderer from the rope he so richly deserved, fired the little mountain communities from Rich and Bidwell Bars to Chinese Camp and Big Oak Flats.

4

In Nevada City a property owners' law-and-order committee met and took an action which I believe was unique at the time: it appointed a secret deputy, to be paid by private subscription, to take up the trail of Henry Plummer and either return him to Nevada County for trial, or see him dead by gun or gallows or natural debility, wherever found. The selection of this deputy, necessarily, had to be made with care.

Some men would have regarded such office as a paid and protected excuse to dry-gulch Plummer in the name of personal notoriety. Others would see in it an opportunity for interesting travel with no thought of coming within a country mile of their deadly game. The individual selected had to be one who understood the assignment; to be one, moreover, of basic intent to support, not thwart, the law. It was a moment of sobering pride when I learned the committee had voted seventeen to three to send me.

Fortunately, I had not a great many important arrangements to delay my departure. I did need an excuse for leaving town so suddenly, one that would contain no hint of the nerve-tingling assignment just tendered me by my fellows. Then, too, I had also to borrow a sound mount and secure a more powerful pistol than my little Elliott Patent Remington pocket model. Beyond these things, my only other duty was to say a plausible farewell to the young lady with whom I had been keeping company that summer, a Miss Felicia Gooderham, daughter of Dr. Samuel Gooderham of the city. All items were attended to by sunset of that same day. It was shortly after eight P.M. when I set out along the Downieville Road.

The purpose of my mission was clear, if its means of achievement were not. There was, however, one thing about the situation which I understood perfectly. That was the thing which had been so indelibly built up in my mind by the events transpiring since 1852. Henry Plummer was not only a devious man; he was a very dangerous one.

My first slender lead appeared in the form of an absurd press report encountered in a stage station up near the Oregon line, called, as I remember, Eagle River.

It was a page-four item in the *Oregonian* headed "*California Papers Please Copy.*"

"*Henry Plummer,*" the account ran, "*the notorious Nevada City (Calif.) desperado was last week taken and hanged at Walla Walla in Washington Territory for the murder and robbery of a miner on Patoosh Creek, near Snake River. Plummer denied guilt for any of the crimes which have been attributed to him by our sister state to the south. He said he had made powerful enemies in California by his in-*

5

dustry and honesty, and been forced to flee for his life to a friendlier place. A handsome man of good education and polite address, Plummer died with exemplary calm, forgiving all his false accusers, as he said, and going with a prayer on his lips for God to bless each of them in His infinite mercy and understanding of human frailty."

Weary as I was, I at once got out my notebook on the subject of Nevada City's ex-town marshal to enter the accompanying dissent from Oregon opinion:

". . . This cannot be the Henry Plummer I know. I suspect this bizarre Walla Walla story has been hatched and planted by the resourceful Mr. P. himself. . . ."

Even so, and despite my stated refusal to believe its former proprietor dead, the ghost of Henry Plummer remained very well laid indeed.

I could get no further track of him in Oregon nor for that matter in Washington Territory. I scouted as far north as Walla Walla and as far east as Patoosh Creek, and came up with exactly nothing. He seemed to have vanished without leaving a trace.

After a full month of this blind quartering for a scent, I had to admit defeat. My money was gone, my hunger for the manhunt entirely dissipated.

I returned to Nevada City and reported my belief that Plummer was still alive and had deliberately written his own obituary for the Oregon papers. This view was directly contrary to the one supported by the Walla Walla story which had meanwhile been picked up and played big by the large California dailies. In consequence, the committee heard me out with short patience, and a great deal of subsequent suspicion. Presently, they accused me outright of taking a vacation at their expense and during a time when I already knew Henry Plummer was dead and justice fully done.

The implications were intolerable, the atmosphere unhealthy. I resigned at once and made belated shift to defend myself.

Under the circumstances there was but one reasonable course a man of courage and honor could take. I resolved, forthwith, to take it. That night, on a fast horse and under cover of first darkness, I left Nevada City.

2

Between the late fall of 1858 and early autumn of 1862 I roamed the northwest wilderness from the rain forests of

Washington through Idaho's timberlands to the buffalo pastures of high Montana, and back again. I hunted and fished and prospected a promising section now and again, even stopping to set up a sluice or two where the gravel panned rich and quick and the other elements of living were easy to come by.

Along the same road, as necessity demanded, I took regular work. Now it would be a golden autumn gathering cattle for a pioneer rancher of the Bitter Root Valley, now a silver-white winter tending store in Deseret, now a green spring herding sheep along the Humboldt, now a smoky-blue summer mule-packing supplies from San Francisco out the old emigrant road via Hudspeth's or Myer's Cutoff up through Nevada to Twin Falls on the Snake and thus northward to the isolated Idaho and Montana settlements, trading all the way to Fort Benton on the Upper Missouri. And whatever it was, I took from it a far greater profit than the scant wages involved.

When I left Nevada City in October of '58, although certainly a person of some slight character and education, I was a pale, thin and bookish youth who would not have weighed 140 pounds with a sackful of old horseshoes in either hand. When I rode into Fort Benton that last, late summer of '62, I was a man grown.

I then weighed 185 pounds, was dark-skinned and stringy as a square of trade-plug, had saddle calluses up to my elbows, smoked black seegars for breakfast and drank any brand of whiskey without blinking.

By now I knew that if your belt gun was not one of Sam Colt's new single action .44's, you were wasting the space in your holster. I had, too, learned a bit about pointing the latter weapon in a hurry.

Other than these hardening changes in attitude and experience, I had grown a fierce red-spade beard and affected, generally, the raffish, high-booted attire of the frontier soldier of fortune. That riders of this suspicious look were apt to be taken for commercial highwaymen, I well knew. Further, I frankly enjoyed the dramatics of the doubt. I had gained my manhood in many thousands of hazardous trail miles since leaving the Mother Lode country and I was overtempted, as are most physical weaklings grown strong, to play the swaggerer.

It was in this questionable temper that early September of '62 found me stranded in Fort Benton.

An unseasonal Montana blizzard had closed the mountain passes to the west, preventing our mule train from making the return journey to the coast. My employer was induced to sell his mules for Indian meat (the red rascals would eat it in preference to fat buffalo!), and take passage down-river on the last packet leaving for St. Louis and the eastern settlements. Yielding to his friendly suggestion, I decided to accompany him.

I had not been home to Kansas City since leaving it when it was called Westport Landing. At that time, as a lad of eleven, I had journeyed with my parents out the old South Platte Trail to Oregon in the so-called "great migration" of 1843. My father had been killed in the subsequent Cayuse uprising of '49. Mother had gone back to Missouri and I, with her blessing, down to California to try my luck in the rush set off by the historic glitter in old John Sutter's mill-race. I had not seen her in all the intervening years and was now suddenly anxious to do so; a practical demonstration, I am afraid, of the tardy conscience which comes with advancing years.

In any event, I had, in addition to the nostalgic urge, a more substantial reason of economic nature to turn me homeward. The previous summer of '61, I had panned out a very rich pocket on a little alder-choked Montana creek. I had been carrying the dust with me ever since. It was both a considerable sum and a bothersome weight. As the present month marked my thirtieth birthday, I decided to cash in my little stake, retire from the risky life of the frontier and invest in some sound business back east.

Accordingly, I weighed in my poke with the American Trading Company which, fortunately, had a Bank of St. Louis franchise and could pay off in easily stowed treasury notes. Packing my new fortune of federal bills in a hastily purchased moneybelt, I booked passage on the *Yellowstone Belle* and started down to the mooring to board her and seek out my friend.

I never set foot on the first cleat of the gangplank. Halfway down the low bluffside trail to the landing, I got the sudden feeling that I had been followed away from the trading company's assay-office window. By the time I had crossed from the bluff trail's foot to the crowd now beginning to go aboard the *Belle*, I had picked out my birds from their milling cover.

There were two of them. They were both tough, hard-looking cases, with the taller one seeming to be somehow familiar in general bearing. This vagrant impression continued to bother me as I drew near the welter of frontier freight stacked on the bank for loading aboard the little packet. Directly, I determined to have a look at my followers' features, close up. I ducked behind an eight-foot bale of buffalo robes and waited for them to come along. At this point I was not overly concerned, only mildly excited by ordinary curiosity.

8

Soon enough, my trackers came abreast of the bale. Seeking eagerly ahead for the quarry they had momentarily mislaid, they did not see me pressed against my shaggy screen. I, however, had an excellent look at them and was very quickly glad they had not yet realized I was lost rather than mislaid.

The shorter of them was the most classic murderer I had ever seen. Yet his brutish scowl and heavy physique did not disturb me one-tenth so much as the refined elegance and pleasant smile of his slender companion.

I decided in the next moment that I did not want, after all, to visit my mother in Kansas City. I would not, in fact, have set foot on that presently loading steamboat for all the mother's love in Missouri.

In the footpad world the easiest way to murder a flush mark is to tap him behind the ear and slide him over the rail of a river streamer on a dark and moonless night. The teams of notorious toughs who had successfully worked this criminal conspiracy since the days of the bloody Harpe brothers, were without number. A skillful pair of partners could lay you on the deck, turn out your pockets and put you over the side in less time than it would take to light up a damp cigar. And of this particular team's professional ability I had no doubt at all.

Of the member with the apelike skull, I knew nothing and cared less. Of his graceful, gleaming-toothed accomplice, I both knew and cared quite a lot. Four years had not changed him as they had me. I recognized him on the instant, and my heart beat so furiously fast I thought it would smother me.

That was Henry Plummer down there at the gangplank smilingly sorting out the boarding passengers for the man with the red-spade beard and the bulging new moneybelt.

While I watched Plummer and his friend down at the mooring, I was also kept busy in another direction.

The *Belle's* deck crew were dismantling my various hiding places without regard for my pressing need of them. As quickly as I slid behind a new bale of hides or box of moccasins, it would be picked up and carted aboard the boat. I was eventually saved only because the upstream freight being discharged to supply Fort Benton through the winter was piling up as fast as the frontier produce was being torn down. Taking advantage of a newly built pyramid of salt-meat barrels, I looked desperately about me for some more permanent refuge. As I did, the nearest, most obvious retreat of this description eliminated itself. The *Belle* was "upping plank."

Tensely, I watched her back out in the stream, swing her blunt bow northeast, and slip off silently down the eight-mile

9

current to disappear around the bend toward the mouth of the Marias. My feelings in that moment were as uncomplicated as a four-finger peg of Montana tanglefoot. I had my hackles up, my belly in, my teeth together. I was scared.

In that day there was literally no law in the Three Forks country. A man's life and property were as safe as his personal ability to defend them. The wagon roads, footpaths and goat tracks of empire were used at the traveler's risk. The crude new towns and crumbling old trade settlements were little better. Murder was as common on main street as along the lonely mountain mule trail.

Middle Western morality made for some rule in Oregon. The stern religion of Old Brigham's saints protected Utah and the Great Salt Lake basin. Judge Lynch held jurisdiction in the Colorado mines and Justice Gallows Tree in the Mother Lode of California. All around the frontier compass from Montana there were the bright beginnings of community life under organized social order, but in Montana herself there was nothing. Only the law of gravity prevailed there: a man was shot, he fell down. I had no great desire to example myself to prove this matter of criminal fact.

But as Plummer and his desperate-looking pal now turned from the deserted mooring to scan with wolfish care and coldness the tangle of discharged Fort Benton freight, it seemed that I had very little choice.

If I stayed at the company post, they would stay with me. If I left it to take the snowy trail toward home, their tracks would overlay mine within the hour. I would never get across the Idaho line.

Then, just when I was despairing of a way out, I remembered the unwritten law of the outnumbered: if victory is impossible, negotiate. Shrinking farther back into my ambush, I eased the .44 in its frost-rimed holster. Seconds later, I stepped out behind the prowling Henry Plummer and put the naked steel into the small of his back.

He elevated his slender hands, spoke out at once in that soft-tongued way that was his deadly trademark.

"Name your game, friend. You have the deal."

"Turn around slow," I said. "And keep your hands high."

"Five-card showdown, she is," he smiled, and came easily about.

I waited with the gun now in his belly to see if he would recognize me. He did not appear to do so.

"Well, friend?" he said.

I moved around behind him, putting the Colt into his left rib ends. "Call your partner over here," I told him.

"What partner?" he asked.

I put the muzzle of the .44 to his temple. *"Call him,"* I repeated.

The delicate eyebrows arched. He cocked his lean head away from the cold touch of the Colt's tongue. "Jack," he called out into the thickening swirl of the snowflakes, "come over here. I want you to meet an old friend of mine."

I took a sudden chill, and not from the whipping of the blizzard wind. But a searching glance showed me he had not meant the remark literally, and I managed to control my shivering.

The moment his trailmate padded into view, he saw the situation and raised his own hands to my weapon's request with a professional's quickness.

"Now, then," I demanded of both of them, "what's this all about?"

Plummer shrugged.

"Perhaps you can tell us," he said. "My friend and I were just down to see a mutual acquaintance off on the *Belle*. We're ranchers from up Great Falls way."

"You're murderers and ruffians from up no way," I corrected him quietly. "You never saw a ranch unless it was to kill its proprietor for his money or a fresh horse." With the challenge, I stepped back and holstered my Colt to show my acceptance of them on that outlaw basis. And to indicate, hence, my own membership in the same trade.

Henry didn't buy it. I saw the instant change in his eyes. There it was, clear as glass—the old familiar shooting of the dark surface shadows across their innocent gray depths.

"You're a damned fool," he said evenly, "to talk to me like that with your gun put away."

He had a point. I palmed the Colt back out with a wrist-flick four years in the learning. Its art was not lost upon Plummer. I saw that by the shift of his black lashes and the little tightening at his eye corners.

"Agreed," I said. "Let's continue as we were."

"All right," nodded Plummer. "How about starting with you. What's your name, friend?"

"Sutter," I offered, using the first identification that popped into my mind, that of my maternal grandfather. "Dade Sutter, out of Sonora."

"Any kin to old John Augustus?"

"None kissing close."

"That Sonora, California?"

"Is there any other?"

He eyed me a shade too long and too close.

"You talk reckless, Sutter. I don't like that."

I gave him back the hard look.

11

"And who," I asked, "might you be that it ought to scare me that you don't like it?"

He *liked* that. I saw the tightness go out of his eyes. "Name's Plummer," he said, completely surprising me. "Henry Plummer of Nevada City, California." He paused a moment, then concluded almost hopefully. "Being from those parts, yourself, perhaps you've heard of me."

"Well, I should reckon!" I laid it on. "Who hasn't heard of Henry Plummer?"

At once the shadows were shooting his eyes again, and I knew I had overbet a bad hand.

"Who indeed?" he asked softly, and he was watching my face like a faro dealer watches the faces of the tiger buckers when the luck is running high against the house and the next card out of the box might break the bank.

"We heard you were dead!" I blurted. "It was in all the papers. Everybody believed it."

"Everybody did not believe it," said Henry Plummer. "There was a newspaperman in Nevada City . . ."

"Oh, him," I interrupted, sensing the urgent need for another risk. "You mean McCandles?" I shoved the bet clear in. "Yes, I heard about him. There's always one like that to make things tough for our kind."

"There's something about you . . ." Plummer began, but I cut him off again, knowing full well I wouldn't be a great deal interested in hearing him develop that theme much further.

"Never mind me!" I laughed uncertainly. "Did you hear what happened to that damned McCandles? He got old Doc Gooderham's daughter in a family way and they ran him out of town. Why, man, that was four years ago. Where you been?"

Plummer's gray eyes were framing a dangerous next question. I shoved in another stack of chips, knowing I had to. "I was just through Nevada City last month. Heard the yarn in the barber shop, or maybe it was Dakin's Hardware. We come up the Grass Valley way with our mules for a change. Figured to try Donner Pass. It's a shade lower than Carson or Ebbetts or any of the other south passes. We reckoned being a little late in the year we might be in for an early snow."

"Yes," said Plummer, "those early snows are hell."

He was not thinking about early snows any more than I was. Pretty quick, he proved it.

"I'm glad to hear about Cul McCandles," he muttered thickly. "But for him and his damned dirty lies in the paper, I would still be operating a fine bakery business back there. He ruined me with his printed slanders against my good name and I'll see him in hell for it one day."

12

I did not care for the way he stared at me while making the threat, but I had to plunge ahead. I was into the midstream of my bluff now. If I stopped and tried to back out, I would be swept under and off down-current before I could explain how to spell Dade Sutter.

"If he's a newspaperman," I scowled, "he'll be there in hell one way or another. There never was a one of them didn't live by writing filthy lies about honest men and making murderers out of good clean boys who wouldn't do a low thing or a legal wrong to their worst enemy."

Plummer looked at me with a new and friendlier interest. "Sutter," he said unexpectedly, "what you doing this winter?"

"Nothing that won't wait," I said.

"You want to throw in with me and Jack Cleveland, here?"

"Depends. What's the job?"

"Biggest thing of its kind ever worked anywhere."

"Where do I come in?"

"We need capital."

"Mine, eh?"

He nodded, waiting me out expressionlessly.

"When do we start?" I asked.

"Tonight."

"Where to?"

"Place called Bannack. Ever hear of it?"

I denied it, although of course I had.

"Bannack," he said deliberately, "and the whole of Grasshopper Creek above and below it for more miles than they yet know, is stinking, rotten, stumbling-deep in sixteen-dollar dust."

"That big?" I queried doubtfully. "In *Montana?*"

Plummer jerked his head, light eyes blazing.

"The richest single strike," he rasped, "made anywhere since Jim Marshall hit into the Mother Lode at Sutter's sawmill. I, my friend, am going to sluice out every solitary foot of it from upstream gullet to downcreek gut-end, and do it without touching a long tom, a rocker, or a riffle box. Now what do you think of that?"

"A good trick," I stalled, "if it can be done."

"It can be done," he grinned. "And done without we stake a claim, or jump one already staked. We don't lift a pick or rattle a pan. We don't work, we don't sweat, we don't starve. Yet come clean-up time next fall we take out more dust than any ten-claim-filers in Montana. Last time around, my friend. You want in or out?"

"Talk," I said boldly, "never sunk a shaft nor shot a powder charge. Now you've said quite a bit, but you haven't

13

told me a damned thing. Let's get down to the case ace. What's your big idea?"

He stared at me, losing his grin.

"Your method of operation," I clarified quickly. "The way you mean to go about making this granddaddy cleanup of yours."

"Oh," he nodded unblinkingly. "The best way there is. One that's worked sure and simple ever since Cain used it to salt Abel away."

It was my turn to stare.

"By God, you can't mean it!" I said.

"Oh, but I do, my friend," he assured me, shrugging it off as though we were discussing something no more monstrous than the easiest way to screen a gravel bar.

"We'll run it like a business. Wholesale and on overnight order, for anything from ten dollars' worth of dust to a smelter wagon full of bullion bars."

3

Old Fort Benton sat on the south bank of the Missouri above the confluence of the Teton. The best trail southward in foul weather lay on the north bank of the parent stream. We set out from the fort that same afternoon, September 7, crossing over by an old Hunkpapa Sioux ford a mile or so upriver. The wind was north-northeast, quartering our course with increasing bitterness. By the four o'clock twilight there was a foot of snow on the open trail, drifts of two and three feet building in the swales. In a snug cottonwood draw cutting the north-bank bluffs down to stream-level, we made camp only minutes later. It was black dark before we got the fire built and the horse blankets hung up to dry around it.

By common consent, as men will do when partnered off by chance, we at once fell into the working arrangement best suiting the talents of each.

In our case Plummer was to be the cook, I the bottle-washer, and our faithful, surly dog Jack, the general roustabout. Since the latter's chores included bedding down the horses and getting enough wood to hold the fire through the night, Henry and I were given a little chance to get better acquainted while the brute was yet stumbling around in the outer darkness.

For a few minutes, he busy with the bacon and fried bread, I with getting down our blanket rolls and making our rough beds, we talked only by covert glances.

"Well," said Plummer finally, by way of ice-breaking, "it's a hard life but a healthy one."

"You can have it," I shrugged noncomittally. "I much prefer the bright lights. Straight whiskey, streetwalkers and sinful serenading are my meat. I never did care for roadwork."

He studied me sidelong a minute.

"Being on the road has its risks," he admitted.

"Yes," I nodded. "And the greatest of these is that sooner or later you run out of roads."

"How's that? What do you mean?"

"Let us not waste time, my friend," I replied. "We were both in Fort Benton on the same errand. If you were not heading down the river to give your heels a chance to cool, I will buy the bug-juice till next January. As for me, the only thing which kept me off that boat was you. Now we've both changed our minds and are staying over on borrowed time. I suggest we stop watching one another and get on with our work. The sooner we make this big cleanup of yours in Bannack, the better. I, for one, want to be back in Fort Benton for the first boat out following the breakup next spring. Any questions?"

It was another gamble, forced by his continuing study of me. He had not quit trailing me with his eyes since leaving the fort and it was clear that he was still trying to remember where he had seen me before. Even clearer was the afterfact that if he did succeed in making the memory connection, he would leave me behind in the drifting snows of this lonely little draw—with my boots on and a bullet hole in the back of my bumbling head. This type of good-bye did not suit my selfish purposes.

Fortunately, or so he made it appear, it was not on his agenda either.

"No," he laughed, "no questions. You and I see things through the same keyhole, my friend. We'll ride to the end of the line together."

If, at that precise moment, I could have foreseen the simple, terrible accuracy of his statement, I would have put him under gunpoint, called in my horse, swung up and escaped into the outer blast of the blizzard. However, the human eye is not for future seeing.

"I trust that is a profitable fact," I agreed carefully. "Two gunhands are better than one in this business. And I've a notion yours and mine are better than most."

I was simply reminding him of my own proficiency, not praising any he might possess. It was another attempt to smoke him out, but he would not smoke. He merely nodded acknowledgment of the missed try, and said, "Meat's done; call in that damn fool, Jack, will you? He's horse crazy. He'll stay out there all night petting and fussing with those miserable crowbaits if we let him."

15

I went out and got Cleveland and we ate in silence. Afterward we each had one of my cigars and Jack turned in as soon as he was smoked down to the lipline. I cleaned up the supper things after a bit, then sought my own blankets. Plummer stayed up.

Before lying down with my hat over my face, so that my eyes could remain open while my posture suggested slumber, I dug my leather-bound journal out of my saddle pocket and made the following entry:

> ". . . P. is still watching me across the fire. He is thinking about something and that something is me. He must have the rare human instinct of smell. He is like a dog separated young from a former master. His nose tells him we have met before, but his eyes refuse to tell him where. . . ."

It was scarcely a soporific thought, yet such were the compound wearinesses of the trail that no will could keep me long awake. My last drowsy picture was of Henry Plummer's calm gray eyes counting my breaths from beyond the curling smoke that separated us. I remember thinking, my God, you can't just lie here and let him murder you in cold blood; then I was asleep with my left hand knotted around my moneybelt and the .44 Colt, unholstered and on the half-cock, naked in my right.

Nothing happened that night. I awoke with the Colt still in my hand and Henry's foot in my blanketed ribs.

"Rise and shine, my friend," he called down to me cheerfully, giving me a friendly half-roll with the arch of his boot. "Coffee's boilt and bacon burnt. Come and get it or I'll throw it to the woodpeckers."

While it was not the season for flickers, I took him at his word, wolfing down my breakfast while he and Jack Cleveland, already fed, made up the bedrolls and brought in the horses. Shortly we were set to go.

We started out in sunshine, the blizzard having pulled back up northeast during the night. But inside of two hours it blackened up again and began to blow from all four quarters. The snow had not come on again but we were all well used to Montana weather and knew it could not be sixty minutes behind the wind.

Presently Henry pulled his horse in.

"How far by your trail," I asked him, checking my hammer-headed roan alongside his ewe-necked claybank, "is this Bannack that we're bound for?"

"By the river," he said, "to which we're held by this damned snow that will be piling up to our horses' bellies by noonhalt, and following the Jefferson from Three Forks

16

down to the Beaverhead and up it to the Grasshopper fork and the diggings, I'd guess three days over 200 miles."

"*Arrrr!*" growled our tame ape, Cleveland. "I don't cotton to it, by God. When the wind blows boxy like this, you can get buried out there."

"He's right," said Plummer to me. "We'd best start looking for a hole."

"It can't hold this early in the game," I demurred, not caring to be wintered in with these two. "This is only the first week in September. It's bound to break away before the big snow hits. I say let's give it a gamble, at least down to Wolf Creek."

Henry seemed not to have heard me. He clucked to his claybank and sent him on ahead. The switching wind caught up his words, slapping them across my face. "You'll follow or get left behind, Mr. Sutter. The choice is yours."

I did not tarry to guess what he meant. He was not talking about leaving me to find my own way, free-choice. That was as sure as the snow was sticking in my nose and ears. I pulled my knotted scarf high to cover my mouth, hunched my neck into the roached collar of my wolfskin coat, turned my raised shoulder into the wind and followed Plummer's dimming form through the driving flakes. Behind me I could hear Cleveland's growling laugh and the grunting of his horse as it dug in to tail mine into the storm. Half an hour later Plummer pulled up again, this time pausing to peer, neck thrust, at a signboard siding the trail.

It was a new sign and, considering the fact that it was posted along the road to nowhere, right square in the middle of nothing, rather intriguing.

VAIL'S SUN RIVER FARM
TURN HERE

Beneath its well-made lettering a bright red arrow directed the interested traveler to turn hard right up the north bank of a sizeable branch of the Missouri which came in from the northwest at this point.

Plummer looked at Cleveland.

"You ever see that before, Jack?" he asked.

The brute shook his great matted head. "What does it say?" he replied.

His master read it off for him and, when he shook his head again, turned to me. "How about you, Sutter? You ever hear of Sun River Farm?"

"Never," I said, in entire honesty. "I didn't know there was such a thing as a farm in this country. What do you suppose it is?"

"I don't know," nodded Henry Plummer. "But I propose to find out pretty damned quick."

He threw his horse to the right, buck-jumping him through the growing drifts to hit high, hard ground beyond the sign. There was no discussion on this decision. Our "chief" had made his point during the previous pause, and well he knew it. Cleveland scowled at me. I scowled back. We put our mounts after Plummer's.

I looked back as we got them through the low spot, up onto the windswept rock of the Sun River Trail. Already their footsteps were filling. In another ten minutes not a mortal trace would remain that "Dade Sutter" had ever passed this way, or that Black Jack Cleveland and Henry Clay Plummer had flanked him in the passing.

4

We sat looking down on the place like three wolves skulking above a lone settler's cabin deciding on the best way to go down and kill his milk cow or cut the throat of the shoat he had fattened against the October frosts.

We were crusted with snow. The ceaseless wind whipped more of the stuff continuously off the bare spine of the ridge above Sun River. The sun was an hour down. There was no more snow falling. Above the whistle and cut of the ground flakes, the night sky was a polar black, the stars glittered with arctic brilliance. I had never known it so cold for early fall.

Below us, cupped in a shawl of hills thrown shelteringly around a looping bend in the river, its oil lamps welcomingly awink, the fragrant wood smoke streaming away downwind from its rock chimney, snuggled a low, shake-roofed, prosperous-looking frontier ranch house.

The lead wolf turned, white teeth gleaming in the darkness of the wind-whipped ridge. "Last one down gets to do the dishes," he grinned, and put his weary claybank over the edge of the drop-off.

"*Arrr!*" snarled his burly trailmate, kicking his clumsy-footed black horse down the slope in headlong suit.

Left alone upon the ridge, the third wolf shivered and tucked his tail. He looked longingly back through the night toward the distant Missouri and possible freedom. He scanned the naked ridge north and south, quickly, desperately. Then he did what he had to do, and what his companions had known that he must, or freeze. He put his snow-caked roan over the lip of the dropping trail and cascaded him, stiff-legged and haunch-sat, down the roof-steep pitch of the granite decline. At the bottom, he reined him up and headed him for the chinked-log horse shed, looming ahead in the window light of the ranch-house kitchen. A fur-coated figure came out of the house, swinging an unhooded hurricane lantern in friendly beacon. A sheep dog ran barking up through the snow, his tail cutting happy circles in the glowing warmth of the opened door. My roan stumbled to a grateful stop in the straw-littered shelter of the barnyard, his rider so numb with the cold he could not for a moment move his off-leg high enough to get it over the saddle's low cantle to dismount.

On the ground, I had strength enough to swat the roan across the rump, sending him into the squat warmth of the windowless shed, before turning for the open square of beautiful yellow light beckoning across the frozen earth of the stable lot. A moment later I was in the kitchen, with the impossibly wonderful smells of fresh, hot bread and smoking coffee wrapping their fragrant arms around me like those of a lover long denied. I let them gather me in, surrendering without struggle to their strengthening embrace, gladly giving over the floor of courteous response to our host's natural curiosity, to the ever-qualified Plummer. I was asleep before I heard Henry's first ten words of gratitude, and almost before my aching backside settled into the rough pine chair alongside the gaily ginghamed kitchen table.

And that was how, on the blizzardy night of September 8, 1862, I came to Sun River Farm.

At the moment I held it to be a heaven of friendliness and wood-stove warmth; an oasis of firelit safety in a sea of frozen wind and sculptured snows.

Within twenty-four hours it was to become a hell of jealous hatred; an ice-bound island of eerie danger amid a rising flood of deadly suspicions.

The catalyst was one as old and lethal as Eve. Her name was Electra.

I awoke with a start. The half-gloom around me was close and warm with the resinous odors of the cedar fire. For several moments, while my eyes adjusted to the low-key lighting, I lay quietly, studying my position; this, before making any move.

I was bedded on a pallet of prairie hay and clean blue ticking. My wrappings were two blood-red Hudson's Bay blankets and a beautifully tanned cow-buffalo robe. My boots and buckskins lay with my wolf coat, piled in the nearby corner. My snug sleeping place was a small raised alcove dug into the dirt bank against which the house was built. It overlooked the main room of the place by perhaps five feet, and was reached by a low-bannistered staircase built of split log risers and pine plank treads.

Looking out from this toast-warm vantage, I was impressed with the seeming prosperity of the Vails, our well-bred and generous hosts here in this far-off corner of the wilderness. Before falling asleep at the table, I had been too exhausted to note much other than their gentility, unusual for pioneers in a land so remote and rough as this one. Now I was seeing the physical evidence to support the earlier social assay.

The central room below me was no less than twenty feet square, a perfectly enormous room for that day and place where the average complete cabin was not that large.

Off it gave the rear bedroom, the spacious farmhouse kitchen, and a covered areaway to the attached horse shed and hayloft. Its walls and low ceiling were solidly paneled in western red cedar, its floor planked and pegged in hard yellow pine. In one-half of its far, dimly-lit end was a desk and some other office equipment (clearly Vail's place of business) and in the remaining section a curtained-off boudoir which, from its French dressing table and frilly wardrobe hangers, read "young lady" as plainly as I could see the intriguing evidence beyond the presently pulled-back curtains. Since we had met only Vail and his good wife at supper and had not been told there was a house guest there ahead of us, this prospect assumed immediate, keen interest for me. It was all I could do to slow my eyes long enough in their eager search for the missing lodger to see that the remaining considerable space in the room was tastefully taken up by an assortment of settlement-made living-room furniture most rare and genteel for that raw frontier time, including what must certainly have been one of the half dozen pianos in the entire territory.

Then my glance had reached, passed by, and leaped back to the huge, cross-room fireplace.

There, and in that way, I first saw Elly Bryan, sitting in an old-fashioned maple rocker bathed in the soft rose light of a cedar fire one Montana midnight.

I must have made some slight noise watching her there from the living-room loft, for she came around, poised and startled as a yearling doe, her luminous eyes widening as they met my narrowed ones.

As I made some move to arise and come down to her, she motioned up to me in a negative way, holding her slim finger to her red lips in clear warning to be quiet. Before I could so much as guess at her intent, she had gathered her dressing gown about her, glided lightly across the pegged plank floor and up the low stairway to my warm retreat.

The next instant she was seated across from me on the fringe of the buffalo robe. We both waited, saying nothing. The indication must come from her, not me, and she seemed to know this.

While she hesitated over it, her lovely face slightly, almost shyly, averted, but her dark-shadowed eyes watching me with a sidelong, steady boldness that set my imagination afire, my senses would not stop the feasting upon her which they had begun at the fireplace. She was so near to me now, that I could have reached out and touched her without straightening my arm.

In the heated air of the alcove the perfume of her loosely-clad body (she appeared to have on only the ankle-length, princess-collared gown) was as sensuously arousing as the outward look of her was schoolgirlishly sweet and simple. Clearly, she did not know what to do now that she had come to me; yet certainly she understood and was gambling with the primitive instinct which had sent her there.

A man does not have to be an alley cat, nor a woman a creature of the streets, to speak this silent language of natural desire, particularly when their normal appetites have been honed by enforced loneliness and the resulting overstimulation, for isolated months on end, of inherently healthy love-thoughts.

This exquisitely formed Elly Bryan was no wanton. But she was all woman and she had been alone too long. The same, in a male sense, could be said for me. We were simply two high-blooded young people brought together by the design of pure accident; and not, certainly, motivated by the desires of impure thought. Or so, desperately, I tried to tell myself.

Yet, with all my cool common sense, with all my studied insights and due moral considerations, the Montana ranch girl's reaction to our moment of surcharged stillness caught me completely unprepared.

One second we were seated across from one another on the buffalo robe, exchanging hopeful but still doubtful and uncertain looks. The following instant she had reached out her slender hand and placed its pink fingers hesitantly upon my cheek, and all logic and cool thought were driven out of me as with the force of an iron fist.

I seized the hand, crushing its soft palm against my mouth. She cried out low and soft, like an animal in sudden hurt, and came in toward me with the same sinuous movement in which her other hand swept downward to slip free the slight pinnings of her negligee. When the garment fell away from her she was crouched over me as innocent of cover as she

21

had come into the world. Then she had writhed beneath the buffalo robe, bearing me with her.

I was no clumsy virgin. Women, well clad or in their natural state, were no mysteries to me. I would have thought I was above their ordinary power to surprise or intimidate. Yet the sheer physical shock of this one's wordless, instant and total demands, together with the breathtakingly savage beauty of her superb figure, would have made the devil, himself, back up and cry out for a moment's quarter. But my one startled gasp of belated propriety (or was it honest fright?) was crushed out aborning.

The following morning, to my prideful injury, the Bryan girl refused to recognize me.

When I looked at her across the breakfast table with that open-secret smirk which is the obvious delusion of clandestine lovers in public places, she stared back at me as though I had just dropped into my chair from the planet Mars.

Putting my attention back upon my plate of fried venison and corn-meal mush, to cover my confoundedness with the balm that at least no one had noticed, I was denied even that comfort. In dropping my glance from the girl's hostile stare, I got an unpleasant eye-tail impression that Henry Plummer had been watching the exchange without once interrupting the smooth current of his small talk with Mrs. Vail, our host's handsome wife and the older sister of the young savage with whom I had spent the previous midnight.

I determined then and there that I would talk to Elly Bryan at first chance. She was indeed quite young, scarcely seventeen, I believe, and it was possibly her idea of a good joke to tease an older admirer with such deliberate archness. I was never more wrong in my life.

When I caught up with her at last—it was about noon in the horse shed, where I had gone to look to my roan and she to gather eggs from the dozen scrawny hens which roosted and made winter scratch therein—she was still remote as the stars.

I soon enough dropped all pretense of being polite and asked her outright if it were her usual custom to make every wanderer as welcome as she had me.

The blunt query brought some color to both our faces; hers by the implications of my rude comment, mine by the ringing slap she fetched me because of it.

Her quick mind, however, was not confused. She did not by any means surrender herself indiscriminately, she snapped. She would certainly not furnish a list of her experiences, or lack of same, to me or any other questioner. If I wanted to think she was promiscuous, that was my busi-

ness. On the other hand she felt that the man who would re-
mind a girl of his gratitude or, worse yet, as I had done,
chide her for her failure to reflect the like feeling, was no
man at all. She concluded the angry lecture by saying that,
as far as she was concerned, my future at Sun River was
going to be entirely proper—whether I was there another
hour or until the ice went out of the river below Fort Benton
next spring.

With that, she flounced off into the house, hips aswing,
egg basket atwirl, clear voice uplifted in a defiant chorus
of "The Yellow Rose of Texas."

Perforce, I got on with my brushing down of Cassius, my
gaunt and ribby roan whose uncertain love of me was no
less dangerous than his name implied.

I had gotten the strawberry-colored brute for nothing
from a generous widow lady in Orofino the previous summer.
The horse, an unregenerate outlaw, caught wild and broken
with a nose-twitch and a leather-wrapped rifle barrel, had
killed the poor woman's husband but the week before I acquired him. She, kind, good-hearted soul that she was, could
not bear to bring any reprisals against a "poor dumb animal."
Especially one, if I recall her exact words, who had saved
her from the penetentiary by "laying out dear Charley the
very day before she had planned to do it herself."

In any event, he was a devil and fit company for me in
that black moment following Elly Bryan's rebuff.

After I had kicked him twice in the belly and he had
stepped on my foot and bitten me on the arm in return, the
air cleared a little and I was beginning to feel halfway human
again. It was then Henry Plummer chose to show up and
some conversation ensued.

"You don't waste a hell of a lot of time, do you?" he
opened quietly.

It was at once clear to me that he had not broken off his
surveillance of Elly and me with his interception of our
breakfast-table exchange of looks. She had not been gone
over three minutes, and here he was, Johnny on the prying
spot.

My first inclination was to play coy with him. My main
thoughts in connection with him and Jack Cleveland were
still devoted to breaking up the uneasy partnership at the
earliest opportunity. Meanwhile I did not want to do or say
anything which would put him on the alert as to that intention. My moneybelt with its burden of new bills still weighed
heavy about my anxious middle. I knew that it was the price
of my life. The first minute either of them could engineer an
excuse for killing me that would hold up as self-defense in
some distant territorial court or nearby miners' meeting,

23

would be the last minute that I would remember. They would cut the "long green" buckle of the belt before my falling body hit the floor. And I would be left to bleed to death, not only a pauper but a poor damned fool to boot.

Nevertheless, I did not like the color of Plummer's implication. And I let him know as much.

There was nothing but open daylight between us, as I came out from behind Cassius. My right hand was free and brushing my gunbutt. My back was to a stout log wall. Under such circumstances I feared no man, not even Henry Plummer.

"What's it to you?" I answered him back, every bit as quiet as he had been with his acid inquiry.

"Nothing yet," he shrugged. "But I'll give you three-to-one it will be, before this time tomorrow."

"Meaning?" I said.

"Meaning," he repeated, "that beginner's luck doesn't entitle you to any monopolies."

"What the devil are you talking about?" I demanded.

"You got to sleep in the house last night because she took pity on your 'poor tired face' and made Jack and me tote you up to that damned alcove. Tonight it's your turn in the hayloft, that's all. *Comprende?*"

Like most Californians he salted his speech with occasional condiments of "mission Mexican," and I *"comprended"* plenty in this case.

But the complete cheek of it, the consummate, ill-natured, lecherous audacity of it, stopped me cold.

I shook my head unbelievingly.

"Do you mean to stand there and tell me," I said carefully, "that you accuse me of having seduced that girl last night, while warning me that you intend to do the same tonight?"

"That's the general picture," he nodded.

I took one step forward.

"Well, sir," I told him, "I will see you in hell first. Do you understand that? If you so much as touch Miss Elly, you outlaw scum, I'll kill you."

Eight years ago Henry Plummer already had earned his name as a pistoleer. His Nevada City reputation, on the eve of his flight to Oregon, had been that of a man who could draw and get off five aimed shots in three seconds.

Yet he stood and he took my come-on and he never batted a curling black lash nor moved a fingertip of his suspended gunhand. The only sign I saw was the old one of the dappled shadows clouding his still gray eyes.

" 'Miss Elly,' is it?" he said bemusedly. "And 'outlaw scum' no less! Interesting. Very interesting . . ."

24

He let me sweat, while he took his time with the concluding nod and the slow-breaking smile which accompanied it. "You know, Sutter," he said softly, before turning his back on me to stroll off across the stable lot, "it still sticks in my mind that we have met before. That we know one another from somewhere, and not just passing well, either. It's coming to me, my friend. I feel it in my marrow bones. Like the Indians feel the big snow. Or the overnight chinook that melts it. Wait up a bit, my friend, wait up. The weather's about to change."

5

I was now in trouble.

One outlaw doesn't call another "an outlaw"; especially an "outlaw scum." Plummer had pulled me neatly off-base. We both knew it; he the moment I made the slip, myself some five minutes later when, as was my newspaperman's habit, I began going back over my story, checking my facts.

The next move was mine. While I was thinking of what it might possibly be, a shadow fell in the stable door.

It was a very shapely and slender shadow.

"Would you like," laughed Elly Bryan, "to go snow-shoeing up the ridge? The wind is down and the sun will be through in another twenty minutes."

Her voice had the sound of silver sleigh bells. The high color of her face mirrored exuberant, beautiful health. Her violet eyes held the dance and sparkle of the sun on mountain water. Who could resist her?

"Well . . ." I began uncertainly.

Again, quick as light, she waved the magic wand of her smile. I was destroyed.

"Of course!" I laughed excitedly. "Do you have a pair of shoes for me?"

"Up here," she motioned, "in the harness room. They're Indian shoes. Light as a feather, strong as a thigh bone. Or at least that's what Old Jubal says. He's the old buck who makes them. Vail calls him a thieving Bannack and won't let him in the house, but I've had him in the kitchen a dozen times and we're great friends. I like Indians, don't you? They're so simple and easy to understand. Sort of like children, I guess you'd say."

I nodded, thinking to myself that this was quite logical reasoning in her case. Children the world over like and trust other children. But out loud I made small talk while we got on the Bannack shoes. Presently we had them laced and started out across the stable lot and along the foot of the ridge, climbing to the north and the apron of hills sheltering the Sun River ranch buildings.

After zigzagging straight up for about 500 yards, I had to call a halt. A man uses a different set of muscles on a horse. I was saddle-tough, but foot-tender.

Elly greeted my plea for a moment's mercy with another burst of her silver-belled laughter.

"Oh, I think we'll make out just famous!" she said. "That's why I like older men. They give a girl more of a feeling of equality."

I put back in the side pocket of my wolfskin coat the briar I had been about to load. "Now," I said, "we'll just see about that equality. I don't know about Montana, but in California where I come from, you still have to be free, white and nonfemale to vote for President." I kicked the snow out of my webs. "Let's go," I challenged, flinging a contemptuous arm upward toward the craggy lookout she had designated as our objective. "Winner names the bet and loser pays off on the spot."

"Don't talk any more!" she warned, behind the ringing clarity of laugh number three. "I want you in condition to settle your debts up there. And at your age . . ."

She left it there, darting off up the slope like a puff of smoke. I was after her on the instant, age or no age. I felt younger than springtime. What were mountains, much less hills, to conquer for a prize like this golden-haired creature of pure delight? I soared upward, swift as an eagle, my heart beating high and wild with the excitement of the chase.

Presently, however, it came to me that it was not the excitement but the altitude which was leaping my pulse rate. And not the giant vigor of youth but the condemned windbreak of incipient middle age which was making me puff like an ailing donkey engine.

That was high country, and boyhood was as far behind me as the hope of hitting heaven. I cut my gait to a plodding stagger. By the time I reached Elly's side, far above, I was breathing better and beginning to believe that my ribs were going to keep my heart from breaking free of my chest after all. But I had lost my manly brag by a full five minutes. And I could see, by the undiminished sparkle in Elly's eye, that I was not to escape the agreed penalty.

Yet the climb had sobered me. With time to think, I had remembered that I had other problems to face than that of playing snowshoe tag with the prettiest girl in the Idaho Territory—as the Montana folks were then tending to call their wide open empire of grass, gold and grizzly bears. As I sat with Elly Bryan, warmly sheltered from the wind in a cleft of the lookout rock and following the fling of her slender arm as it pointed out the tremendous panorama below us, I was not thinking of girls, but men. Grown men. And dangerous ones. Like Henry Clay Plummer.

"Before you collect your bet," I pleaded, when she paused for breath from her prattling description of the farflung wonders of the Upper Missouri drainage basin spread below us, "I've got a serious favor to ask of you."

"Name it," she murmured, "and it's yours."

From the way she said it, her violet eyes not laughing now, her wonderful mouth set in sudden soberness, I decided to go the whole distance with her.

I stood up and took her by the arms.

She came up off her rock to face me, breathing deeply.

I shook my head and, as she had misread my intent only the instant before, she now understood it and corrected her own reaction. "What is it, Dade?" she asked softly. Then, before I could think to manage it, she answered her own low question. "You're in trouble . . . !"

"Yes, Miss Elly," I nodded. "Bad trouble."

I was not so entirely absorbed with my situation that I did not know she had called me Dade. Nor did I miss the delicious thrill it gave me to realize it had slipped out without her noticing it. Such wondrous signs are the benisons by which lovers live. But my own immediate living was not about to be made safe by emotional tongue slips. I was eminently satisfied that Henry Plummer was not interested in the sign language of love.

"It's those two I'm traveling with," I went on quickly. "Plummer and Cleveland. They're outlaws, Elly. Professional murderers and working road agents. They mean to take my money and my life, and God knows what they may not do to you and your good folks down yonder, once they've put me under!" From there I rushed on, giving her the whole story of Henry Plummer and William McCandles up to the present stroke of evil luck which had brought me to her home in his company. When I had finished, warning her not to use my real name, she disengaged herself from my grasp and sank down again upon her rocky bench. Her face was as troubled, I thought, as only a child's can be when trying to solve the problems of a beloved but not too bright grownup.

"I know, I know . . ." she sighed. "He is an evil man."

I took a sudden chill from the soft emphasis.

"Why do you say that," I asked, "in just that way?" But I knew before she answered that he had already been at her.

"I met him this morning," she said, "just after he left you in the shed. Do you know what he said to me?"

"What?" I scowled horribly.

She laughed, the memory evidently delighting her girlish vanities.

"That he was looking forward with every possible anticipation to taking your place in the living-room loft tonight; that he had just let you know as much and considered it only gentlemanly to advise me in turn."

"He *what!*" I gasped, half-suffocated.

"Informed me," she murmured, low-voiced, "that he was going to sleep with me tonight."

I took it in my teeth, growling wordlessly over it, as a bear will do with a spawned-out salmon. He has caught it and he is hungry, but the flesh is pasty and of evil flavor and he cannot decide to swallow it or spit it out.

"And what," I seethed thickly, "had you to say to that?"

"Nothing," she shrugged. "What is there to say? Can you answer a man like that with words?"

"There are other answers."

"You asked me what I *said.*"

I looked at her, my heart leaping in relief, swelling with gratitude. "And who?" I grinned in an entirely different tone, "*will* be sleeping in that alcove tonight?"

She was on her feet, light and quick as a lance of sunlight. "You, my love," she smiled, reaching on tiptoe to find my lips. Then, seconds later, as we tore our mouths apart that we might bring our bodies even closer together, and laughing it very softly, "*Alone, my love, all alone . . . !*"

Our descent was marked by two more halts, not for breath but for a twin brace of her impulsive, smashing kisses.

All women have bodies equipped essentially the same. All of them have, in some degree, an amplitude of the secondary sex characteristics. All of them, at least mechanically, understand the application and use of these gifts toward the practical enslavement of man. But most women do not, in their entire physical lives, learn how to kiss.

A wicked kiss will raise more hell in a man than any number of average blanketings. And Elly Bryan, somewhere in her seventeen years, had learned to kiss as wickedly as any woman alive.

Her lips left you weak. Unstrung. A male shambles. Your mind would hold no thoughts but those of her body, your ambition was reduced in range to the point-blank prospect of the next bedding. And yet, perversely, this was not a wanton or a wicked woman in any sense of either word. She was, right then, and for all the time I subsequently knew her, as unconscious of her sex as any other totally healthy female. If she swung her hips more maddeningly than most, it was simply a way of walking as natural to her as the gliding grace of a young puma. If she tossed her pretty head and batted her lovely violet eyes to a noticeable extent, it was only the ageless instinct to flirt, somewhat magnified, which motivates every woman from six to sixty. And if she spraddled her long legs and flaunted her silken rump more fractiously than your maiden aunt, then it was no more than a human demonstration of the same coltish fire that puts the spirited foal to sun-fishing and buck-jumping across the clover field when the spring sun sends the life-sap higher than can be borne by standing still and swishing one's tail.

No, my crazy, sudden love for her aside, and the dark memories of her later tragedy disregarded, Electra Lee Bryan was a good girl.

As moral as most who were so soon to set themselves in petty judgment of her, she was more clean of mind and courageous of spirit than any of them. What she did, she did in complete innocence. She atoned for it, in the end, in the only, cruel way a woman of natural honor and iron rightness, who has inadvertently fallen by the way, is allowed by her vicious sisters to repay fully a so-called debt to society—by self-banishment and flight, without public rebuttal or the decent chance to defend a fate no more of her conscious choosing than of theirs.

But enough—no, too much—of that.

At the panting moment of recovery from that third kiss on the last slope above Sun River, my mind was hardly concerned with forecasting the future. It was far too busy trying to scratch the hard surface of the present.

"Elly," I said, "I want you to listen to me as carefully as you ever listened to anybody in your life. You must do exactly as I say, if I am to have any chance at all, do you understand? Plummer is a madman. He has the instincts of a wild animal. He catches every sign, reads each glance, sees any least move out of the ordinary. He is watching me now and if either you or I make one false step, I am as good as done for."

"All right, Dade," she said, completely serious. "What must I do?"

"You must first answer a question," I told her, reaching for her slim hands.

"Yes?" She took my fingers, squeezing them hard.

"Do you love me?" I blurted awkwardly.

She pulled my hands passionately up to her lips, kissing them fiercely. In the same wonderful moment I felt the hot splash of her tears upon them.

"Oh, yes, Dade! Yes, yes . . . !" Then, with that sudden,

startling honesty of hers, the tears were gone and she was saying as calmly as she would "good morning," that at least she thought she did, since she had never felt the same way about any other man and had certainly never expressed herself to the same extent she had with me.

Thrilled as I was with her quiet assurance, I had to put my pleasure aside for a new and compelling reason.

Down below, Henry Plummer had just come out of the horse shed and was standing looking motionlessly up at us.

"Wave to him!" I ordered tersely.

She obeyed instantly, backing the gay gesture with a sun-flashing smile which I am sure must have squinted Henry's gray eyes, even at the distance.

"I'll talk while we work on down," I nodded. "Laugh when you answer back. Say anything that comes to mind, but remember two things—laugh and listen."

She returned the nod and we started down.

Down by the shed, Plummer did not move. His eyes never left us in all the long, sliding way to the trail at the bottom of the ridge. They were still on us as the clack-clack of our snowshoes hit the frozen clay of the stable lot, and we paused to kick them off before crossing on over to come up to him.

"Your sister wants to see *you*," he said quietly to Elly Lee. "And *I* want to see you," he finished even more quietly to me.

Plummer led the way to the horse shed.

I followed without question and, worse yet, without any idea of the nature of his mysterious summons. All I felt, for sure, was that he intended, very directly, to disclose his intention to me.

When we were safely inside he swung on me with the old smile turned up all the way. "Sutter," he beamed enthusiastically, "I've done an honest day's plowing while you've been over the hill with the farmer's daughter!"

The meaning of the phrase was no different then, than now, and I scowled my dislike of his unwanted familiarity in applying it to Elly and me. I wasted my hard look on him. When Henry Plummer wanted to be pleasant you couldn't discourage him with a rifle butt. "Go on," I grudged, jaw set.

"Well," he waved, "it's all set for the three of us to hibernate till spring. I've been working on the wife. She's got a soft leg and a willing ear."

"What the hell are you talking about, you infernal scoundrel!" I shouted. "I'll not listen to any more of your damned lies, do you hear, sir?"

"Oh, you'll listen, all right, Mr. Sutter. The way I see it you've got no choice."

30

Plummer had to be a superb bluffer to have stayed alive all these years. But I had learned a little about reading faces in my time at life's tough table. I didn't think, right then, that Henry had the desperate look of a man hoping to brazen out a busted flush.

"All right," I threw in. "I'm listening."

"It seems like Vail's got to go to Lewiston soon's the trail's open. That'll be right quick, judging from this sun. Now the missus doesn't take to the idea of being left without a man around the house. I talked her into hitting up Vail for us to chore-out our keep for the winter. He bought the deal. I'm to cook, you to keep house, Jack to fetch the wood and feed the stock."

I nodded, hard-eyed, adding only the one condition.

"What about the girl? What I said this morning still goes. You so much as look her way, all bets are off."

"I don't think," he answered slowly, "that you will have to worry about her."

"Tell me more," I gritted.

"Well, in the first place," he shrugged, "I've found myself something a little older and better broken in."

I never believed then, or later, that he had gotten to Elly's sister, but it was no time for moral heroics.

"And . . ." I prompted angrily.

"And," he echoed pleasantly, "I rather doubt that you're any longer in a position where worrying will do you a great deal of good. *Comprende, amigo?*"

"No," I said flatly, and in utter truth I did not.

"While you were gone," he smiled, "I took the liberty of moving your things to the hayloft."

"You son of a bitch!" I rasped.

"While shaking out your blankets," he went on, unperturbed, "*this* fell out."

With no more warning than that, he fished in his pocket and brought out my diary. He tossed it to me without looking at it, and I caught it automatically. *"If you ever publish any of that,"* he smiled, as friendly as though he were still half-owner of Hyer's Empire Bakery and we were talking, these four years gone, on the boardwalk of Nevada City, *"I'll expect my fair cut."*

He said no more, nor did he need to.

It was entirely like him and his weird sense of warped dramatics that he never made further mention of my brief masquerade. Life was a game of imagination to Henry Plummer. To the last, he respected any foe who played it likewise.

And, apparently, he sensed our kindred flair for acting. Yet it was also typical of him that he never failed to hedge a chancy bet. I remembered that characteristic a moment

31

later when, with his footsteps still fading across the frozen ground of the outer yard, I instinctively opened the mislaid diary to its last entry.

It was under date of the present day and not in my hand, although in a chillingly fair imitation of my style.

> ". . . P. caught up with me today. The prospect should remind me of what Shakespeare had to say on the subject of settling old scores. 'When the debt grows burdensome and cannot be discharged, a sponge will wipe out all and cost you nothing.' "

6

I was not misled by Plummer's puckish entry in my diary of his misdeeds. He was like the smiling patient in the insane asylum—at his most dangerous when suddenly playful. Of course he meant to kill me. The only questions were how, where and when.

But I was not primarily concerned with my ability to protect myself. It was the much more difficult, because so much more unpredictable, matter of how he would move against Elly with me out of the way, which bothered me. And of how I might possibly defend against that move while still alive.

In the first place I could not trust Elly. Plummer was an absolute Lucifer with the ladies. To deny him that talent would be absurd. He was tall, he was lean, he was graceful. He was well mannered, smooth, villainously handsome, careful of his dress and speech with strangers, an impeccable gentleman for the public, the best of good company in private and, withal, simply irresistible when he chose to be charming—which was always, where a susceptible young woman was involved.

He had the damned stud animal's instinct of being able, seemingly, to scent out the vulnerable ones in any company of human females; and to do it with unerring accuracy.

My own similar instincts—any normal man has his controlled share—told me that he had fastened his infallible eye on Elly Bryan. To me this was equivalent to the wolf's selecting the most defenseless fawn from a herd of snowbound deer. Once he had made his choice, the end result was inevitable. The fawn might make the most desperate effort to escape but she was doomed from the first jump.

So I knew that Henry meant to try for Elly. This literally sickened me. I was violently in love. I had fair reason to believe that, to the limit of her youthful ability to judge the returned feeling, Elly loved me. I was completely ready to offer my life in the defense of our threatened future. But I knew that with a wily professional like Plummer, I might all too easily spend my blood for nothing, leaving him not only in possession of the emotional field but of my money-belt as well.

At this point my mind hung fire on that latter, forgotten point. The moneybelt, of course! Here was the whole crux of the matter. As a professional, Henry must give it first consideration. My thoughts flew back to his cold-eyed plan to apply the methods of Cain to the cleaning out of Bannack's gravel bars. With the memory, hope leaped up within me.

The game was still on. It was a $16,000 deck, and the deal was mine.

My lead play was to lay a line of clear tracks straight away from Sun River. Where the money went, there went Henry Plummer and his shaggy-haired henchman, Jack Cleveland. Only one tactical problem remained—minor but pressing—to stay alive long enough to plant the lure.

It was now past time for noon dinner. Henry was full fed, for I had just now seen him come out of the kitchen door employing his gold toothpick out of sight of the ladies, as would be his genteel way. His surly partner had preceded him, hitching up a team to the drag sled and going with Vail down into the woodlot to cut and haul stove kindling.

As I watched Plummer, Elly came out and joined him. They talked a minute, then I saw her nod and he went into the house and came back out with his rifle. They started down toward the woodlot, following the packed trail of the drag. As they passed the shed door, laughing and carrying on like they'd been raised out of the same litter, I caught enough of Plummer's drift to make out what was up. Earlier, he had seen a fat buck down in Vail's young fruit orchard. Fresh meat was wanting at the moment and perhaps Elly would be good enough to come along and keep him company while he made a deer-set down yonder with an eye to venison chops for supper.

Since it was clear she was willing to spend the time with Henry, I could only suppose she meant to improve it by seeing what she could get out of him that might benefit me. I still had something to learn about women, especially this woman. At the moment, however, the opportunity created by this unexpected employment of both my watchdogs could not be ignored.

I had wanted, above all, to tell Elly why I was going and to charge her to wait for me. There was now no chance for this. A note containing the information and the plea, left with her sister, would have to suffice. There was a weakness here of needing to trust the sister, a most attractive if somewhat flighty older woman, but the risk of delaying my departure was immeasurably greater than this unavoidable small hazard and so I got on with my gamble to draw Henry Plummer away from Elly Bryan.

I composed my good-bye to the latter and, in a moment of complete foolishness, dashed off a companion piece for Henry. I folded and addressed both notes and left them, with precise instructions for *separate* delivery, with Mrs. Vail.

She, good creature, sensing a love affair and being normal woman enough to delight in being involved, promised faithful attention to the assignment the moment Henry and her sister returned from the orchard. As well, she packed me a delicious lunch to take along, prattling the whole while about how dull and different things here at Sun River were from what they had been back in the Middle West corn country from which she and Elly had come, and how much they both missed the bright lights and good times of the settlements, and how she was working on Vail to give up the farm and try his luck closer to civilization and on and on until I simply had to take up the lunch and walk out on her.

She followed me out, demanding that I be sure to remember that I would always have a friend in Virginia Vail and that if there was anything she could do to help things along with Elly, I had only to tell her what it was. I reminded her that she could render me the greatest possible service in that direction simply by seeing that her sister got my farewell note, and swung up on Cassius as quickly as I could. Virginia Vail was a good and a vivacious woman, well bred and well educated. But she was one god-awful talker and I was very thankful to be getting the other sister. I last saw her waving me a warm farewell from the windswept stable lot. Then a turn in the river trail cut off my view of the snug Sun River buildings. The full force of the upriver wind struck us, and Cassius and I leaned into it with a will.

In the end, I was glad enough to be gone. I had done what I could to secure my young love's safety by leading her would-be seducer away from her. My note to her would assure her sympathy with my motives while at the same time guaranteeing her faithfulness against my return.

That she would wait for me I was absolutely certain. That Henry would follow me I would have bet my life. A man of his consuming ego could not be expected to resist taking up the parting insult I had flung him in the form of Geoffrey Whitney's sixteenth-century taunt concerning the revolting quality of easy marks:

"The fool that far is sent,
Some wisdom to attain,
34

Returns an idiot, as he went,
And brings the fool again."

I was, to tell the truth, feeling very well satisfied with myself as I put the roan up and over the backbone of the high ridge above Elly's home, and on down its far side to continue the river trail eastward. The going was firm underfoot. The unduly warm sun was dropping the lightweight snowpack six inches an hour. When Henry read my caustic farewell verse and stomped cursingly for the horse shed and his bony claybank to come after me and the irresistible bait of the moneybelt, my cup of cleverness would be running long over.

The good start led to a good continuing.

I made the Missouri and the confluence of the Sun River with the Bannack and Three Forks trail before dark. I rested the old roan long enough to load and smoke a pipe, and to take another look at the still intriguing Sun River Farm sign.

I finally let it go with a head-shaking grin. Although I had spent the most exciting and instructive twenty-four hours of my life there, I had forgotten to ask what kind of a farm it was. Moreover, I never found out.

Seconds later, with twilight closing in and a gaunt shadow of a gray wolf softly mourning the departing day from his lookout on the northern hills, I turned the roan southward. With that turning, I had seen my last of the sheltered little valley and its cozy ranch.

Had I known this at the time, not Henry Plummer nor a dozen like him could have kept me from turning back. As it was, daylight found me thirty miles south of the Sun River crossing, and still traveling.

That morning of September 9 was one of those you will not believe unless you have lived in high Montana.

It was clear as rinsed crystal, still as the poised forefoot of a stalking coyote, fragrant as the breath of pine-filtered sunlight.

The roan and I were resting on a little bench of last summer's hay swept free of snow because of its exposed way of standing out from the raggedly wooded flanks of the Lewis Range. The roan was grazing free (he might kill but would never leave me) while I made a smokeless Indian fire of dry grass and cedar twigs by which to boil my coffee.

Yet on that flawless morning in mid-Montana I can promise you I was not thinking in terms of cloudless skies, smokeless fires, nor even the matchless aroma of brewing mocha.

My mind and eye were far too busy studying the fall of the wild land north, east, south and west away from my high and lonely perch to be bothered with such trivial wonders.

Five miles southwest, at the three-cabin settlement of Wolf Creek, the Missouri reversed itself a full quarter of the compass to flow from due southeast. Directly below my vantage it coursed swiftly through the ten-mile jumble of low hills known locally and euphemistically as Holter's Pass. This barren area was a trackless badland reaching from the last abutments of the Lewis Range to the first headlands of the Little Belt Mountains. Immediately to its west, some fifteen miles crowflight, reared the dominant crest of the Great Divide. Over there lay the easiest pass across the spine of the continent within fifty miles north or south; the historic Lewis and Clark gap, at just over 6,000 feet.

My choice of continuing routes, then, was elemental. I could go down the Missouri Road to Three Forks. I could swing west over the Divide to hit the headwaters of the Blackfoot, following that stream down its canyon to the old Deer Lodge Trail in from Lewiston.

There was no chance, either, of deception in the choice. The snow would be gone by tomorrow, leaving the ground soft as a green sponge for days to come. Cassius was a 1,100-pound horse in a day when 900 was considered heavy. Worse yet, he was newly shod. He would leave in our wake a line of unlucky horseshoe prints engraved as deep and clean as the President's face on a five-dollar bill. No, the only option lay in selecting the better terrain for survival, the superior track for the running fight or, by luckier chance, the purely strategic retreat.

In my case this figured very quickly to be the Deer Lodge Trail. It was more mountainous, more timbered, more canyoned, altogether more "comfortable" than the Three Forks route.

Well above the Forks the Missouri spread out into a country where you could, as the natives put it, "See three days behind and a week ahead." It was buffalo and wild horse range pure and simple. Its grass was short and thick, its timber thin and sparse. It was patently not the place for a traveler who had just picked up two unfriendly shadows he would like to shake.

At least I took leave not to think it was, as I shaded my eyes northward for a final consideration of the twin dots which had been growing steadily bigger along my backtrail during the past half-hour.

A Western man may occasionally falter across such a five-mile view in calling infallibly for you the correct identity of a particular rider. He will never fail to give you the exact cut and color of the horse beneath that rider.

I was a Western man and this was a very clear morning. One of those two dots back there was a cobby, coarse-boned black; the other a rangy, wall-eyed claybank. It was time to go.

7

All that day, since the roan was fresh and was, in fact, a better horse tired than were the black and the claybank rested, I was satisfied to ride straightaway with no concern about Plummer and Cleveland coming up to me as long as there was light to see by.

Furthermore, the nature of the trail precluded any flanking circles on their part. The Lewis and Clark road over the Divide would pass no wheeled traffic whatever from Wolf Creek to Deer Lodge. Moreover, it was cut through a country which brooked no turnings away from the established track, not even by a man on horseback. At least it brooked none in the higher part of its canyon, from summit westward down the Blackfoot to its south turning toward Clark Fork. So I had no worries save to sleep light and build no fires at night.

By taking occasional sightings from high places in the trail I was able to keep a good account of my friends through the morning and early afternoon. They were not gaining and not pushing to do so. That pleased me no end —for the moment. But when the sun began to slide west and the short autumn day to slip into its swift twilight, the quality of my pleasure began to curdle. Off northwest, where the very best of Montana's brute weather was bred in the Aleutians and spilled down the icy flume of the Canadian Rockies to flood all over the Idaho Territory, a blizzard blackness was building up behind the mountained forests of the Flathead and the Kootenai. There was remaining to me perhaps as much as an hour to get under cover and dig in. But the prior point to that was that Henry, with his damned "Indian feel" for the smell of snow, had sensed the coming storm while the sun was still aclimb and the morning sky without a cloudlet bigger than a cotton boll.

It was now apparent why he and Cleveland had been in no hurry. With the blizzard certain to strike that night, Henry and his friend had only to wait along a bit. By next morning nothing without wings or snowshoe webs would be moving in that narrow pass.

And in deep snow the odds would favor them, two to one.

Decision again. Run? Fight? Surrender with conditions? Gamble on the storm? Set up a cold-blood ambush and bet on Henry and his pal blundering into it? Double back, take a drop on them and offer under gunpoint to get out a new deck and deal a fresh hand all around?

The choice narrowed grimly. I could not kill any man from cover. They would know that of me, even in our short acquaintance, since the murderer can tell his kind and separate with unerring instinct the merely brave from the purely brutal. Neither could I, in simple sanity, hope to live through another working partnership with Plummer. He now had to kill me for more than my money. With the revelation of my true identity his own life stood in the gravest peril. Should I come before him now, no matter the settlement, he had always to fear that his Nevada City reputation would have preceded him. This he could not tolerate under the circumstances of his disclosure to me of his plans for the gutting of Bannack.

Henry had been extremely fortunate, through the years, in "going to earth." True, he had been spotted now and again since his clever plant of the Walla Walla execution story. There was the matter of that rich and famous Washington lumberman's lovely bride in '59; a suicide, as I recall, following Henry's usual success in the seduction of other men's wives. Then, the long chase and cornering of the culprit by the irate husband in early '60; with the famous gunfight in that Snake River border town wherein Plummer's partner, "Cherokee Bob" Talbert was killed and Henry escaped by a miracle of misfire on the lumberman's second shot. After that, Henry had "taken to the road." Lewiston's ladies of purchasable virtue knew him through the summer of '61 and Orofino's for the winter of '62. That summer he and a casual friend botched a job of trying to dry-gulch one of the Tracy & Company's pony express riders between Lewiston and Salmon River. Fleeing the scene (his random pal was buried there), Henry took a grazing ball from wrist to elbow of his pistol arm. Seeking medical aid in Orofino, he had to shoot an inquisitive saloon keeper who was either new to the country, or to Henry, or both. The man took a notion to die, and did so. Word of this came to Henry via one of his omnipresent "friends," and the hero of my Nevada City journal at once jumped the territory. In this most recent flight he had fallen in with Jack Cleveland en route to head-of-navigation on the Missouri at Fort Benton, where fate had crossed our trails and decided us all to turn back and give Montana's golden wheel one more spin.

Now, having disclosed his plans to me and presuming that no other save Cleveland knew of them, Henry must assure himself of my silence somewhere short of the Grasshopper Diggings. Either that, or see his Bannack ambitions frustrated. Knowing him, I had no doubt what his present thinking would be. But knowing what Henry *would* do and what I *should* do, were rarely different birds.

I decided in the end, the end being a matter of some sixty seconds after I first smelled snow, to keep running. There might be little chance of beating the storm. I saw none at all of coming out ahead of Henry.

In deciding to go on that night I was gambling the whole route: 100-to-1 that the pass wouldn't drift in tight before I got out of it: 500-to-1 that if it did, I could still figure some way to outflounder my enemies anyway: 1,000-to-1 that it wouldn't snow at all and I would make a clean getaway under cover of darkness and the threatening weather.

There was another set of odds, too crazy even to quote; an utterly impossible 10,000-to-1 or worse, that I would stumble into a life-saving camp of friendly strangers at the exact bend of the down-plunging Blackfoot where Henry Plummer was closing in on me from behind just as the blizzard wind had blocked the trail ahead with a six-foot wall of shifting drift. Later that night I put it down in my diary as a miracle.

At the very moment a thing happens, we are apt to credit either pure luck or personal ability. My own precise reaction, on seeing ahead through the blinding whirl of the storm the fleeting wink and twinkle of the firelight, was, as I recall, a joyous shout of *"By God! we've made it!"*

What it proved to be was the "impossible" camp of friendly strangers. The firesiders were two in number, terse in address, tough in appearance. When I had slid off the roan and gasped, "Gentlemen, I'm W. C. McCandles of Nevada City and I'm in trouble," the stockier of the pair stood up and nodded, "John Bozeman, Bannack; J. M. Jacobs, the same." His companion acknowledged the introduction with a grunt, moved only enough to take the pipe out of his mouth and spit into the fire. "You look like you'd been wolf-chased, friend. What's your hurry?"

"Wolf-chased is the word," I said. "And I'm glad to hear that 'friend' in your remark."

"It's always a pleasure," waved Bozeman, "to have company on the trail."

"I'm happy to have you say that, for there's more coming," I replied, jerking my head toward my incoming course.

"Eh?"

"More company. My wolves, remember?"

"Ummm. Who might they be, and how many?"

"Two. Henry Plummer and Black Jack Cleveland. Road agents and murderers to my certain knowledge."

Jacobs spat again. "Rough times, these, and getting rougher. Gold does that to a country. How much you carrying?"

It took me a little quick, but I had no choice. Henry Plummer was coming. "Sixteen thousand dollars," I said. "In bills."

"Well," vouchsafed Bozeman, "you've come to the right bank. We'll take your account. Set down and dig in."

He motioned toward a blackened pot of stew meat simmering on a warming rock by the fire. At the same time, Jacobs poured me a smoking tin of coffee, and got up. "Here," he invited, handing me the cup, "help yourself. I'll look to your horse."

"Watch him," I warned. "He's mean."

He nodded and went for the roan. I watched him to see that the ugly devil was going to let him come up, then turned gratefully to Bozeman. "I'm mightily beholden to you both," I told him. "But please take care with those two rascals. Plummer will charm you blind. You will think warm butter would not run in his mouth. That he would not hurt a flea nor harm a housefly. That he is the very soul of honor, the dot on both "i's" in integrity, the glass of true-blue friendship and the mold of never ending faith. And he will kill you for a fresh horse, a clean shirt or an uncrushed cigar."

"Plummer," nodded my young host. "It seems that I have heard the name."

"And will again before the winter's out," I said.

"What?"

"He's bound for Bannack."

"Oh."

In the little stillness between us, I was conscious of the cry of the wind out beyond the alder and the evergreen walls of the snug campspot. In where we were, only a few stale flakes of snow sifted down through the thick overhead lock of needles and spruce boughs which closed us in. It was quiet enough to hear the fire snap and hiss, as Jacobs lanced it with a third stream of spittle. Then we heard a horse whicker faintly uptrail, and the muffled cry of its rider hallooing the fire. Bozeman cupped his hands.

"Come along in," he called. "Reins free, hands likewise."

"Careful," I advised him for the last time, "this is a real tough brace of birds."

"They're flying downwind, Mr. McCandles, looking for a place to land. They'll not flare on us."

"All the same . . ." I began nervously, but was cut off by a soft-voiced order from behind me.

"Two steps to the left, Mr. McCandles. You're blocking the way."

I looked around to find Jacobs standing just beyond the

far firelight, a short-barreled side-hammer shotgun at the hip-ready position, his watchful glance staring past the stocky Bozeman and me, toward the sound of the approaching horses.

I nodded, stepped aside, palmed out my Colt. There was a muffled thunking of dislodged snow and the uncertain shift of bulking shadows in the heavy stand of sapling spruce up-canyon of the fire.

"Here they come," said Bozeman sibilantly.

Seconds later, Plummer and Cleveland broke their mounts free of the timber.

8

"Cul! Cul McCandles! This is real luck! I was beginning to think we never were going to come up with you. Good Heavens, man, do you always travel as though you were being pursued by cutthroats?"

I was still too stunned to answer. All I could think of was his monstrous, unbelievable gall. But I had seen nothing yet.

He turned with a flattering little bow to Bozeman, not waiting for me to unmask him.

"I'm Henry Plummer, sir," he introduced himself. "Perhaps you've heard of me."

"Perhaps . . ." admitted Bozeman, receipting the ingratiating bow with a curt nod.

"In that case you have no doubt heard that I am a rapist, a rascal, a ridge runner and a road agent. Sort of an inhuman wolf in sheep's clothing!" he laughed.

"Something like that," agreed Bozeman.

The latter was looking from me to Henry now, genuine puzzlement in the questioning glance. Behind me, I felt Jacobs' eyes also leaving our slender guest, to study me demandingly.

"Well," said Henry, "it is true I have been on both sides of the law. My friend, Cul, can tell you that. He can also tell you that I have always denied any criminal intent and have been the victim of the vilest slanders. I have been hounded from pillar to post for the past four years and all because of a youthful mistake into which I was led by a designing older woman and for which I was officially pardoned by the Governor of California. All a matter of legal record, sir, as friend McCandles will gladly substantiate."

Bozeman and Jacobs were openly watching me. They were waiting for, nay, they were asking for an explanation. I couldn't give one. Plummer had me in the position of the innocent accuser who has been trapped by perjured witnesses for the defense. Moreover, he knew it. He stood there, gray eyes glowing, sober face alight.

Behind his master, Jack Cleveland was just smart enough to stand head hung and awkward, the very picture of the unpolished gem, the diamond-in-the-rough of humble but touchingly honest origin. The tableau was too much for Bozeman and Jacobs. Nor can any discredit for the confusion be placed to their account. Plummer had never faced braver men but he had already fooled brighter ones.

"Well," said young Bozeman to me, "it seems we have been given two stories."

"Yes," I conceded bitterly. "Mine and the other fellow's."

"What do you think we had ought to do?"

"Whatever you wish. You've heard both sides."

"I don't like guessing games," frowned Bozeman. "It sounds like a draw to me. Somebody's lying but it's not my business to decide who. One thing, though, impresses me. You claim this man was chasing you and he admits it. Where's the sense in that? I mean the sense to back up your feeling they were after your money or your life?"

His honest puzzlement struck a spark in me. Of course! Where was the sense in that? If not to do me ill, what had inspired their admitted pursuit? Here was Mr. Plummer's little mistake and I meant to stick him with it then and there. "You might ask Mr. Plummer that question, rather than me," I nodded tersely. "I'm sure he'll have an answer for that as glib as the rest he's given you. Come on, speak up, Henry," I challenged him angrily. "Tell the gentleman what it's all about. Just why *were* you chasing me?"

The injury in his fine eyes was as hurtful as the look with which the faithful dog receives the boot of the drunken owner. But his brave smile was quick to replace the shock of an old friend's treachery.

"Oh, sure, Cul. I'm downright miserable about it, though. Everybody thought that you and her—well, you know . . ." He dug in his heavy blanket coat and brought out the rumpled piece of note paper. "I didn't want to push it on you tonight, Cul. Thought maybe you could take it better after a good night's rest. But could be it's better this way."

He held the paper out for me to take and as he did so the firelight struck its familiar shape and manner of folding. I froze in mid-reach to take it, my fingers paralyzed.

"You better take it, Cul," said Henry Plummer softly. "It's from Elly. I'm sure sorry . . ."

I took the note. My hand dropped woodenly to my side. I didn't bother to open and read the returned missive. I didn't have to. I had written it.

It was the note I had left with Mrs. Vail for Elly Bryan and which, somehow, Plummer had gotten ahold of. At the moment, in the depth of my hurt, I could think of only one way in which this might have happened—that Elly, callously amused over my passionate expressions, had shown the note to Henry and then, either forgetfully or deliberately, failed to get it back from him. In any case, he had it from her and I had now to face the clear, if brutal, implications of the fact.

Plummer had cuckolded me with Elly Bryan. Showing me my own love note to her was simply his cat-and-mouse way of letting me know he had done so. But his action in tailing me away from the Sun River ranch had not been motivated by any such refined cruelties. He was still after my moneybelt and my life beyond it. He knew it and Jack Cleveland knew it and I knew it. At the moment nothing else mattered.

"Thanks," I said belatedly, and put the note inside my wolfskin coat. "Maybe some day I can repay you in kind. *I want you to remember that, Henry.*"

"No," he said, innocently avoiding both my meaning and my murderous look, "I aim to forget it, and so should you. I hold no grudge for your hard words, Cul. Tempers grow short on a winter trail and snow stirs up a man's nerves. I know how you feel."

He knew how I felt, all right. The son of a bitch. I felt like a gut-shot buffalo sinking in a blue mud wallow while his herdmates thunder past to safety. I could see and hear and feel everything that was going on around me, yet I couldn't move to save myself without going deeper into the muck.

"Mr. Plummer's right," I heard Jacobs say, and turned to see him move out of the shadows with an inviting wave.

"A good night's sleep will set us all straight," he continued. "Get down, gentlemen. There's meat and coffee left and more can be put on."

Seeing that he had laid the shotgun aside, I was left to assume he had been hoodwinked by Henry's incredible pose. For the moment, therefore, there was nothing I could say without risk of further damage to my case. My best course was to keep my own counsel, waiting for Henry to be his own worst witness, a habit well demonstrated by him in past performances. Hence, I nodded in tacit agreement to Jacobs' suggestion.

"If you will excuse me," I pleaded, "I will turn in." I gestured toward the note in my inside pocket. "Affairs of the heart can be exhausting, gentlemen," I added by way of

43

logical explanation. "Particularly to the loser. This whole thing has been something of a shock to me, as I trust you will understand and appreciate."

Whether or not they did comprehend, they at least showed compassion. I sought my blankets amid a full round of sympathetic head-bobs, even the loutish Cleveland daring to add his doglike growl to the group regrets. True love spurned or unreturned is a subject all men, even brute men, regard with deep feeling, and upon which, no matter what his own lofty or swinish experience, each believes he is an exceptional authority.

So it was with my four friends. They were quite tender with me in that hour of spiritual need. And I could gladly have done in the lot of them for it, the gullible Jacobs and Bozeman no less than the villainous Plummer and Cleveland.

Instead my fate was to be made to lie there for over an hour listening to Henry Plummer compound the purity of his past life with the driven snow of his future intentions. It was nauseating but marvelous. Western history lost a great hero when the genes of criminal heredity decided Henry should be delivered with a twisted mind rather than a withered arm or a clubfoot.

That night, however, history was fifteen months away, waiting for Henry on the frozen flank of a gold strike not yet dreamed of. And I had to hear him seduce my good hosts with the same shy smile and soft voice which had killed God knew how many men, since poor Joe Vedder paid the price of invading the privacy of his own boudoir.

By the time he had finished, I knew quite a few things about Henry I had never imagined. I shall not list these revelations other than to say that their burden amounted to an amazing admission of youthful waywardness terminated by a sober, straight-eyed oath that his one remaining aim in life was to repay society by going back to his old profession of law officer, whereby he might save other youths the hard life and blighting cruelties inherent in such an innocent spate of wrongdoing as his enemies had forced him into.

It was a master stroke, destroying at once the only possible weapon I could use against him then, or with which I might threaten him later in Bannack. And no more effective poison to the better judgment of honest men has ever been invented than the soulful protestation of wrongful persecution forgiven of society by the blameless victim of criminal bias and public libel. Henry's dramatic pledge of reformation had in it all the limp, sudsy bathos of the drunkard's oath, or the wastrel's vow to get a steady job and support his poor consumptive sister and her five fatherless children. But Bozeman and Jacobs were pioneers, not philosophers. Such simple men had no chance with cold-blooded liars like Henry Plummer.

When the latter paused for breath, they gave him their own true short story in return for his rambling fabrication. They were headed east on an exploratory hunch of young Bozeman's that they might find a wagon route from the States to the northwest territories that would shorten Bridger's historic South Pass trail by several hundred miles, and not need to cross the main Rockies in the process of bringing freight in and out the Montana camps.

In its intense quiet way John Bozeman's missionary zeal was even more compelling than Plummer's incredible confidence come-on. I found myself listening to him, spellbound.

Montana, he told my two pious footpads, was destined to become the Texas of the north. Its vast buffalo pastures would soon be dotted with longhorn cattle driven up from the Lone Star State, and its complete transformation into a beehive of mining and ranching riches awaited only the termination of the present terrible conflict of the Civil War to insure fulfillment of the prophecy. Bannack would, by its preëminence of golden wealth, be the capital city of this coming empire, and all things of a nature to advance the ambitious would flow to and from its fabulous hub. Meanwhile, far-sighted men must know that the freight wagon, not the gravel rocker, would make them rich. A fortune awaited the first to pioneer and exploit such an overland trade route as his charts and estimations assured him could be found through the Powder River lands of the Wyoming Sioux and Cheyenne.

It must not be imagined that any such undertaking was for the hesitant or timid. The race would go to the tough and the swift. There was no time to waste.

Bannack, in this first short season of its mining life, promised to weigh out $500,000 in dust. Indications were that next year's take would be nearer $5,000,000. There were only 300 men on the creek now but more were coming by the minute. By the following fall there had to be no less than 3,000 people living on the Beaverhead drainage alone. God knew how many more thousands still other new strikes would bring in. The point was that the big killing, as always, would be made by the men who mined the miners. It was the supplying of these hard-eyed merchants of the fifty-cent fresh egg and the twenty-five dollar hen that laid it, with the goods to sell for the gold that would otherwise go begging, that impelled Bozeman to seek out his trade route.

45

Those who would take an honest profit must work doubly fast to get theirs before the vulture hoards of con men, swindlers, crooks and cardsharps showed up to pick the body politic of its last lean ounce of hard-earned dust.

At this point Plummer coolly remarked that he had heard of Bannack but had had no idea that such opportunities for advancement existed there, and that he was tempted to change his plans and try his luck in the new camp. Both Bozeman and Jacobs rose to this blatant bait, urging him by all means to do so. As a matter of fact, they proposed that we all travel back with them. The unseasonal snow had blocked the passes and they could not now go on over the Divide but would return instead to Bannack, there to await a second opportunity of better weather. If we were interested we might throw in with them or, as our fancy dictated, stake a claim and try our hand at mining. The end point was there was simply no way to lose in Bannack.

It was touching to watch Henry weaken and give up his "former plans." But he managed it. Twenty minutes later the camp was quiet. When I was assured by their heavy breathing that all were indeed asleep, I got out my leather-bound journal and scratched in it by the dying light of the fire, this uncertain summation:

> ". . . P. has cornered me again. He has got me where I am damned if I do and damned if I don't. Yet to Bannack I intend to go, for if he has made it safe for himself he has made it the same for me. He cannot now come at me and still enjoy the immunity built up by his weird tale to Bozeman and Jacobs. I am put in the remarkable position of being better off for their believing Plummer's lies than my own truths. . . ."

At this point I broke off to stare into the outer night, the entry unfinished, my thoughts turning darkly on the next thing I must record—the strange fact of Plummer having delivered to me my own impassioned note to Elly Bryan. Had she lost it and he found it by evil accident? Had he slyly stolen it from her, suspecting its content and thinking to use it against me? Had she, poor dear, upset by the note's vagueness of reason for my departure and forgetting my stern warning about trusting Henry, shown it to him in the forlorn hope he would know something about my destination I had not dared, or cared, to tell her myself? Or, indeed, was my first bitter impression that she had given it to him in a moment of capricious female cruelty, the ugly and entire truth?

The restless questions prowled on through my weary

mind unanswered and without end. As they did so, I had a strange and sudden premonition that I was being furtively watched; no, more than that, being studied unblinkingly, without attempt at cover or dissemblance of any kind. I peered across the fire to find Plummer's gray eyes wide open, his sensuous lips unsmiling.

"If you're wondering what to write about the girl," he murmured, his voice no more than a whisper above the wind, "write this: *'the next time I trust a woman, I'll make sure not to trust her with Henry Plummer.'*"

The next morning the snow was still coming. Bozeman said we would now have to hurry to get on down to the Deer Lodge Trail, and would need some luck if we made it.

We set out without waiting even to boil coffee. For three hours we bucked the drifts along the Blackfoot, each man breaking trail with his mount for about ten minutes at a time. By ten o'clock when we stopped to have our coffee, we were safe. We had lost 2,000 feet of elevation, but were a mile or so above the Deer Lodge Trail. The snow here was no more than fourteen inches on the level; it was light and dry, and the ground beneath it smooth and hard. The horses had no trouble once we struck the main track and we made forty miles south in the next twelve hours of fairly open going.

That night around the fire you would have thought we were five of the best friends ever met. Well, four of the best, anyway. Jack the Beast was still not fit company for white men. Plummer was the absolute life of the party.

I had to keep mentally pinching myself to prevent falling under his damnable spell. His main aim, I saw, was to draw out Bozeman and Jacobs on the subject of Bannack and the general gold-strike history of the territory we were in. He approached this in exactly the careful way a businessman would investigate the prospects of a trade area in the county seat of which he proposed to invest his savings.

In Henry's case, of course, he had no money of his own with which to speculate. But he was a busy man and could not afford to waste his one great asset and surpassing talent (commercial murder) on a barren community. The gravel had to run pretty high-grade to interest Henry Plummer. Time was money to any successful operator, and if he could make more on the road than settling down to city life and the sedentary limitations of a permanent street number, then my friend Henry was not about to spend his winter in Bannack, Montana.

Quickly enough young John Bozeman, that indefatigable

salesman and first promoter of the new bonanza, assured his town of Mr. Plummer's business. In the process, he got me hooked as well.

As I drifted off between my warm blankets, still listening to him spin his prophetic web of the wonders that would appear in Montana Territory within two years, I had made up my faltering mind at last. I would go on to Bannack, make some good connection there, get established, pack up at first opportunity and go north to Sun River to settle my suspicious fears and satisfy my worried mind as to the strange case of my wandering love letter. This decision to go back and have it out with Elly Bryan had been turning in me for twenty-four hours. The moment it was made, all the bitterness, all the doubt, all the suspicion went out of me and I slept like a blissful, breast-fed babe.

But new careers aren't built on one night's rest, or one hour's resolutions.

Neither Henry nor I came off too well in our first winter as Bannackians. Our excuse was the standard one which Montanans still curse: the weather.

The previous winter of 1861-62 had started off like a blessed bleating lamb and wound up like a bloody wounded lion. All autumn long, clear up to Christmas, it had been bluebird beautiful. Then December closed with the worst storm on Northwest record. It isolated upwards of 800 miners and ranchers from the trade routes with little or no provisions. The snowpack was eight feet deep on the open level. Men were soon eating their saddles and shoes, drinking "Montana tea" boiled from the inner bark of certain pines and firs. In far-off Walla Walla, 700 miles down the dead-frozen Snake, flour sold for twenty-four dollars a pound. In the icebound camps of southern Montana men starved, died, devoured one another. It was not until late May that the ice went out of the rivers and the roads were once more open.

It was natural that this bitter memory should cause Montanans to be overwary of the coming winter of 1862-63. As they were reminding themselves of this fact, September closed and we came to Bannack.

What happened after that was a direct reversal of last year's deadly pattern: the worst and coldest autumn on record, followed by the finest and earliest spring to be remembered.

We had no sooner gotten down off our jaded mounts in midtown Bannack than it came on to snow again and did not let up for six solid months. The trails north were closed within forty-eight hours of our arrival and did not thaw out again until late March. There was very little movement anywhere in Montana, none north of the "Gate of the Mountains" gap, between the Lewis and Clark Range and the Little Belts.

For better or for worse, I was as isolated from Elly Bryan as though Sun River Farm were located on the banks of the Irrawaddy, somewhere in Rangoon.

9

But the luck of William Cullah McCandles was due to change. It went from just plain bad to unbelievable.

To begin with there was as yet no newspaper in Bannack. As a matter of fact, I don't believe there were any newspapers in the whole of Montana at that time. The very first one, if I recall correctly, was the one started in Virginia City, January of '64. I don't rightly remember what they called that one, and I don't think anyone else does either, but it predated the Bannack *News Letter* by a good three months. Of course the first *real* newspaper was the *Montana Post* gotten out by old John Buchanan and M. M. Manners over at Virginia City in August of '64. I recall that first issue like it was last week. It was August 27 it came out and was nothing but four pages of what a hell of a trip Old John and M. M. had just had on the Yellowstone from St. Louis to Fort Benton, and what a hell of a news service they were aiming to supply the camps with once they really got the presses rolling. It sold for fifty cents a copy. They ran off 1,000 copies and sold 964 newspapers in the first thirty-five minutes they were in business.

Still, at the time I hit the diggings, there was no regular paper being published and hence no place for me to practice my profession.

Of course, I could not let this disappointment do me in. I was a man of considerable means. If my journalistic talents were to be denied, my financial ones were not. I unbuckled my moneybelt and went to work.

Within ninety days I had succeeded in cornering the entire worked-out gravel market of southern Montana. It cost me every cent of my $16,000 but by the end of the year I owned every worthless claim on the creek, from discovery half a mile either way.

Also by the end of the year there were some 500 people in town, most of them miners. This meant jobs for non-miners, particularly those with stout backs and failing brains. I wound up clerking in the unique general merchandise emporium of an itinerant New Mexican freighter from Santa Fe, one Manuel Otero Jones, a fellow of mixed temperament and marked destiny.

At the moment I was interested only in his money: $1.50 a day. Yes, that is what he paid me. But these were not the sinful wages they might appear. With them I got my bed and board, a quite appreciable item. If one would for a moment think not, let him consider that three square meals a day, that first winter of the Bannack rush, would stand any man half an ounce of dust. A dry place to sleep, even a bale of straw busted in the musty bottom of a parked freight wagon, like my makeshift retreat, went at anything from five dollars upwards to fifteen dollars, depending on such extra luxuries as a canvas top, sheepherder's stove and blue granite commode *with cover*.

While I was keeping books and sweeping out for Jones & Company I did not lose track of Henry. His luck, over all, had not been much better than mine. He made out by dealing blackjack and faro up and down "saloon row" and by cadging a variety of free beds from a sequence of working girls who could resist his bedside manner no more successfully than their sisters in a dozen camps before Bannack. But viewed dispassionately Henry was not prospering. Those first months he barely kept himself in clean linen and good cigars. To him who felt a soiled cuff a thornier crown than starvation, and a cheap smoke a perdition fouler than besmirching a blood sister, these were critical days indeed. In view of them I can state categorically that, as of the turning of that year (1862), Henry Plummer had not in any practical way implemented his impossible plan for the sack of Bannack. This to refute those historians who like to imagine Henry came to the Grasshopper Diggings with his ring of road agents in full operation and with a great record of success already achieved around Lewiston, Orofino and Salmon River. The fact is he came to Bannack without a dime and ninety days later he had maybe three dollars to his name.

All the same, he was at work in his old established way— ingratiating himself with the citizens who counted. He acted like a man without a care in the world, and a conscience cleaner than a new collar. All the while he was laying about him with his warm gray eyes and shy sweet smile, making friends and building up confidence.

He lived in "Jeff Davis Gulch" with the rest of the Confederate sympathizers and general run-down dirt-poor Southerners. But we knew he didn't mean to stay there. He had his eyes on uptown "Yankee Flat," where all the money was and where most of the boys who had "struck it" were building permanent shacks. Yet, like I say, neither of us had hit any real color up to New Year's of '63.

Then, along in March, things began to work loose for me.

As usual with the major changes in the course of one's life, the preliminary movements to this one were innocently simple.

About the fifteenth the weather broke. It started off with a forty-eight-hour chinook. For the first eight hours the wind rattled the ridgepoles. It was a real gully-duster. Then for the following forty hours it just hummed along steady and soft and sweet with that impossible smell of sudden spring which any old Montanan can accurately describe and no newfangled meteorologist satisfactorily explain.

The snow didn't melt, it just disappeared. It went down a foot the first night and by month's end every main trail in Montana was open.

Some time before April Fool's Day, however, fate sent out her second feeler. Under date of March 27 I find an entry in my journal of the Plummer-McCandles feud which records, among other facts, the interesting one that my employer had just fired me.

His reasons, he claimed, were not personal but historic. He was going to Denver to bring in another string of wagons for the spring trade. He was taking along a bag of the coarse Bannack dust, which he proposed to put in the front window of the Rocky Mountain Bank labeled "from the Grashopper Diggings." It was his opinion that the Colorado color was playing out, and he predicted a stampede that would "bust Bannack wide open" when the Denver boys got a look at his Montana sample.

I didn't argue with him, just took my pay and got out the quickest way I could. I had no immediate plans but destiny was taking care of that. She let me know it ten days later.

It was the warm windy night of April 8, 1863, which found me composing and putting down in the diary my happy good-bye to Bannack. Only the hour before I had used my accumulated wages to get old Cassius out of winter hock down at Ben Henderson's hay yard, and to buy a good stout pack horse. My excited intention, of course, was to take the trail for Sun River Farm and my six-months-frustrated showdown with Elly Bryan.

The entry documented my soaring eagerness.

As well, it held some cryptic warnings.

In both cases it constituted a clear record of a man thinking with his heart rather than his head.

". . . Hail and farewell to 'Bozeman's Bonanza'! I leave in the morning with James Stuart and a party of other well-known men from Bannack, who are going north on a spring prospect. I am lucky to have their company, for we hear the Crows are active up there and hence it is wise not to travel alone.

Henry Plummer was invited along, I understand, and refused on grounds of urgent business upcoming in Bannack. He arranged to send George Ives in his place. I don't think I know him.

We start at first light.

It has been so long—I wonder what Elly will say when she sees me . . . ?"

10

We were up and away from Bannack at sunrise of as fine a day as ever came over the Tobacco Roots.

Stuart, a pioneer statue of a man, was our captain. S. T. Hauser was his lieutenant. George Ives, Henry Plummer's friend, was the camp hunter. Of the others I remember not a name or set of initials, but we were a well-met group nonetheless. We numbered fifteen, inclusive of myself, and there was not a low fellow, a work-dodger, a rain crow or a camp drifter among us. Spirits were very high.

My own pulses were pounding with near-audible fervor. My temper hovered midway between that of a bull elk in the velvet and a rambunctious bear cub; rough and rutty on the one hand, full of the empty-headed sap of springtime on the other. By the time we had been an hour on the trail I had composed at least a hundred lyrics for the opening aria of my big reunion number with Electra Lee Bryan at Sun River Farm. Come noonhalt there was still no holding me. I was going all five gaits at once, with my tail flirted up sassy as a gingered saddlebred. It wasn't until nightfall and first camp that I settled down and came to hand. And only then because I was utterly worn out with the pure joy of my renewed love.

That third forenoon we were to meet by prearrangement another party of six prospectors from Deer Lodge. This was the Fairweather-Simmons outfit originally out of Elk City on the South Fork of Clear Creek over across the Bitter Roots in the Idaho country. They had been through Bannack earlier and gone on to try their luck at Deer Lodge. When they heard about Stuart's proposed sortie into the unexplored Yellowstone drainage they were eager to come in on it. Some makeshift planning back and forth had set up a tentative rendezvous for April 11 at the mouth of the Big Hole River just below the confluence of the Stinking Water and the Jefferson.

We made the meeting place on schedule, about ten A.M. As the others were not yet there, we set up camp in expectation of their momentary arrival, planning to push on after noon dinner. But we were ahead of ourselves.

No company came in from the east.

We ate alone, cleaned up the dishes, unpacked the mules, put all the stock out to graze, settled down to smoking and talking.

After a bit, there still being no sign of our Deer Lodge friends and the talk wearing thin, George Ives drifted around to me and suggested that he and I go "run up" a little fresh meat. There had been good elk sign all along the morning's trail and the thought of long yearling veal broiled rare over alder charcoals was enough to interest me.

I nodded to George, got up and shucked half a dozen shells into my Winchester and was ready. He called over to Stuart that we were going to work up the Big Hole a ways and would keep our eyes out for the missing party as we went, looking meanwhile, of course, to down a second-year calf, fat spike bull or young barren cow in the bargain.

Stuart warned us to watch our shots when in heavy cover, as he did not want to start out with any tomfool hunting accidents. George laughed at that and I didn't blame him a great deal as it was somewhat like warning a sourdough prospector not to salt the bacon. Still there was a little something quick and crazy in that high chuckle of his. I decided to let him watch out for the elk, while I watched out for him. After all, he *was* Plummer's man, and might very possibly have been sent along by Henry with orders to "accidentally" drop me at the first clear chance.

I deliberately lagged back and got behind him as we splashed across the Jefferson and set out east along the south bank of the Big Hole. He didn't seem to notice it or at least gave no sign that he did, keeping up a good pace and not once looking back to check on me.

Shortly I gave up the notion his laugh had been in any way unbalanced, or that he meant to shoot me in the back, and allowed myself to relax into the beauties of the day. In good time we jumped our elk. There were five cows with nursing calves and two long yearlings left over from last year's crop.

The cows went into the river brush in three stomping leaps. Their babies flattened to the ground in the high swale grass where they stood. The brace of brown calves bounced off uphill, flags jerking, big ears flared. I pulled too late on mine, saw the dirt spurt left and low for a clean miss. I threw the lever for my second shot, but before I could get the breech closed on the fresh shell, Ives fired twice.

My calf went down like he had been belted between the eyes with a slaughterhouse hammer. I knew I didn't need to look to see if Ives had put his own calf on the ground but I did anyway. I was in time to see the poor brute stumbling to its knees fifteen yards further up the slope than mine. While I watched, its dying momentum carried it lurching onto a steep rockslide. The loose material gave way, cascading Ives' calf down into the Big Hole river brush.

The latter waved good-naturedly to me and started sliding downhill to find and skin-out his game. As I squatted to slit open the gut of my calf that Ives had shot, I made a cautious note. For all his crinkly grin and bubbling laugh Plummer's "substitute" was a superlative rifle shot. It would do me well to remember as much.

This mental marking was broken into by the hair-raising sound of an angry bear's squeal arising from the willow thicket into which Ives had plunged in pursuit of his calf. I grabbed my rifle and jumped for the talus slide.

This was a bad time of year for bear. Just out of hibernation they could be a real handful. If you hit one in just the right mood, you had yourself just about the meanest, mistempered bundle of nerves in the animal business.

At this point in my descent I was about halfway down the slope, not yet knowing if George were in trouble or not. As a matter of fact, he was.

He came rolling out of the brush just as I struck the bottom of the slide. His limbs were asprawl, his body limp. He was clearly unconscious. Furthermore, he had hit the main vein.

He had not only got himself a bear, but a grizzly bear and a sow grizzly bear and a disordinately unsocial sow grizzly bear at that. The enraged brute came bombarding out of the scrub, up-reared on her hind legs and looking for George. As she spotted him and dropped back to all fours for the charge, I got her in my sights.

She had taken five shots before she went down to stay. Even then, her great hairy arm, reaching for George, had come so close in falling that it had laid open his hickory jeans from waist to ankle.

Letting them both lie I went down and dipped a hatful of river water which I sloshed generously in George's face. He came up on one elbow, spitting dirt and gravel and spluttering water. Seeing the proximity of the bear, the extent of the rent in his trousers and the fact of the powder-smoke still wisping from my Winchester barrel, he came wobbling to his feet with the right answer.

"I reckon I owe you one, friend," he said. "That cussed sow meant to put me under."

"There's nothing owing me," I denied shakily. "She probably wouldn't have stayed with you."

He shook his head. "The calf must have landed squarely on her. She rose up out from behind it and swiped me one just like that. I never even saw her till she squealed right in my ear. I still don't know how or when she clouted me," he grinned, "but God A'mighty knows she sure did!"

"You were lucky," I nodded.

"No, the hell with that," he denied soberly. "I'm into you for a stack of blues, McCandles."

"Well," I said, looking around nervously, "we'd best get on with our skinning. Papa might be around here somewhere."

"Not likely I allow. But we'll get along with it like you say." He reached down to pick up his fallen rifle. "Now what do you imagine was eating that old devil to bring her to lay into a man like that? I didn't see no cubs."

"She's got a pair nonetheless," I guessed. "She's rib-gaunt and looks to have been nursing heavy."

"No, dammit," he insisted, "I didn't see no cubs."

"That might be it, then. No cubs." I walked around to one side of the bear, moving her huge leg with my boot. There it was, the teats clottingly lumped and poisonously inflamed.

"Breastcake," I nodded to Ives. "She's been unsucked a week or more. Lost her young ones to something."

"Leave it to me," laughed George Ives. "Sparrows sing for some people, but I dassn't look up to an orchard warbler for fear he'll splatter me like a Salt Lake seagull."

He was feeling right again now, his head cleared, the shock weakness out of his leg muscles. He stepped around the dead grizzly. His warm brown eyes found mine, as his big hand went lightly to my shoulder. "I want to tell you something, old-timer. I cotton to the color of your whiskers. You can remember that."

"Well now . . ." I began to remonstrate modestly, but he cut me off and dead serious about it, too.

"No, now you listen to me, I mean it. I done plenty things in my time I wouldn't care to have my mother catch me at. One I ain't done, though, is let down on a friend. And you bite off a chaw of this for keeps, Red. I ain't about to begin with you."

I got the sudden feeling he wasn't just talking. He meant something definite, if not dangerous. I left off my token examination of the bear.

"What do you have in mind, partner?" I asked him very carefully.

He caught my eye again and held it hard. "You know your friend Henry Plummer?" he said.

"Quite well," I admitted.

"Not quite well enough, I'll wager."

"Go on."

"Well, he ain't your friend Henry Plummer, he's my friend Henry Plummer. You wash that color?"

"No, you'll need to sluice it again."

"All right. Plummer's out to put you under."

"Is that all?"

"Nope. I'm being paid to do the putting."

"Well," I said, "that's more interesting. What's been keeping you? We're three days out."

"True," he grinned, walling his eyes in that quick, wild way he had. "And six miles downwind of a sound asleep camp."

"It's what I mean," I snapped.

"I know, I know," he said defensively. "Dammit all, I meant to drop you today—you know, accidental shot, just like old Jim said—then this infernal bear . . ." He broke off, shaking his head in frank disgust.

"George," I told him cynically, "you're true-blue."

"Well now, that ain't my fault either." The wall-eyed grin was back at once. "Mother just brung me up to do the Christian thing."

"Thanks," I said.

He laughed. "Praise God and pass the plate again!" He spread his long arms as though in ministerial blessing of my sentiment. "Amen! Hallelujah! Glory, glory!"

I swallowed uncomfortably and took another long look at George Ives.

There was no remaining doubt but that he was touched. Yet his was that inspired brand of insanity peculiar to all truly great outlaws, classic mountebanks and extraordinary mayhemists. That mad mixture of pure evil and impossible errantry which has fascinated the literary mind since villainy was invented. And which will always make crime and punishment a more absorbing subject than good deeds and gold medals.

Ives was of that perfect mold. He was a murderer, make absolutely sure of that. But he was never, by any artistic or professional measure, a *common* one.

"George," I worked cautiously back to the point again, "you've still not told me what it is that's bothering you."

"I did so," he said. "It's you saving me from that damned bear. I can't do you in now, damn you."

"I don't mean that. It's not the job, it's the details of doing it that are bothering you, I'd guess."

He thought a moment, frowned hard, nodded seriously.

"That's so, Red, and here they are. Plummer sent me along to see that you didn't do either of two things; get to that girl up to Sun River or back to the Bannack diggings alive and kicking. Now it's just as simple as that."

"All right. Did he say why?"

"Only that he wanted you out of the way the same as Cleveland."

"Cleveland?"

"Yep. Sure, now, you remember poor Jack? The faithful dog?"

"I see," I said softly, and I was not just using a figure of loose speech. I did see. All too well. On January 14 past, Plummer had shot down and killed "faithful Jack" in so-called self-defense. Now it was clear it had been premeditated murder and equally clear that it was presently my turn to be likewise "legally" put away.

Henry had only been hibernating. He had not for one minute abandoned, or thought about abandoning, his plan.

He was getting set to move fast now while Stuart, the head of Bannack's decent crowd, and the other prominent citizens with him, were out of town. As the opening gambit he meant to get rid of the second and last of the two original "earwitnesses" to his coldly plotted design for "cleaning up" along the Grasshopper; which same would naturally be me, Cullah McCandles. Now, however, because of a freak twist of hunting luck and a quixotic kink of fairness in the criminal mind of George Ives, I was momentarily spared. And not alone that, but forewarned and brought up to date as to the continuing nature of my Nevada City nemesis' plans.

"George," I told my benefactor, as I reached out fervently to take his ready hand, "we both owe each other one!"

"Sure!" he laughed, quick and crazy as a cuckoo clock. "Now we're all even and can start over again. Happen I might yet earn old Henry's pay for putting you under, providing you don't sleep too light!"

With that, he chucked me a left fist in the side that left my ribs tender for a week, hitched up his torn breeches and bawled, "All right, by God! Let's get our meat cut out and packed. Take only the saddle, liver and loin. Rest's dog food far as I'm concerned or you'll ever live to care, eh, Red?"

Acknowledging the probable likelihood of the happy thought with a pale smile, I started off up the hill to get my elk. As I went, I turned my eyes demandingly skyward with one of my rare references to any power past that of a .44 slug. "Why me?" I groaned. "With 500 other stupid sons of bitches to choose from in Bannack. Why did you have to pick on me to side that rolling-eyed idiot down yonder?"

All the next day, Sunday the twelfth, Stuart kept us waiting at the rendezvous. When, by late afternoon, the Deer Lodge party had not appeared, he called us all up to the fire. "If they are not here by sundown, men," he said, "we must assume something has happened to their arrangement and be prepared to move on with first daylight." He paused significantly. "I want to get on through this Crow country before the new grass is well up."

There were no questions, nor dissents. We all knew what he meant. When the grass got up the ponies got fat. When the ponies got fat the braves got sassy. When the braves got sassy the white man got scalped. It was that uncomplicated.

The wait went on. One, two, three hours; still no halloo from the banks of the Big Hole. The time eased by lazy and quiet. With the meat hung and all the stock on graze there was little to do save sit around and worry. Which was fine for me. I needed the exercise.

What did George Ives now mean to do about Plummer's orders to murder me? Could I trust his oath as to never "letting down" on a friend? Or did he mean literally his parting laugh about sleeping light?

It was the devil's own decision with an edgy one like George. But I finally found in his favor. He would, I guessed, avoid the act if he were given an adequate excuse for doing so. The next problem became the physical description of an adequate excuse. That, I knew, was my child.

The answer did not come to me until after supper, and not then until after the third tamping of shag-cut. But the three pipes were well smoked. They made me wait to approach Stuart until all the others had sought their blankets. In this way necessary caution was served.

"Sir," I opened earnestly, "I've been thinking."

"A good habit," he replied, talking around the stem of his battered briar, "and reasonable in price too."

"Sir," I began again, determined to go through my lines as I had rehearsed them, "it seems you may well have to go on in the morning without your friends from Deer Lodge."

"Aye, that's a fact."

"Well, sir, it strikes me as a mortal shame for those fine men to miss the trip by what may prove to be a matter of hours."

"As well it may be two days, or a week, or not at all," he observed dourly. "There's no telling what's come amiss with

58

a party of men in the mountains." He still hadn't bothered to remove the pipe. "You realize that, of course?"

"Yes, sir, I realize that. But what I had in mind was this: as the sole free agent in your company I am the logical one to remain behind and wait for the Fairweather outfit; that's either a few hours or a few days or whichever, sir. Furthermore, I'd be entirely happy to do it."

"Why now that's very good of you, McCandles. But . . ."

"No 'buts' to it, Mr. Stuart!" I laid it on thick, sensing that here, indeed, I had stumbled on the perfect way of cutting myself adrift from "Long George" Ives. "Please say no more about it. Believe me, it's the least I can hope to do in return for your generosity in permitting me to join your fine group. And as far as any trouble goes, there simply is none. I can easily catch up to you, traveling alone. That is, should they fail to appear within a reasonable time."

Now he took down his pipe.

"McCandles, I appreciate this." He thought about it a minute, nodding to himself. "But do you remember why it was you sought to attach yourself to this company in the first place?"

"Well, there was some talk of the Crows. But we haven't seen hide nor hair of anything that looks like one of their war parties."

"Exactly. Now how long have you been in this country?"

"Four years off and on."

"And how many Crow war parties have you seen in that time?"

"Why, none at all, now that you mention it."

"Precisely."

"Precisely what, sir?"

"Precisely no war parties. Now see here, McCandles, your not seeing Indians and Indians not being there to be seen, are two entirely different streaks of color. Kindly remember that as long as you are a member of my company."

"Yes, sir," I gritted. "Was that all?"

"Aye." He put his pipe back for three or four puffing nods, then took it down again, pinning me with its tooth-pitted stem. "You're a Scotsman, eh, lad?"

I admitted it, reserving only my German-Swiss grandfather.

"I thought as much. Cullah's a Highland name."

"But not so 'high' as Stuart," I suggested politely.

"Aye," he agreed, and lapsed into smoke-wreathed silence.

I waited, sure his mind had wandered afar into the mountain mists and nodding blue bells of his parent heath. But James Stuart's keen mind was hardly of the straying sort.

"McCandles," he said at length, "good night."

Then, as I arose to go, clearly frowning my pique at the brusque dismissal, he added softly, "Cullah, lad, if you're ever in real trouble in Montana, think well of that emblem on your finger. It will see you through. Your friends are everywhere."

I had seen him glance at my Masonic ring and had, of course, noted his own. Nonetheless, and lightly, I dismissed the fraternal advice. I had ever been a reluctant "joiner," and was a Mason mainly by family custom and mining camp persuasion. Moreover, I had as yet no reason to suspect the true strength of the Scottish rite in Montana. Much less had I any present warning of the grim part Freemasonry was to play not only in my own future but that of the entire territory.

Accordingly, I returned James Stuart's lodge-brother counsel with a curt nod, and promptly forgot it.

Going to my bedroll straightaway I was not at all conscious of the fact that I had just parted with a most remarkable man; certainly one of the four main pillars of pioneer Montana.

At the time I thought only "what a grand old fellow he is," and rolled over and went to sleep chasing visions of Elly Lee Bryan along the flower-banked shores of sparkling Sun River.

11

I was captured by the Crows on the morning of the fourteenth, exactly twenty-four hours after Stuart moved on. There were no heroics involved on either side. One moment I was sitting there in the April sunshine enjoying my breakfast of broiled elk liver, the next minute there was a tall shadow blotting out that sunshine and spoiling my appetite.

I looked up to see a perfectly huge chief standing about three feet behind me. He was on foot but his pony was near by. Not fifty feet from my fire, watching solicitously to see no harm befell their headman's mount, were about thirty of the toughest looking Indian horsemen I had ever seen.

Fortunately the party was in good spirits, although their heavy paint, full armament and lack of baggage animals indicated they were definitely on the prowl.

The Crows now ran up my two horses. While they divided my pack outfit and squatted down to gamble for the horse with a game of "hand," they graciously indicated I might keep the roan, and welcome; at least until they needed some fresh wolfbait or a feed for the camp dogs. I made a silent vow that Cassius would show them they had a bit to learn about judging horseflesh, and was very glad they considered him unfit for Indian duty.

While my pack horse was being won, the tall chief came over where I was saddling the roan. He had a little chap with him not over five feet, six inches and looking like a jockey alongside his own towering bulk. This wise-faced brave he introduced by the direct method of fetching him a clap on the back that must have separated his shoulder blades and grinning, *"Ho-hah!* Him Little Crow." Then he smote himself an equal blow on the chest and added blandly, "Me Red Bear. Him, me, we chief Absaroka. Who you?"

Relieved to know from his crude English that we could at least have the advantage of communication, I told him a fairly straight story. This course was indicated neither by inherent honesty nor native modesty but by the direction from which the Crows had come upon me. They had clearly been tracking our company and with their marvelous skill at this game would already know nearly as much as I did about the Bannack party.

The bigger Indian nodded repeatedly as I went along and when I had finished said he was glad I had a straight tongue and that I should be too because he and Little Crow had decided to kill me if I lied. What they meant to do with me otherwise he did not say, and I got the impression from Little Crow's scowl that Red Bear had done most of the "deciding" in the matter of sparing my life.

A brave named Yellow Dog had now won the pack horse. Little Crow, who seemed to be not so much a fellow chief as an assistant chief to Red Bear, ordered the march resumed.

At this point there was a slight delaying discussion which opened my eyes and shrunk my stomach. It seemed there was some option in the matter of which white party to chase. Back a few miles at the mouth of the Stinking Water they had ridden around a smaller band of travelers who had, to all appearances, been camped where they were about a week or more. Some of the Crows were for taking care of the easier chore first—there were only six men in the Stinking Water camp—before riding on to attack Stuart's company. This minority opinion was voted down by Little Crow who seemed very angry about the latter group of whites going up through his country. He said the Stinking Water men would wait. They could get them later, after they had gathered in the "big band" from down in the Beaverhead Hills.

This would be Stuart's party of course. The other would as surely be that of his friend, Fairweather. Obviously there had been a confusion of rendezvous rivers, the Deer Lodge group waiting at the mouth of the Stinking Water while the Bannack men camped at the confluence of the Big Hole. It was a singular example of the luck of the footloose. By something like five miles, give or take a bend or three in the river trail between the two camps, five family fortunes were founded and the history of Montana made over.

For the better part of two weeks the Crows trailed my recent companions eastward toward the Yellowstone River, never quite finding the opportunity to attack due to Stuart's constant watchfulness.

Finally, after a hot argument between Red Bear and Little Crow, the latter rode off with about twenty-five of the braves, leaving the former and four companions in camp with me. When they had gone Red Bear asked me if I would like to see a little fun, as Little Crow and the others had gone off to brace the white brother in broad daylight, a most uncommon practice for the Crows who were famous for their night raids. Since the white camp was just over the hill, we could ride up and have a very good view of Little Crow's reckless challenging of the invaders.

I jumped at the chance, being naturally in favor of anything which might result in a chance at escape.

We reached the hilltop in time to see the two dozen mounted Indians riding swiftly in toward Stuart and his men, who stood arm-to-arm around their fire which was built against the bank in a protective bend of the Yellowstone.

I must say I have seen some cool customers but never a one to top James Stuart. He ran the prettiest bluff you will find anywhere in the history of Indian fights, and he made it stick.

Instead of running, diving for cover, crossing the river or even bothering to bring in their horses, he ordered his followers to stand there with their rifles up and ready, not moving a muscle in any other direction.

The surprised Crows brought their ponies to a sliding stop, quieted down their whooping and yelling, looked at the white party distrustfully. What the devil was this? No running? No shooting? No desperate scattering for cover when the red man thundered up with the warwhoop ringing?

This was not fair of the white thieves and not according to the rules of the game in any decent way at all. Why, a man might be excused for thinking they actually meant to argue about it, and outnumbered nearly two-to-one, at that!

Little Crow got down from his pony and stalked forward to parley the matter. A dozen of his followers trailed him, bent-legged and stiff-spined. The rest stayed mounted.

It was a very short talk. We could translate its burden very clearly by the hand signs used on both sides.

"You will turn back here, or we will kill you," was Little Crow's salutation.

"If you are still standing there by the time I count the fingers of one hand," replied James Stuart, "we shall fire into you from this distance, eye-to-eye."

Fourteen white rifles meant fourteen dead Crows at that point-blank range. The diminutive Absaroka chief knew this, and more. He knew he had made a serious tactical blunder.

He had counted on these fools stampeding. They had stood still. Well, there would be another day. This one was already lost. But the next one would be a different matter. Woe betide the next white party to come under the guns of Little Crow and his Crazy Mountain Absaroka!

With that threat the embarrassed Indians backed off. When they returned, it was apparent Little Crow's stock had fallen sharply. Red Bear reminded his braves that he had advised against the daylight maneuver and hoped they were now satisfied he knew what he was talking about. They were.

We now turned around and went back after the Fairweather party which we knew, through our scouts, had been tagging along the Stuart trail about four days behind us.

The Crows had been careful to parallel the latter trail instead of following in it, this so as not to alarm the smaller group of white men trying to catch up with their advanced fellows. It was the early evening of May first, when we saw ahead of us the tenuous smoke of a campfire on the Yellowstone. We were at this time about fifty miles east of Pompey's Pillar, traveling along the south bank and back away from the stream in a region of sharply cut-up hills.

The white camp was not the only one near by. By midnight no less than 200 new warriors had drifted in out of the dark to join our original thirty. In answer to my query Red Bear informed me that the main Crow village, "heap big, many lodges," lay just down the Yellowstone from the prospectors' fire. Had they gone on another three miles, the huge chief said, they might have blundered into his home lodges and been already dead. As it was, he saw little enough chance of saving them, though he meant to do so if he could.

This surprised me, but I only nodded and he went on. He had succeeded, he claimed, in getting Little Crow to agree to capture them first and consider the matter and, if need be, manner of their deaths later on. He impressed upon me the fact that he knew the danger of killing white men these days. Times had changed, he said, but he was having trouble convincing his people that this was so. They still favored Little Crow's feelings on the subject. Which feelings were, simply, to shoot any white man found traveling north of Three Forks. Red Bear well knew the eventual price of such a policy. Other tribes had already paid it. He could name the Blackfeet, the Piegans, the Bloods and Gros Ventres for a few. Still others were yet trying to pay it. One thought immediately of the Sioux, Cheyennes and Arapahoes in this latter group, he said. It should be clear, from such examples, that no Indian could expect to find a profit in fighting the white man, he concluded, but the fact was that many of them still did and that Little Crow was such a one.

I was understandably intrigued with these views of Red Bear, but before I could explore or exploit them our reinforced war party was moving off to invest the site of the white camp.

On the following morning, the second, Fairweather and his companions awoke to find the low hills around them literally alive with Crow warriors. They had the good sense to stand still and so gave Little Crow no excuse to start shooting. Before the sun was an hour high we were all prisoners in the Crow camp, which indeed proved to be a big one. I counted close to 200 lodges on the way in, and that would mean very nearly 1,000 Indians. Prospects now looked very poor for "white color" along the Madison.

I had been taken into camp ahead of the Fairweather captives and was placed in a lodge across the village from the one in which they were imprisoned. Hence, they knew nothing of my presence, then or later.

All that day the camp teemed with excitement, the squaws, oldsters of both sexes and the button-eyed children making a constant noisy parade past the lodge which housed the six white men. By contrast, I got no notice at all. I put this down to the fact Red Bear placed me in his own tepee and that thus, as a "guest" of the chief, my privacy was considered on an entirely different basis than that of my less fortunate fellows.

As well, and by the same token, my personal safety was a great deal better guaranteed, I imagined. My seclusion was an almost certain case of Absarokan "political asylum," arranged by my host to give himself time to cool down the killing temper of his less intelligent fellows and, in particular, to offset the arguments for immediate action of the white-hating Little Crow. So, at least, I argued hopefully with myself while, across the village, the meeting which would decide all our fates went on hour after suspenseful hour.

I had no news through the day of how things were going in that meeting, nor did I get any until Red Bear "got home" from it that night. This lack of information was particularly interesting considering the fact that I got on very well, while the chief was away, with the youngest of his three wives. She was a slim-legged, luscious-bodied little thing, happily fascinated with my red beard and "pretty bright hair." However, her interests proved strictly nonpolitical and I got nothing out of her but several hours of sparkling-eyed entertainment.

Her towering mate, on the other hand, had a great deal on his mind when he stalked in through the lodge flaps about an hour before sunset. He was, he said, losing his fight to save the lives of the white men, mine included, and he wanted to talk to me about it.

By this time I did not believe him. I had been from the first suspicious of his claimed effort to spare the Fairweather party and myself. True, I had held some hope through the day that he meant well and might persuade his fierce fellows to let us go. Now I was satisfied he was lying, although for what reason I could not imagine.

I could not resist the temptation to inquire nor, indeed, the opportunity to uncover any last possible chance that he was telling the truth. Knowing his proud race revered personal honor, I deliberately challenged the sincerity of his representations.

Again his answer surprised me. Yes, and in its simple honesty, humbled me.

Did I think, he began, that his heart was truly good for the people who were invading his hunting preserves, cutting down his forests, digging out his hillsides, dirtying his stream beds and plowing up his buffalo pastures? Had he said anything to give me that impression? If so, he was truly sorry, for this was not what was in his heart at all.

He had never said he liked the white man. He did not say so now. In his heart he hated him no less than did Little Crow. It was only that he saw things more clearly than his small fellow chief.

Red Bear had longer eyes than Little Crow. He saw ahead only disaster for any Indian people who invited war with the white man. He had already told me that, and that was all he was telling me now.

It was his conviction that the Absaroka must not become involved in any big medicine dreams such as were currently disturbing the sleep of the Sioux and the Cheyenne. Those tribes would follow the Blackfeet into oblivion. But if the Absaroka would listen to him, they might survive to see their grandchildren walking the white man's road. There came always a time when it took more courage to stop than to go ahead. In Red Bear's opinion that time, for his people, was now. And he still meant, despite my small faith in the honor of his word, to do all that he could to protect me and my friends. I was not to hope for too much, but at least I could know that his tongue was straight and that he was talking for us.

Toward that end—he interrupted my stumbling apology to advise me—he had brought me something which he hoped might contain some information useful to the next day's final arguments over our fate. This "something" turned out to be the "trip log" or "trail journal" of Henry Edgar, one of the Deer Lodge men. Red Bear had seen him writing in it as he left the meeting just now. Thinking it might furnish evidence harmful or prejudicial to the case of the six white men, he had taken it from Edgar to keep Little Crow's "side" from getting their hands on it. It had only this moment occurred to him to have me read it for him in the hope it would tell us something helpful.

I include here only a selection of entries whose dates and continuity I copied into my own record after Red Bear had rolled up in his buffalo robe. They tell a terser story, I believe, than I could manage in their place.

"April 14:
". . . All well. Today looks better, clear—but cool. Meat wanted. Bill and Simmons started for sheep and got one. Watched all day for Stuart but did not see anyone . . ."

"April 15:
". . . Morning looks well. After breakfast Bill and I took our guns and started for a tramp down the river. *What is that?* Shod horses' tracks! We took the trail for a mile or two to find, if we could, how many there were and where they were going. Came to the conclusion it was Stuart's party. Back to camp; too late to move . . ."

"April 19:
". . . Fourth day following Stuart east. Now think we are no more than three days behind them and will overhaul them very soon. Camp here is on Madison where they crossed. Simmons, who reads signs like an Indian, says we are but two days back . . ."

"April 23:
". . . Good morning, good country, all looks well. Game everywhere. Sheep, elk, deer, antelope, duck. Crossed Yellowstone-Missouri Divide today. A grand country. No charts but we know it pretty well by 'general feel.' . . ."

"April 26:
". . . Now we know where we are! Simmons was right. Two days! How do we know? On a bush by their firespot ashes we found a note with date Apr. 24. Forty-eight hours and we shall be up to them . . ."

"May 1:

". . . Simmons alarmed. Out scouting to one side of our advance, he cut across heavy Indian sign also following Stuart. We are camped in some small hills without a fire. We have not put our tents up. The horses are what they are after, Simmons says, and we have them on stakes close in. We have also set a guard. The horses are very restless. They will not eat . . ."

"May 2:

". . . We are the 'guests' of the Indians. Crows. They took us this morning, no shooting. We have talked the matter over and agreed to keep together, and, if it comes to the worst, to fight while life lasts. We are in a big lodge. All the young ones are around us and the women. What fun! We got plenty to eat; Indians are putting up a great big lodge—medicine lodge at that. Night. What will tomorrow bring forth? I write this—will anyone ever see it? Quite dark and such a noise, dogs and drums! . . ."

When I had scanned these brave words I did not quite know what to tell Red Bear. There was nothing here which would help him in his fight to save the white men and, on the point of admitting as much to him, I thought of something. A little flattery might fire him up for his return to the council fire and was no more than his due reward, besides, for his efforts on behalf of my countrymen and myself.

Actually, I never was able to understand the Fairweather party's lack of appreciation for Red Bear's part in its defense, and Edgar's attendant failure to include mention of this debt in his journal always puzzled me. In the end I was left to conclude that my white friends were not aware of the Crow chief's actions at the time, and that later they simply forgot to acknowledge them. It was that or, perhaps more honestly, just another example of the relentless refusal of the white pioneer to believe that any Indian was capable of any good.

In either event the problem at the moment of reading Edgar's entries in Red Bear's lodge was that of remedying them, in translation, to the point where a kindness could be tendered the latter at the same time that a service was rendered the former. (*And* his six fellow prisoners, not forgetting William C. McCandles!)

Perforce, I got on with the courteous deception.

"They say nothing here," I told him, putting the slim volume aside with the necessary falsehood, "except that they owe their lives to a splendid chief named Red Bear.

"They say they honor this chief, but do not think he can dissuade another named Little Crow, who seems both more eloquent and more popular with the tribe, and who is clearly determined to see them all put to death."

"*Ho-hah!*" growled Red Bear. "We shall see about that! Little Crow popular? A better speaker than Red Bear? Bah!" He pulled himself to the full of his enormous height and stormed out of the lodge, still growling and muttering to himself.

The following council argument lasted through that night, all the next day and on into the second night. Henry Edgar's description of that second day in the Crow camp, which I did not see until later, is set down here for the reason that it tells graphically what I could see nothing of for myself, but could only judge from the heavy shouts and vast insults coming from the medicine lodge.

In the same spirit of reporting accurately a circumstance to which I was a present but "blind" party, I use in direct sequence Edgar's wonderful entry for the final, third day in Red Bear's village; both entries made after my success in persuading the chief to return the "little talking book" to its owner as a token of his, Red Bear's, continuing effort and friendship for the white brother.

Here, then, is the trenchant and redoubtable Henry Edgar on the subject of Absaroka Indians as viewed, firsthand, May 3 and 4, 1863, in formal council gathered; question under grim consideration—to cut or not to cut the throats of Mr. Edgar and his five friends:

"Simmons tells us we are wanted at the medicine lodge; up we go. Bill says, 'Ten o'clock, court now opens.' We went in, the medicine man sat on the ground at the far end; both sides were lined with the head men. Red Bear and Little Crow, the two chiefs of the village, sat beside the medicine man. We were taken in hand by an old buck; in the center of the lodge there was a bush planted—the medicine bush —and around and around that bush we went. At last their curiosity was satisfied and we were taken outside and told to remain there. We had a good laugh over our cake walk going out. Bill swears if they take us in again he will pull up that medicine bush and whack the medicine man with it. We tell him not to, but he says he will sure. An order comes again, and we go in and around the bush. At the third time Bill pulls up the bush and Mr. Medicine Man gets it on the head. What a time! Not a word spoken; what a deep silence for a few minutes! Out we go and the Indians after us. We stand back to back, three facing each way; Red Bear and Little Crow driving the crowd back with their whips, and peace is proclaimed. Red Bear mounts his horse and started in on the longest talk I ever heard of; I don't know what he is talking about; Simmons says he is talking for us. He began the talk about noon and he was still talking when I fell asleep at midnight. . . ."

"All's well that ends well. We were told this morning what the verdict was. If we go on down the river they will kill us; if we go back they will give us horses to go with. A bunch of horses were driven up and given to us. I got a blind-eyed black and another plug for my three; the rest of the boys in the same fix, except Bill, he got his three back. We got our saddles, a hundred pounds of flour, some coffee, sugar, one plug of tobacco and two robes each for our clothes and blankets; glad to get so much. It did not take us long to saddle up. Simmons asked us what was best for him to do, stop with the Indians or go with us. I spoke for the boys and told him he had better stay with the Indians, if he was afraid to risk his scalp with white men. He stayed. We got away at last. Harry Rogers was riding by my side. I asked him what he thought would be the outcome. His answer was, 'God is good.' The Indians told us to cross at the ford and go up the south side of the river. We met an old Indian woman and she told us not to cross the ford. She made us understand that if we did we would all be killed. When we came to the ford we camped and got something to eat, and when it was dark saddled up and traveled all night; took to the hills in the morning; we were about forty or forty-five miles from our friends, the Indians. . . ."

12

My first intimation of what had happened came along in the early afternoon.

I had spent a very pleasant morning teaching Red Bear's tiny wife the intricacies of telling time. I owned an old stem-winding pocket watch of German silver, once belonging to my foreign-born grandfather. It was an ingenious affair of Swiss manufacture which struck a miniature fairy bell on the hour. A striking pocket watch in those days was not something one could buy in every general store. Even urban white men were intrigued by my museum piece, and the wonders it wrought with Lisa Red Bear was her childish faith and delight in the fact (supplied by me) that unless she pressed her ripe lips to mine, on the hour, "the little iron sun" would not make its magic sound.

Of course this was all in the spirit of fun on my part, as what normally healthy young man is going to miss out on any clear chances to taste a new and lovely pair of lips? Lisa regarded it in the same way. At least she did for the first two demonstrations. On the third one her soft bare arms went around my neck and—well—it was time to put the watch away. This worked out rather fortuitously for both of us I should imagine, as we might otherwise have had to call off the game on account of darkness; same being caused by the sudden looming of Red Bear's huge bulk in the lodge's entrance the very next moment.

As it was, I think we were saved by the fact that the Crow chief had just come in out of bright sunlight and had not yet adjusted his eyesight to the inner gloom. For the way his child-bride rolled back away from me and to her feet, blushing and giggling and smoothing her doeskin camp dress, must surely, were this not the case, have alerted the most trusting spouse. However, I must say one never knew with Indians. One time they were perfectly capable of insisting that you sleep with their favorite squaw as a matter of minimum courtesy to an honored guest: the very next they might puncture your spleen with a skinning knife for looking sideways at the ugliest old hag in their harem. It was one of the things which always inclined me in the Indian favor. I have always loved surprises and they were full of them.

In this case, however, the surprise was not a pleasant one. Red Bear had brought disconcerting news. He did not like what he had to tell me, but he would try to be brave about it. Would I try to be the same? Good.

Start off then, he said, with a little cheerful tidbit: he, Red Bear, had succeeded in buying off the prisoners. They were just now gone safely out of camp, all five of them.

All *five* of them? I did not need to state the question in words; my startled expression did it for me.

Yes, he nodded, I had heard him right. One of the six white men had decided that his chances were better if he stayed in the village. He seemed to think that the Crows were going to chase after his friends and kill them, as soon as they turned them loose. He had told his friends this, as his excuse for staying with the Indians, but his friends had not believed him. They had looked at him with bad hearts, and Red Bear did not blame them. The Crow chief did not like a man who would desert his friends in a time of danger.

To tell the truth, I did not know what to think of Simmons' peculiar action myself. It was a puzzler to begin with and, so far as I ever heard, remained one to end with. The usual explanation behind such occasional defections lay in the timely and deliberate acquisition of some susceptible squaw's favor, the latter then interceding for her new white love and, generally, being allowed to "walk off" with her doubtful prize.

Whether Simmons saved his hair by this method or whether, indeed, he saved it by any method at all, I never learned. Years after, I did hear a rumor that a white man of his description was living with a younger sister of Little Crow's—a clubfooted girl who had known some difficulty in attracting a mate among her own people—but squawman talk of this kind was always going around the settlements and I personally give it little credence.

At the moment of Red Bear's report on the council's decision, moreover, I was not nearly so interested in the price Simmons may have paid for his life as I was in that certainly paid by Red Bear for the lives of his five former friends. Something told me the latter figure had been an exorbitant one. It had.

To secure Little Crow's agreement to the release of the Fairweather party, the huge chief now told me, he had been forced to promise *not* to let me depart: he had, in effect, he reluctantly admitted, *traded my life, five-for-one to Little Crow, for the lives of my friends!*

I was stunned. I could not believe that I had heard him right, and told him so. He assured me that my ears had been uncovered and that I had understood him correctly. Little Crow owned me now and would be coming soon to claim me. How soon? That same night. Within the hour.

What did Little Crow mean to do with the white brother? Ah, that was the bad part. There was a burning pole being erected, even now, in front of the medicine lodge. A dance circle was being marked off around it. Wood was being brought in and piled up. Yes, it was all being done for the white brother with the red beard.

Eh? What was that? How did it feel to be burned?

"Bad, brother, very bad. The happiest thing which can happen is that a man's heart fails him at the first heat, and so he dies before he sees his skin begin to peel off and his fat hiss into the climbing fire."

I looked at him a long, cold-bellied minute.

"I know a better way to die than that, *brother*," I told him, tooth-clenched. "Give me back my rifle and one bullet."

He crossed over to me and put his red hand on my shoulder.

"Me sorry," he said. "Him no good."

And with that he turned his back on me and stalked out of the lodge without another word or backward look.

Well, I still had one chance. Lisa, the Indian girl. The little soft-lipped charmer with the woman's body and the child's mind. She I could possibly corrupt. At least I had her to hand where I could work on her.

Turning from my barren appeal to her craggy-faced mate, I broke out my best gleaming smile and dug in my hunting-shirt pocket for Grandfather Sutter's old reliable Swiss squaw bait.

I was left with my smile spread wide and my Swiss watch dangling. The girl was gone.

They had me chained like a dog. Around my neck was a collar of crudely forged soft iron, lined with buffalo hide. This was fastened by a rusty wagon-box padlock and from it a length of lightweight trace chain, still charred from the fire which had gutted the covered wagon whose tailgate it once lowered, ran to a green cottonwood stake mauled two feet into the hard ground.

I had chain enough to walk around freely on all fours. I could not stand up, nor could I crawl far enough to see out the door of the lodge. Save for the darkening strip of sky visible through the smoke hole overhead, I may as well have been buried in a cave. My only means of getting free would be to get that stake out of the ground. To accomplish that with my bare hands was impossible. I had found this out by trying it until my palms were like pounded meat, my fingers stripped of skin.

As the smoke hole lost its blue to the gray intrusion of twilight, then turned velvet-black to show the lone twinkle of the first star, I gave up the idea that I was going to get away either by my own or anyone else's efforts.

My main hope all along had been the girl. But when full dark struck and the drums began to thump over by the dance square, I decided the rest of it was between me and that reference up yonder, whom I had last approached with regard to sticking me with George Ives as a self-elected camp pal.

I set my jaw and began to shake a mental fist skyward. I didn't even get the first surly growl out. There was a slithering rip from the darkness to the rear of the lodge. The side-skins parted and Lisa Red Bear stepped through them behind the slitting glide of the knife. While I glanced swiftly upward to beg a generous God's humble forgiveness for my angry doubts, she stole by me to check the guard out front. She was back in an instant, smiling her satisfaction with the arrangements so far.

There was no talk. In the first place, none could be risked. In the second place, neither of us spoke more than six words of the other's tongue. We made do with that most wonderful and eloquent of all languages, that of the hand sign.

She had with her the big wood maul used to put down tethering stakes and the like. Hefting it, she made clear to me that I was to make a slight noise—a scuffle—to bring the guard in. He was alone out there and since he had just come on duty, would not be changed before the ceremony. When I nodded that I understood, she slipped to the door.

It went like a merchant's hand over a bolt of imported silk. No sound, and slick as the inside of a willow whistle. I scuffled the lodge floor with my feet, made a low noise in my throat. The guard was inside the entrance flaps in two long strides. Halfway through the third stride he was stretched flat by the accurate, solid "ka-chuck" of the maul going home behind his left ear. Once his face bounced in the dirt of the fireside, he did not move. Grinning proudly, Lisa bent over him.

It now became apparent why we must have the guard. On a heavy copper wire around his neck, he carried the key to the ancient padlock.

When Lisa got my dog collar off, she pointed to the unconscious brave, circling her own slender throat with a delicate forefinger to indicate the logical extension.

I patted her on the head—she barely reached above my elbow—like one would reward a good child or a favored spaniel, and dragged the fellow over and locked him up in the collar. When he was chained, Lisa took an eight-inch stick about one inch in diameter and a stout buckskin thong out of the pocket of the man's hunting shirt she was wearing. Stuffing the buck's mouth with a big wad of mattress moss pulled out of Red Bear's pallet, she jammed the stick crosswise between his teeth and cinched it cruelly down upon his tongue with the rawhide drawn up around the back of his head. This was my first introduction to the "Absaroka hackamore," a superlatively efficient gag, albeit one which occasionally suffocated its unfortunate wearers.

I was in no position, however, to question my young friend's lack of moral compunction. If that guard-buck strangled, he strangled in a fine and worthy cause—mine.

I patted Lisa again and indicated somewhat nervously that in my opinion it was well past time to go. She shook her head, giggled, patted my watch pocket. This was no time to haggle. I grabbed out the damned thing and handed it over to her, again pointing the exit slit in the rear wall. She handed the watch back, once more shaking her dark head.

I glared at her. She laughed happily. Pouting her glistening lips she touched first them, then mine, with a cool finger tip. Then, closing her eyes and turning up her lovely face, she put her hands behind her back, poised herself on tiptoe and stood there waiting like a mischievous imp of twelve. I kissed her, and like no imp of twelve, and we got out of there.

13

Red Bear's lodge was on the north edge of the village, which in turn was on the north bank of the Yellowstone. The site lay in a sprawling, open loop of meadowland backed by low hills and heavy stands of lodgepole and bullpine. It was no more than twenty yards from the knife-slit rear wall of the chief's dwelling to the inky black of the timber. We were under cover in less than a minute.

The darkness was not stygian: it was something about three caverns back from that. I made no objection to Lisa's taking my hand and leading me through it at a dogtrot. I got whipped cruelly about the face with small limbs but I was getting spurred from the rear by the pulsing beat of the Crow drums building up for my bonfire, and so had no difficulty keeping up.

After about ten minutes of this blind marathon through the timber, we came into a small pothole meadow. Here in the starlight the blackness lessened a bit, and here Lisa called a halt.

I felt her little finger on my lips warning me to be still. I nodded, joining her in listening for sounds of pursuit. There were none. But there were some other noises.

I cocked my ear. Horses. Near by. Snuffling and stomping. And beyond them, somewhere, the sound of running water.

Alarmed, I tried whispering to Lisa. It was no use. Her ten-word English vocabulary was not up to the demand, and the darkness was too thick for hand signs. Again I had to trust her, following along helplessly as she took my hand to guide me on across the small meadow. When we reached the far side I saw beyond the thinning timber, the starlit run of the Yellowstone. Near at hand, in an alder thicket I heard again the stamp of the horses. This time there was the jingle of a bit chain and the squeaking of a leather girth and I knew my Indian miss had somehow gotten out of the Crow pony herd not only a mount for me but a saddle and bridle as well. The second animal, I assumed, would be either a spare so that I might ride relays, or a pack horse. I was right with minor reservations.

There were three, not two horses, and two of the three were saddled. The third was a pack animal. And very well packed at that.

If I had missed the significance of the arrangement to my surprised count, I would have caught it a moment later from the glistening smile with which Lisa led out the three hidden animals. I had been wasting my time standing there composing my grateful farewell while she went to get my ponies.

They were not my ponies, they were our ponies. This was no good-bye, it was a beginning. Lisa Red Bear was going with me.

If those statements appear rather bald and unadorned, that is the elemental way they went through my mind: one, two, three—just like that—she had me trapped!

But I was here in no better position to argue about her accompanying me than I had been about the kiss in the lodge. I swung up on my mount, not even surprised by this time that it was Cassius. How she had gotten the miserable brute to stand for saddling I will never know. All I knew at the moment was that from then on nothing, absolutely nothing that this graceful slip of a red child might come forth with, was going to ambush my expectations. She was clearly capable of anything.

We set off east along the Yellowstone. My companion was in no hurry, which I thought strange and let her know as much. Moving along the open river bank was quite another matter of illumination from the cave-black foothill track by which we had circled through the timber to get out and around the village. Hence we could catch one another's hand signs fairly well, aided as we were both by the direct starlight and its gleaming reflection from the riffling surface of the Yellowstone.

By the time we had a little lather lacing the inner rub of our horses' rear quarters, Lisa Red Bear had brought me crudely up to date. She had made up her mind to run away with me the minute she heard her oversized mate announce in the lodge that he had traded my life to Little Crow. All the arrangements for the ponies had been made by her mother, who could do this sort of thing with no fear of being suspected by Red Bear since tribal custom forbade a man to look upon his mother-in-law or her to speak to him, or either of them to have any social intercourse with one another whatever.

I could not help but think, even in the extremity of my situation, what a delightfully logical law this was. But my approval of the Crow denigration of mothers-in-law was a bit premature. Meanwhile, Lisa's story went on swiftly.

The matter of the ponies had no more than been disposed of when Little Crow's sister let drop at the riverside washing place that her brother had no intention of honoring his bargain with Red Bear. As soon as darkness came down to hide their movements, he and a number of braves meant to ride up the river and wipe out the freed white men when they crossed the Yellowstone in the morning, as they had been instructed to do when leaving the village.

When the gossip came to Lisa she had at once sent her tough old mother trotting off upstream to the white camp at the upper ford. Her equally tough young daughter's instructions were for her to warn the white men that they must break their camp as soon as it was dark, and flee the night through *along the north bank*. By no means, if they valued their lives, were they to cross over to the south bank as Little Crow had advised on turning them loose.

My lithe red guide had complete confidence both in her mother's integrity and Little Crow's crookedness. The one could be trusted to see that the whites stayed on the north bank, the other to stick to his plan to sneak up the south. If all worked well—and we would know very soon if it had—we should come upon the track of the fleeing white men with first daylight, some thirty miles from Red Bear's village.

It did not occur to me to wonder by what agency we were so soon "to know" whether or not Lisa's mother had succeeded in carrying out their mission. By the time it had, we were already at the upper crossing and it was too late.

The infallible agency was, of course, "Mama" herself.

The Crow squaw was waiting for us in a clump of willows close by the place where the regular trail went over to the south bank. She came trotting out of her cover, strung together about two yards of Absaroka talk for Lisa's benefit, scrambled up on the pack horse, jerked its lead rope out of my startled hand and beamed at me, *"Hopo!* white son. Let's go!"

With that she led off up the Yellowstone, belting the poor pack horse with the rope end and sing-songing a Crow chant in a spirit obviously as light-minded as though she were stringing bear claws or beading moccasins back in the snug safety of her village lodge.

Since Lisa followed her without hesitation or explanation of what she had said, leaving me alone upon the banks of the brawling Yellowstone somewhere under five miles from the proposed site of the McCandles barbecue, I was faced with a decision: to trust and stay with my Indian rescuers, or to strike out at once upon my own?

I stared nervously up and down the river, thought I had never seen such a black and ugly stream and wound up peering through the night after my departed companions.

What were they up to and what should I do about it? Did they intend to desert me? Or was the choice mine, and should I avail myself of it to get shut of them? Were they bluffing me, or was I bluffing myself? Did they know I would follow them, and want me to do so? Did I have any real choice not to, since I did not know the trail? And if that *was* my only choice—to trust and stay with them—was the addition of the obviously feeble-minded older squaw to our company too great a price to pay for a local guide?

It came to me abruptly that there was no real comparison between receiving Little Crow's arrows in my rear and accepting Red Bear's mother-in-law on my front. I winced at the thought of the former, scowled at the prospect of the latter, and so was able to resolve my hesitation in something less than five seconds. There was a time, I told myself, for live cowards to outrank dead heroes.

With the decision, I dug my heels into Cassius' startled

flanks, shook out his reins, gave the roan his ugly head and some muttered instructions to "move." He did, and caught me up with the two squaws in fifteen jumps. I smiled at Lisa, she smiled at her mother, the latter turned and beamed beatifically on her "new white son."

Frantically, I questioned Lisa to make sure I understood this welcome. No, the slender beauty assured me, there was no mistake. Mama liked me fine. Moreover, I would learn to return the affection in time. Meanwhile, her mother's slight added weight would be no handicap to the pack horse. We had a good start on Red Bear and Little Crow, and there was no reason in the Indian world why we should not make a very happy family.

The old woman could cook and sew. I, Red Beard, could make weapons and bring in meat. Lisa would share her white love's blanket and make memorable to him every waking moment he spent upon it. These conditions guaranteed, what other things in life were there? Eat, hunt, sleep, make love. Could Red Beard name another? Red Beard could not.

For lack of a better answer he nodded and rode on, scowling as all men have ever scowled when brought to the altar bound and gagged by their own overplayful brilliance.

Above the ensuing happy shuffle of unshod Indian pony hoofs along the loamy river trail ahead of Cassius and himself, he was suddenly conscious of the very loud ticking of Grandpa Sutter's solid silver pocket watch.

Seizing the cursed instrument, he was about to fling it from him into the swiftest water of the passing Yellowstone, when, perversely, its tiny chime struck the darkened hour. It was the smallest sort of a silvery little sound, but the ear of an Indian can hear a mouse sneeze in dusty grass. Instantly, Lisa's happy laugh echoed. As quickly, she spun her pony around, reined him up alongside Cassius, tilted up her shapely head and pouted her red lips. Red Beard did what he had to do.

When he was done with it, he put the watch very carefully back in his pocket and told Cassius, the strawberry roan, to get along up the trail and never mind walling his eyes so wise and wicked—a man meant only to see what time it was in the first place.

Contrary to my own wishes, we did not at once move to come up with the fleeing white men. Indian logic prevailed upon Caucasian impulse.

Little Crow might be following swiftly from the ford. If he were, it would not be wise to join up with my pale-faced friends just yet. That would be like the crippled doe taking up with the wounded buck being trailed by wolves. Again,

77

Red Bear may have decided to investigate further the matter of his missing mate. If so, he would have a much more difficult time finding us, who were being very careful about our tracks, than the white party who were not. Above all, discretion, as well as cowardly self-interest, pointed a course of hanging back on the Fairweather party's trail and waiting to see what might develop by way of pursuit.

This wild-animal wariness made sense. Moreover, I was having the time of my thirty-year-old life.

It must be remembered that during those early sixties the Yellowstone Valley was a virgin wilderness, practically untraveled by white men. Famed Luther S. Kelly, the dashing Irish army scout who knew it better than any man who ever lived, did not set foot in Montana Territory until 1868. And even as long after that as 1876, Captain John G. Bourke, Crook's doughty adjutant, referred to it in his notes as "a trackless *terra incognita*," concerning which there existed very little useful information and absolutely no accurate charts.

If, thirteen years later, the United States Army found it "trackless," one can only imagine what it was in '63. It was a paradise on earth, peopled only by the vast herds of ruminant game, packs of predators, colonies of fur-bearers, shoals of sporting fish, flocks of water and upland fowl, whistling, beautiful bands of swift wild horses and, always, the carefree, nomad High Plains Indian. Here came, in season, the various tribes of the Crow, Gros Ventre, Piegan, Blood, Blackfoot, Arapahoe, Cheyenne, Shoshone, Sioux and Mandan to follow the buffalo whither he might wander through Montana's endless pastures. Here came, winter and summer, only the wild birds and the beasts of the field and the proud, untamed red man who was their brother and their keeper. It was a land as deep in Indian legend as it was shallow in white spoliation. Viewed as I was privileged to view it, through the eyes of Indian age and youth combined, it was a revelation of rare excitement and tender beauty.

Forgive the emotion if you will: let us go on to say in belated summation that, after my first twenty-four hours with them, I had precious little inclination to leave the company of Lisa Red Bear and her light-minded mother for that of William Fairweather and his retreating friends.

Now it must not be imagined that I had forgotten Elly Bryan. I most certainly had not. My thoughts were ever with her and my mind actively engaged at all times on the problem of returning to her at the earliest opportunity consistent with the minimum precautions of traveling safely through Crow country. These latter interests were being best served by our present course of hanging to the flank of the Fairweather party, which was heading back for Bannack with all speed; I must make a rendezvous with them for the purposes of re-outfitting myself for completion of my interrupted journey to Sun River.

As to any associations I was enjoying with Lisa which might reflect upon my loyalty to Elly, there simply were none. I was loving the nomad life, but not the nomad. And so passed the swiftest three weeks ever to disappear beneath the shifting sands of a happy man's memory.

On the night of May 24 we camped high on a beautiful ridge overlooking the Madison River. We had that day come over the Yellowstone-Missouri Divide, and were very weary. But we sat up late, nonetheless, for it was to be our final night alone. From her study of the horseprints of the Fairweather party made just before the day's last good light had gone, and seeing them as they were, firm and deep and sharpcut in the damp bank loam of the river-crossing below our camp, Singing Bird had said we were now but a two-hour lope behind the Deer Lodge men. Tomorrow, even dawdling by the way, we must come up with them by sunset. My feelings of sadness and regret at this information were genuine.

As I sat upon a lookout rock jutting from the face of the granite bastion atop which Singing Bird had advised we halt, so that we might with morning's light study our backtrail after the cautious Indian habit, I was suffering a very real sense of impending deprivement.

My gains of association with my little Crow family were in no way important save as enjoyable memories of an adventure shared by as strange a set of bedfellows as were ever made by Indian war or white politics.

Singing Bird, Lisa's mother, was well named. From dawn to dusk she whistled and sang and gave forth with the most amazing variation of perfect bird imitations conjurable from one human throat. Nor was this bright habit in any way tedious. She did not carry it on continuously, but only as some wild bird would speak to her, or as her own consistently sunny disposition demanded some little outlet in cheerful song. While she was admittedly a flighty one, her pixie intellect was amazingly sharp by certain and surprising turns.

There was for example the time, some days back, when I had asked her about the origin of Lisa's name, which was surely, one must admit, of peculiarly non-Absarokan design.

On that occasion Singing Bird had at once and soberly launched into the best capsule description of Manuel Lisa I had ever heard.

She took the famous Spanish trader of Old New Orleans from his early days among the southern Osages to his historic

79

forty-two-man expedition of 1807 up the Yellowstone, with its establishment of Montana's first trading post, Fort Ramon, and through the halcyon years of the beaver traffic when he had as many as 500 men working in the Upper Missouri country; and she did it all in less than fifty swift signs and the few dozen simple Crow words I had picked up in the past weeks. That done, she had added the fact that her father, Tall Elk, had trapped for the Spaniard some ten years. In appreciation for the faithful service Manuel Lisa had given him a pure white buffalo robe. Upon this robe she, Singing Bird, had borne her only daughter and when the old man had seen the child there he cried out that she must take the name of his benefactor and so that was how the girl had come to be called Lisa.

As for that capricious child of nature, herself, there are no words of proper delineation: nor are there any to outline exactly the way I felt about her.

I think that she, herself, said it best when, in that final twilight hour above the Madison, she came softly and without greeting to sit beside me upon the lookout rock and to share, beneath the candle-wink of the night's first-lit star, my silence and my solitude.

After a long, quiet time she simply took my hand, put it to her lips, kissed it through the silken caress of a tear and left me there in the darkness as she had found me.

14

The next day, the twenty-fifth, we crossed the Madison and went west a little ways to the foot of the Tobacco Roots, where we found the past night's camp of the Fairweather party. Following their trail, we went on angling southwest from there up into some rough country which marked the joining of the Tobacco Root and the Gravelly Range, and started dropping down along a little creek on the other side. This looked to me like it ought to be a tributary of the Stinking Water. Shortly, from a high place, I saw that it was, as I could make out the course of the big stream away off where it bent around the north end of the Ruby Mountains to join into the Jefferson.

Pretty quick I noticed something else, as well. Our friends, who had been slowing down to do a little offhand prospecting the minute they got out of the Yellowstone drainage, had stopped up ahead and pitched an early camp in a high-up gulch of this little side creek. I decided from this that they must have spotted some interesting color and were meaning to stay for a spell. This being the case, there was no point in delaying the inevitable. I started my little caravan on down the creek and about noon we came into their camp.

They were some surprised to see us. And more so when I told them my story and introduced myself as W. C. Mc-Candles of Bannack.

They could not believe I had been in the Crow village with them but a few quick questions and answers convinced them otherwise. They remembered Singing Bird, of course, and had not forgotten their debt of gratitude to her. We were made more than welcome and, come sunset that night, we had about as jolly a fire as you can imagine.

The men in that historic party were, in addition to the New Brunswick Canadian, William Fairweather, a rollicking Irishman named Barney Hughes; Thomas Cover from Ohio; Henry Rogers, a native of Newfoundland; the pawky Scotsman, Henry Edgar and a Saint John's River man called Mike Sweeney.

From the list it can be seen that I was earlier wrong in calling it a party of six. With the defecting Simmons, it had originally numbered seven, of course, but no matter the number. They were a good crowd and we got along first-rate.

They, like myself, bless their rough, woman-lonely souls, fell completely for the captivating Lisa Red Bear. It was laughable to watch grown men stumbling over one another, in a prospecting camp 800 miles from the nearest decent civilization, to be gallant to ninety pounds of giggling Indian girl who had never seen a settlement bigger than Fort Benton and who neither spoke nor understood fifteen words of English.

Yet it was a little sad, too, for it made me suddenly conscious of the incongruity of this slim savage in white surroundings, forcing me to think ahead to what I was going to do about her now that Bannack was so near.

However, sufficient unto the day the troubles thereof. For the moment I was content to laze back outside the fire's warm glow and watch my pretty Lisa enjoying the rude court paid her by the six beauty-starved miners. Tomorrow was a brand-new dawn and was sure to bring a solution of acceptable sorts.

After a pleasant talk with Henry Edgar during which we compared journals and as a result of which I prevailed upon him not to include in his diary any mention of me nor of my preceding Crow adventure until such time as I might have found proper solution for the embarrassing matter of Lisa Red Bear, I sought my blankets with every prospect for an excellent night's sleep. Edgar was an understanding fellow and winked broadly when I mentioned the Indian girl in connection with my position as hopeful suitor for the legal favors of a certain fine young Montana lady of local residence and undoubted dim views of sharing her red-bearded fiancé with shapely Crow squaws. The good-natured Scot assured me he would not record a line of the matter until I had made my peace with Elly Bryan and only then with my express permission. Meanwhile he would be grateful, he said, if I might find the time to edit his present notes, as they were nowhere near as eruditely set down as my own. On the exchanged promises, we said good night.

The following day began as ordinarily as a day can. We all got up late, taking a leisurely breakfast and loitering around camp most of the morning. Rogers, Hughes, Sweeney and Thomas Cover went off after a bit to do some half-hearted prospecting. Fairweather and Henry Edgar got to some doctoring they had to do with three or four lame horses in their string, but shortly tired of that, took pick and pan, and set off after the others. Singing Bird had wandered off up the gulch after a pair of wild canaries whose chatter intrigued her; Lisa had trailed behind her, with a mind to take a bath upstream out of sight of camp. Left alone with the coals of the breakfast fire and a quarter of a pot of coffee, I was idling in complete contentment when I saw Bill Fairweather legging it back to camp from downstream.

He had the certain look of a man in a hurry who does not want others to think he is in the least worked up. You sense that in a man, particularly in a prospecting man. I knew instantly that he had found something. He had, indeed.

And to tell you what it was, no words can better Henry Edgar's, as he put it down that night by the light of the most excited fire ever built in the mountains of Montana:

". . . Friend Bill and I won the camp work this morning and in no great hurry to get on with it. We washed and doctored the horses' legs. Bill went across to a bar to see or look for a place to stake the horses. When he came back to camp he said, 'There is a piece of rimrock sticking off the bar over there. Get the tools and we will go and prospect it.' Bill got the pick and shovel and I the pan and went over. Bill dug the dirt and filled the pan. 'Now go,' he says, 'and wash that pan and see if we can get enough to buy some tobacco when we get to town.' I had the pan more than half panned down and had seen some gold as I ran the sand around, when Bill sang out, 'I have found a scad.' I returned for answer, 'If you have one I have a hundred.' He then came down with his scad to where I was. It was a nice piece of gold. Well, I panned the pan of dirt and it was a good prospect; weighed it and had $2.40; weighed Bill's and it weighed the same. Pretty good for tobacco money. We went and got another pan and Bill panned that and got more than

I had; I got the third one and panned that—best of the three; that is good enough to sleep on. We came to camp, dried and weighed our gold. Altogether there was $12.30. We saw the boys coming to camp and no tools with them. 'Have you found anything? We have started a hole but didn't get to bedrock.' They began to growl about the horses not being taken care of and to give Bill and me fits. When I pulled the pan around, Sweeney got hold of it and the next minute sang out, 'Salted!' I told Sweeney that if he would pipe me and Bill down and run us through a sluice box he couldn't get a color,' and that 'the horses could go to the devil or the Indians.' Well, we talked over the find and roasted venison till late; and sought the brush and spread our robes; and a more joyous lot of men never went more contentedly to bed than we . . ."

And there is the way, exactly as told by one of the two men who stumbled upon it, that the richest "single-pocket" placer diggings in the world were turned up.

Two rough and crusty Montana prospectors had shirked their camp chores to "try a pan for luck." One of them had struck his pick into a promising piece of rimrock and sung out to the other, "I have found a scad!" It was as simple as that.

Except for this: When Bill Fairweather's "scad" had been finally mined out, from first creek-bed discovery to farthest high dry gravel, there had been taken from the little brushy gulch above the Stinking Water no less than a hundred million dollars in raw yellow gold.

15

It took the next two days to get the horses doctored up fit to travel and the party started on to Bannack, where it must go to lay in the supplies needed to work its new find. The main work of getting the camp shipshape was done on the twenty-seventh, with the twenty-eighth devoted to staking the claims. The generous members of the lighthearted group wanted to "stake me in" with the rest, but I would not agree, saying that I was not a legitimate member of their or of Stuart's original group, and that I would be obliged if they just left me out of their plans, as I had some of my own which would not wait.

I will not attempt to defend this stubborn viewpoint. It was a combination of my German-Swiss bullheadedness and my Scotch pride. I had never in my life taken a nickel from anyone which I had not earned, and I did not propose to begin with these good and overly open-handed souls.

I must confess, too, that I had no rightful idea of the extent of their strike. I was no mining man. Twelve dollars for three pans was high I knew. Yet I knew, as well, that such washings were usually limited to small pockets. In the grossest error of judgment in gold-strike history, I airily declined the offer of the Fairweather men on the strength of my ignorant opinion that their find would "wash out" in thirty days, like a hundred others before it.

Failing to carry their generous point they pressed me to know if there was not something they could fetch me from Bannack. To this I said yes. There were indeed now several things I needed, since I had announced to them my change of intention to accompany them back to town. I gave them the list—bacon, coffee, sugar, tobacco, the usual standards—and left them to their happy labors, the while I climbed up the gulch in search of solitude. There was some final thinking to do on the rough plan I had in mind.

Briefly, my decision to stay behind had been reached with a view to avoiding taking Lisa into the settlement and, at the same time, to be alone with the two Crow women should there be any "scene" when I apprised them of my pledge to Elly Bryan with its certain necessity of my parting company with them before returning to her. In fact, the main idea of my remaining in the Fairweather camp was to effect the anticipatedly painful business of this parting. And, after that, to start out for Sun River the moment my "Fairweather" friends got back with my supplies.

About a quarter-mile above camp I found my spot. It was a beautiful little amphitheatre formed by a small landslide blocking the creek and creating a miniature lake all surrounded and sheltered by the thick green growth of alders which characterized "our gulch." I selected a seat beneath a clump of scrub pine overlooking this fairy pool and began to rehearse the curtain speech I must next day make to Lisa and her mother.

Oddly enough, I got nowhere. I had come up there quite made up in mind; now no part of my plan seemed to fit into place with the slim, graceful picture of Red Bear's wife which insisted on obtruding itself upon my imagination. Presently I gave up. The damned odium of the chore might just as well be left for tomorrow. It could be made no more hateful by a good night's rest and might indeed be made a good deal less difficult.

I got up and went back down the gulch, nodding to myself. At camp I found everything set for an early morning departure, even the last detail of "naming the discovery" having been cleaned up in my short absence.

It was the gregarious Bill Fairweather who had come up with the winning combination, and he had picked a good one. It was "Alder Gulch."

Bright and early the morning of the twenty-ninth, the boys set out for Bannack. We had a good breakfast of fried bread, antelope steaks and cold water to see them off. And quite rightly it was time for them, or someone, to go. We had used the last of our coffee on "discovery day," had been out of bacon, sugar, baking soda and salt for the past twenty-four hours; and had, none of us, had a smoke since the first week out of Red Bear's village. I envied them a little as I watched them ride out of sight down the gulch. You will never know why. For their rich dust and fabulous luck? Not for a minute. It was the mouth-watering thought that next morning they would be feasting on Salt Lake ham, settlement eggs and Idaho potatoes fried in Oregon butter brought 700 miles up the Snake from head-of-navigation at Lewiston.

However, drooling over their gustatory good fortune was not going to solve my problems. Taking a firm grip on the nape of my wavering gumption, I turned to face the principal one of these. And got the first shock of the morning. Sometime between the last bite of unsalted antelope and the final parting wave down the gulch, Lisa had disappeared.

Singing Bird was doing up the dishes and arguing back and forth with a mountain jay who was watching her and waiting for his morning food-scrap from our plates.

Consulting her, I learned her daughter had *"gone climb him hill make clean"* (walked up the gulch to take a bath) and would be back *"heap quick do me here"* (to help her with the camp work). Not caring to wait that long with my bad news and thinking to catch the girl before she got started on her ablutions—a daily ritual with all plains Indians where possible—I made off up the stream after her.

Five minutes later I was catching my breath above the little alder-rimmed pool—and not from the stiff climb either. For a day of shocks, this second one was a pure beauty. Viewed thus, from pine-scented ambush, not thirty paces distant and clad only in a gown of blue sky and mountain sunshine, the glowing copper body of Lisa Red Bear would have trapped the respiration of any man alive. As for me, it made the world stand still. I was undressed in a moment, down to the pool in another. Calling softly, so as not to alarm her, I spoke her name.

She turned three-quarters toward me, one slender foot still poised, testing the stream's temperature. Again, I spoke her name—and nothing more. She straightened and came toward

85

me, calmly and unafraid. The sunlight danced in her dark eyes. Her slim red arms opened gladly to receive, with the clinging welcome of her sweet lips, her man who had been so unaccountably long delayed in the time of his coming to her.

Lisa was nothing like her civilized white sister. She, the actual savage, was much more deeply shy, far more poignantly tender with her love. With the one the act of love was a full right of equal sharing, with the other it was a limited privilege of total surrender.

Of the two, a man will remember the first with passion, the second with pride. There is no denying the physical excitement of the elemental female, the eternal, the bold-eyed Eve. Yet who will say, having known both, that she is the wearing superior of the quiet one who stands and waits? Who will insist the assault of the huntress is more arousing than the submission of the hunted?

I certainly did not know these answers then, for at thirty a man has yet to learn life's great truth: that as passion is the first thing which will die in him, so pride is the last. Given my free choice of the civilized and the savage loves there in that languorous moment of recovery upon the sun-warmed sands of the alder pool, I could not have made a decision to save my life.

Fortunately, I was not required to. Not on that basis. There was a decision to be made, all right. And one that surely involved the safety of my corporate shell. But it did not arise from either Lisa or myself, nor from the intimate nature of our situation. As a matter of fact, it came from downcanyon and upon the wings of a peculiar birdcall from Lisa's mother.

The moment she heard the distressful, off-key notes—like those of a hurt or highly excited songster—the Indian girl rolled away from my side, reaching for her doeskin camp dress in the same motion which brought her crouching to her feet. I followed suit and without discussion.

The magic hour was over. No lectures were needed to demonstrate the conclusion. Reclothed, we scrambled up the side of the gulch, heading for the downcanyon vantage point of my clump of scrub pine. When we reached it, to peer over its rocky rim into the campsite below, I had the elements of my decision.

Spread in a circle around the fast-jabbering, gesturing Singing Bird, were Little Crow and two dozen scowlingly interested Absaroka warriors. Their ponies stood hipshot and head-down, stained with the dust and lather of long travel. They did not move their trailing reins, save to bite at the black-and-white deerflies or to flick their ears free of the swarming creek-gnats, familiar to every mountain camper.

Their slant-eyed masters listened without interruption to the shrill instructions of Red Bear's mother-in-law, and as they did, the latter's daughter translated them for me.

In essence, Singing Bird urged the newcomers to hurry. Red Beard and her errant child had just left with the white miners for Bannack. They had not been gone an hour. If they did not believe that, let them examine the tracks going down the little stream. Singing Bird was the only one here. Singing Bird and that ugly roan horse of Red Beard's standing over there. See the monster? Across the creek there? He is lame. Look at that bad hock. That is why they left him here with me. All the others are gone. Look for yourself. I have work to do. Out of my way, loafers!

It was a superb bluff; I could have kissed the old lady for it, and small wonder. The only thing wrong with Cassius' hock was a great splotch of antelope grease he had acquired in kicking over our dripping bucket the night before. And the sole reason he had been left behind when our other mounts went along to serve as extra pack ponies, was that neither Bill Fairweather nor Henry Edgar would touch him, let alone try to put a pack on him.

Singing Bird's bluff worked. The Crows already knew Cassius. They dismissed him with a sneer and got back on their own potbellied scrubs. All right, *hopo!* Let's go. If the old woman lies, we will come back and cut her throat. Or maybe slit her crooked tongue, so that she can really whistle like a bird. Small matter. Right now we want Red Beard and the girl.

They turned away down Alder Creek, riding fast behind Little Crow. A hundred yards below the camp a familiar giant figure came out of the brush to join them. Red Bear. Once, just before the final turn in the gulch, Little Crow looked back at Singing Bird. Red Bear never did. The mother-in-law taboo was still sacred. Circumstances did not alter Indian cases.

With that still moment in the rocks above the Fairweather camp in Alder Gulch began the roughest retreat since Hugh Glass crawled away from his grizzly.

Speaking exactly, it did not begin until some ten minutes later—after Lisa and I had slid down the gulch and heard Singing Bird's report—but I date our flight from the first minute I laid eyes on Little Crow; for, figuratively, I was off and running in the space of time it took me to gasp and duck back down behind our upcanyon rockpile.

Yet it was in camp that things really began to move. While I ran for Cassius, Singing Bird was tying up a flour sack containing all our food (about twenty pounds of flour, ten of antelope loin, some wild onions) and Lisa was furling our blankets into a saddle roll. I had the roan ready to travel, everything tied on him good and tight, in five minutes. Thinking that was it, I ordered the two women aboard, saying I would take Shank's mare one way while they kicked Cassius the other, figuring thus to give the Crows two trails to unravel instead of one. This did not wash.

In the first place Singing Bird had not meant to go with us at all. Certainly Little Crow would soon be back and certainly he would have caught up with our friends and found she had lied to him about us being with them. What difference? By tribal law Red Bear could not harm her, nor could he stand by while anyone else did. She was the mother-in-law. The son by marriage might treat her like a dog, but like a dog he had to take care of her too. He could not mistreat her, so think no more about it.

Further, Singing Bird had no intention of admitting that she had helped us away, or that we had even been there.

Of course the Crows would see that the horse was gone. But they knew he was a devil and she would tell them he had pulled his stake and run off and that if they wanted him let them go get him, for she would not chase him five paces except to shoot him for dogmeat.

In any event she, Singing Bird, was remaining behind to do what she could to throw them off our track, or to hold them back from it as long as she could. She was safe no matter how things went. We were not. Where was the argument? There was none.

Lisa kissed her and even I picked her up and gave her a big hug. She slapped me and kicked me in the shins for my trouble, but she liked the idea nonetheless. She was quite a woman, was Singing Bird. In the main I had enjoyed very much having her for a twenty-four-day mother-in-law.

The last we saw of her was when she waved up to us as we rode over the ridge above camp, headed due east and back into Crow country. But we could still hear her cheerful debate with the mountain jays going on for quite a spell after we had dropped over the rise.

Our course was a calculated gamble. By going toward their country instead of my own (Bannack), I might make the Crows wonder which of us was aboard the roan, this leading to a delay while they cast clear around the camp for other escaping trails, either mine or Lisa's on foot. We had nothing to lose and any time we might gain was all to the good. To add what I could to our supply of the latter, I took Cassius over the rockiest, driest, most unlikely going I could find consistent with keeping up a good gait. No use leaving them a straightaway set of prints and, moreover, a wandering set might possibly sell them on Singing Bird's story that the red roan had run away. For the first few miles I even trailed his rope and picket-stake to foster the illusion.

The deception seemed to be working, too. The first day we saw no following movement of any kind along our backtrail. Still, to be safe, we kept going after dark, pausing to cat-nap a few hours early the next morning. By ten o'clock we were moving once more and from then until full darkness stopped only for ten-minute trail breaks to stretch our cramped limbs, or to graze and water Cassius.

That second night we made a dark camp high up on the eastern side of the Madisons overlooking the wild canyon of the Gallatin. We had now come a total of thirty miles as the Crows would fly if they could. Again there had been no sign of pursuit the livelong day and we went to sleep with every hope and expectation that tomorrow would see us certainly free of them and allow me to make my southward circle back toward Bannack and real safety.

With first light, while Lisa broke camp, I shinnied up a granite outcrop to scan our backtrail. The view was superb—for about twenty seconds. Then I saw the dots moving down across a big rockslide we had negotiated the previous dusk. I studied them a moment longer to be sure they were red dots. They were. Now we had a horse race going.

I knew the Crows would never have come this far tracking a stray mount. We had not fooled them, save only long enough to keep them from running us down the first day. So from here on it was up to Cassius to show them that you can't judge a pony by his color nor the size of his big splayed feet. This was the place where my 1,100-pound outlaw plow horse was going to make those Indian scrubs yell uncle —and do it carrying double!

There was absolutely nothing right about Cassius, con-formation-wise, that would let him go a distance of ground in good time. He had the withers of a giraffe, the feet of a caribou, the croup of a dairy cow. His was the body of a camel crossed on a Clydesdale; the spirit of a tiger mated to a cape buffalo; the beauty of a wart-hog wooed by a mudlark. And all he did in the next nine days, over a tortuous steeple-chase course of some 300 mountain miles, beginning near the mouth of the Madison and ending halfway up the Big Horn, was run completely into the Montana dirt the picked war ponies of twenty-six Crow Indians.

From the first day to the last the Absarokas did not make up one mile of the five we had on them the morning I scram-bled down from my granite outcrop above the Gallatin and ran to give Lisa a leg-up on our mutual mount for the first running of the McCandles Handicap.

But with dusk of that ninth day we had made our race.

We were into an open grass country. There was little or no timber. Only low round hills. We still had the Crows headed but we had no place left to go.

Ahead, we saw the dark line of green brush along a sizeable stream which Lisa said was the main Greasy Grass— the Big Horn. Down there, she thought, we might find a place to make a decent thing of our last stand. At least we could get our backs to the water.

At the moment, we were standing on a little rise, letting Cassius blow out and grab a few mouthfuls of the new grass.

I had about decided on a last-ditch gamble: to let the Crows come up in sight and see us both dismounted on the knoll; then to strike Lisa suddenly down, leap upon the roan and ride off as though intent on saving myself. This way, my cornered thinking ran, she would be saved. Red Bear would surely take her back with no more than a good beating at that point. But if she stayed on with me until the shooting began, they might kill her right along with me in the general excitement.

But the race was not yet over. As our pursuers burst into view a mile away, Lisa seized my arm. *"Aki! Aki!"* she cried, pointing not to the oncoming Indians but toward the distant Big Horn. I spun around.

Camp smoke! Eighty miles up the Big Horn? Four hundred miles from nowhere? In the middle gut of Sioux and Cheyenne country?

What chance was there of it being *white* camp smoke? Not much, with one exception—it was a hell of a lot better chance than we stood with the Crows.

For the last time I gave my slim companion the leg-up on the rib-sunken roan; for the last time gave Cassius his homely head and let him run for the river. He made it with a few yards to spare and just as Little Crow and his braves were beginning to lob a few long rifle shots our way. When he slid to his stop, his great clumsy hoofs were practically in the campfire whose smoke had drawn us in on the 100-to-1 odds that its makers might be white men.

One Scotch-burred shout of unbelieving recognition from the bearded leader of the startled group let me know we had come under the wire at even greater odds than I had bargained for.

These were not only white men, they were *my* white men: James Stuart, S. T. Hauser, George Ives and Company; from Bannack, Montana by wandering way of Three Forks, the main Yellowstone, Pompey's Pillar and points south on the beautiful banks of the ever-loving Big Horn River!

This was the turning point of my Indian adventure. We had a very bad, all-night fight with the Crows, resulting in the death and severe wounding of some of our number. Morning's light showed us the enemy mysteriously gone. But Stuart, realizing they would be back and that, in any event, he could not now hope to return through their country as he had come, ordered the expedition to proceed southward toward Fort Bridger with all haste.

Striking the Sweetgrass River, we picked up the old emigrant road, marching without halt, save to sleep and eat, for two weeks and two days, coming thus to Bannack by way of the Bear River cut-off on the twenty-fourth day of June, 1863.

I thought it was the end of a long, tough trail. It was only the beginning.

16

Coming into Bannack that summer morning was like entering a city on the moon. The changes in the two and one-half months we had been away were unbelievable. My ex-employer had done his work well with that sign in the Denver bank window. The Colorado miners had liked the sound of the name of Grasshopper—they and some myriad others from every camp north of New Mexico and south of Great Slave Lake.

There had been 500 hardy souls in Bannack when the snow and I went out in April. God alone knew how many there were that June morning I shouldered my way down Main Street with Lisa at my heels and Cassius plodding along on a loose rope behind us. Thousands, anyway. As few as three, as many as five. And every single one of them out of their heads with gold fever.

The camp was a bedlam. The streets were mud up to a wheel hub or a whiffletree. Sidewalks of riven pine rambled along both flanks of the main stem, laid right down in the mud like corduroy fill in a logging road. Stacks of whipsawed lumber lay dumped everywhere; all so green that when the workman's hammer bit into it, water sprayed like blood from a bullet hole. On every hand buildings were going up. The construction material ran from unpeeled lodgepole pine to hand-split cedar to mill-cut lumber to alder poles set on end in the dirt to canvas stretched on ax-hewn cottonwood frames to actual stick-and-mud huts of Digger Indian design.

Men were everywhere and of every description, save that all had one common denominator—there were no old men. The old men never started or died on the trail. They did not get to the camps like Bannack. That was a thing I remember so clearly and which is so little mentioned by the ones who write about the old times: how very, very young we all were who were there and saw it happen.

Lisa and I forged on through the sweating, good-natured throng. We drew hardly a stare, which in itself is commentary enough on the bizarre origins of Bannack's population, as well as the intent busyness of each individual. I think that when a man with a bright red beard down to his brisket, auburn hair flowing like Samson's beyond his broad shoulders, dressed in strips of rotting buckskin, followed on the one hand by the smallest, most startlingly pretty Indian girl in Montana and on the other by the biggest, ugliest and most weirdly strawberry-colored saddle horse ever foaled—I say that when such a combination can stroll main street of a summer morning drawing no more comment than a pleasant "get the hell out of the way, will you, I'm in a hurry," then indeed you have got yourself a very busy and cosmopolitan little city.

Yet the very first repeated talk of which I became conscious as we went along was the astonishing fact that Bannack was on the downgrade! There was a new camp ninety miles off over toward the Tobacco Roots somewheres. Varnia, they were calling it; though there was a big argument going on up there right now to change that to Virginia because Varnia was the name of Jeff Davis's wife and there were too many Yanks around for that to set well.

Well, that just about took the rag off the bush. I shook my head and wondered a little bit about poor old Bill Fairweather and his bunch, who had thought they had the big strike in their little pocket up above the Stinking Water. A man felt sorry for them in a way, they were all of them such nice, open-handed fellows.

But my main worry right now was to find a place to clean up and to eat and get a decent sleep in a bed with sheets on it. Then a shave and a haircut and a grubstake. And after that some way to dispose decently of the question of Lisa Red Bear: most likely by placing her in the care of the nearby Bannacks.

The latter determination may seem cold-blooded. It was not. It was the kindest thing a white man could do under the circumstances. To keep an Indian girl of her wild good looks in a mining camp would be to see her degraded beyond tolerance, or yourself killed in the process of trying to prevent same. Which, in hard truth, was unpreventable. In that day and place an Indian woman was fair prey. If a comely one could be found and she resisted the finding, she would be raped as surely as a defiant camp bitch by the motley pack of panting village curs. I did not seek such an end for my little Lisa, nor did I wish to die in avoiding it. So the option was to get her out of town and back with her own kind at the earliest opportunity. I knew Black Blanket, the local Bannack chief, for a fine fellow, and was satisfied he would take charge of my Crow ward.

With these thoughts in mind I had spied just ahead a likely-looking log and shake-proof hostelry, the Bannack House, when my horrified glance took in something else, likewise just ahead.

It was a woman. A very young and lovely and smartly dressed white woman. And the last one in the Montana world I would have expected to meet on the streets of Bannack.

There was, however, no avoiding it on either of our parts. The press and crush of the crowd saw to that. The only bolster given me was that I saw in her face the same stricken look that had to be on mine. And so I removed my battered hat and braced my ragged shoulders for the blow.

"Good morning, Miss Elly, ma'am," I bowed, and had the good sense not to say any more, but to wait and see how the weather was going to go from there.

It went cold.

"Is it, Mr. McCandles?" she said.

"Elly . . ." I began.

"I got your note," she cut in. "There's nothing you can add to that surely."

"My note?" I said, stalling for time to think.

"Yes. It was a lovely sentiment. Educational, too."

I thought she sounded more hurt than cynical. I did not understand how Henry had warped her after I left, nor did I rightly catch what was going on in her mind now, but I felt suddenly certain that there was more here than met the ear.

"Elly," I said, "I don't know what you're talking about."

"Oh, don't you?" she accused me. "Well, sir, I am not a fool. Foolish, yes. I proved that with you. But not quite the complete ninny you appear to think."

"Elly . . ."

"It's no use, Cullah." The first name slipped out of her, and now I was sure I saw the dark shadow of hurt in her fine eyes. But she bit her lip and hurried on. "I kept the note, hoping I'd see you one day. I thought you might like to have it back for whipping the next victim. But I see you've changed your brand." She stared hard at Lisa, and nodded. "I suppose it's even more fun when they can't read your clever billy-doos."

I ignored her reference to Lisa's color and illiteracy. A great cold light was suddenly drawing far back in the pigeonhole of my memory marked Henry Plummer.

"Let me see that note," I said flatly.

She laughed, dug into her fashionable handbag and brought it out. "Of course. Good humor never loses anything with age. I really don't hate you, Cullah." Quick as light the change was in her voice and look, her lovely eyes holding mine as she finished softly. "It's just that I *believed* you."

I took the note, my face going white as I unfolded it.

> "The fool that far is sent,
> Some wisdom to attain,
> Returns an idiot, as he went,
> And brings the fool again."

That was all there was: just Whitney's harsh comment on the immutable stupidity of gulls, which I had left for Henry Plummer; and which he, with the fertile genius of maneuver that was to protect him past all belief in the coming months, had somehow interchanged with my note for Elly, passing on the cruel forgery to her.

I set my teeth with the tension of a bear trap and said to her, "May I keep this note, Miss Elly? I've one I'd gladly trade you for it."

"You may, sir, and no trade needed."

I reached inside my grease-stained shirt, bringing forth the frayed note Henry had given me at John Bozeman's fire on the Blackfoot. "It would pleasure me, ma'am," I said, holding it out, "if you would take mine in exchange."

She nodded, throwing an anxious glance toward the entrance of the Jackhammer Saloon, near which we stood. Evidently she was waiting for someone, expecting him to come out momentarily. I gave it no thought, only watching her eyes as I said, "Go on, read it. It's clever and educational, too, just like this one." I put Whitney's verse carefully away in my shirt and stood staring at her.

She opened the note originally intended for her and read it. I will never say what was in that belatedly delivered love letter written to Elly Bryan at Sun River those many bitter months ago, save that insofar as any man can put his heart into twenty lines of impassioned prose I had put mine into that plea for Elly to wait for me.

When she looked up at me, her lovely face was gray with shock. The words which fell from her strained lips were automatic, strangely mechanical, as though she were speaking from the depth of unconsciousness.

"My sister gave both of your notes to Henry, Cullah," she whispered, so low-voiced I could scarcely catch her words. "He got back to the house before I did that day, and Virginia was busy and asked him to find me and give me the note you left for me. Oh, Cullah, Cullah—it was so cruel—so needless —so wrong of him . . ."

She broke off, crushing my note in her hands. Her color was coming back now but she was still shaking her head with patent treachery and the needless heartache of Plummer's act in maliciously exchanging the stinging verse of sarcasm I had left for him with the tender vows I had written for her.

For my part I thought I knew the lines along which she was thinking, and rushed to get into words my own similar thoughts, both to erase the present awkwardness and repair the past damage.

"Well, Elly," I offered hopefully, my voice trembling with the excitement of the implied reconciliation, "all's well that ends well. Now that we know what went wrong and who helped it go that way, we can start all . . ."

"Don't say it!" she interrupted me pleadingly. "Please don't say it, Cullah! There's no use now, it's too late."

"Too late?" I echoed frowningly. "For what?"

"For us," said Elly Bryan. "I was married four days ago."

"You were *what?*" I gasped.

"Married," she repeated in a lifeless monotone. "At Sun River Farm, by Father Joseph Menetrey." Then, so broken-voiced it sounded more like a sob than an actual statement, *"I'm Mrs. Henry Plummer now."*

17

I needed a drink. Telling Lisa to wait with the horse at the hitching rail alongside the Jackhammer, I started in to get it. I got my jolt before I got inside. As I was about to go into the place, George Ives walked out of it. He broke out a grin big enough to cover not having seen me for six months.

"Why, hello, Red! Just the fellow I want to see." He stepped past me to peer up and down the street. "Say," he set out, "did you just now see a good-looking blonde floozie . . ."

"You mean Mrs. Plummer?" I cut him off coldly.

"Why, yes. You know her?"

"Old friends. Why?"

"Henry's inside. Just wanted me to tell her not to wait. He's being detained."

"Too damned bad."

"Yeah," agreed George Ives, "sure is."

His irresistible, wild grin broke again, and he put a big muscular arm about my shoulders, dragging me off to one side and out of the doorway as though he wanted to get me aside for a dirty joke. "Say," he growled, looking around again to make sure we weren't being overheard, "I want to give you a good tip on the local exchange." Once more he leered up and down the street checking the clearness of the coast. "Don't," he advised tersely, "buy any Bannack Preferred, nor invest permanent in Grasshopper Gold Bonds. Understand?"

I did not, and told him so.

"Get out of town," he amplified. "Depart these diggings today and don't go by home to pick up your laundry."

"George," I braced him, "what's up? We've been through a bit since spring and I can't believe you'd steer me wrong."

He shrugged, frowning uncomfortably.

"Just do as I say, Red. I ain't going to go into details with you."

"But, damn it all, George, I . . ."

"Red." The quiet way he said it stopped me short. "Do you know how Jack Cleveland got his? Henry set another fellow up to getting Jack into an argument about *him*. The minute poor old Jack mentioned Henry's name, Henry stepped up and drilled him for defamation of character."

"I don't see what the hell that's got to do with me!"

"Just this, Red—we're arguing."

His point got to me and he saw that it did by the way I stared at him.

"Yeah," he grinned. "Guess who's waiting just inside the Jackhammer's slat doors for me to raise my voice and say, 'What the hell you mean, Henry Plummer's a crooked so-and-so?'"

"George," I said, "I owe you two."

"Naw!" he laughed, all fun again now that he saw I was going to spare him the embarrassment of letting down on a friend. "Make it three! I'm going to give you another. Guess who's got himself pinned back of a little tin star while you and me was off up the son-of-a-bitching river?"

"Oh, good Lord!" I groaned, "not Plummer!"

"In the handsome smiling flesh," nodded George Ives. "And working at it thirty-six hours a day."

"I imagine," I agreed grimly.

"Naturally," grinned my companion. "With him on the job crime ain't got a chance to go nowhere."

"Nowhere," I said, "but where he wants it."

"It's the general idea, Red."

We looked at each other. He gave me just the least perceptible nod, and I knew that he had once more given me full and advance warning of Henry Plummer's plans, and that he had meant to do it, crazy or not. It was just one of those things which will crop up between men for no reason. George Ives liked me. I liked George Ives. We had absolutely nothing in common but that little feeling of unspoken brotherly bond. It was enough to make a very fatal difference in the history of Henry Plummer.

"Thanks, Curly," I said, returning his grin.

I had taken to calling him that in occasional fun and some sort of odd affection on the long trail home from the Crow fight on the Big Horn. It proved a lucky turn, for, he told me, he had been called that as a boy. In any event he now laughed aloud, gave me a giant clap on the shoulder, which spun me half-around, and said, "You're plumb welcome, Red. Now you're pointed right, you'd best start right out walking and don't look back till you're ten miles out of town. And, Red . . ." I had already started my walk, but slowed as he called out the afterthought. ". . . once you've made it out of sight, don't ever turn your back on me again. Win, lose or draw, I'm bound to do my duty if you give me the chance."

Now I stopped and turned, no matter the risk. Duty was a funny word for him to use, and I felt that he had used it deliberately. He had. As I came around, he hooked his thumb in his vest, the movement pulling aside his old black coat and showing me the dull wink of a deputy's star beneath it.

You had to hand it to Henry; he worked fast. We had been back in town less than twenty minutes. In that time he had not only declared the season still open on Sun River sitting ducks, but had issued the best shot in Bannack a six-point pewter hunting permit to bag the legal limit of same.

I nodded to George that I understood the situation. Pausing only long enough to collect my big red horse and my little red hen at the Jackhammer hitching rail, I set off through the mud of Main Street, outward bound from Bannack to points unknown.

Fortunately for my heirs and assigns I didn't quite make it out of town. At the edge of the settled part there was a new fork to the Deer Lodge road. It took off northeastward down the Jefferson and was marked with a sign that said, "VARNIA, 88 MI." As I was sitting there with Lisa on the roan, wondering what to do, there was a hoarse shout from behind and the sound of wagon wheels crunching rock on a sharp turn. I jumped the roan without looking around, and got him off the road just in time to avoid getting run down by a yellow-wheeled, red-bodied Abbott & Downing coach scattering for the hinterlands at a dead gallop.

While the driver was still cussing me I saw one of his passengers lean out of the window and yell up to him. He yelled

97

back, threw on his handbrake, locked his wheels and slid the big stage to a rocking stop.

Out jumped two gents in jackboots, cutaway coats, flannel shirts, hickory jeans, shoestring ties and derby hats—altogether the queerest mixture of mining camp and *boulevardier* haberdashery in my experience—and the two of them came legging it back my way waving and hollering as though they'd just spied their long-lost brother Clarence.

And in a Montana way, we were kin. It was Bill Fairweather and Henry Edgar; by custom of the country and shared adventure, my sworn campmates and common-luck inlaws.

They fell on me and greeted the blushing Lisa with a volley of oaths for which I would have to have punched them in the jaw had she understood English. As it was, we stood up under the punishment and, as a matter of fact, were both right glad to see the rascals. When I could make myself heard, I said, "Boys, you look to me like you have struck the granddaddy hole-in-the-ground. Either that or you are going to the Widow Mulcahey's Halloween party three months early. Whichever it is, you are certainly dressed for it."

"Cullah, my lad," cried Bill, "you have hit it the first swing of the pick. We're rich!"

"Well, I'm glad for you," I said, "and it could not have come the way of better friends. Also," I added, "I'm glad to see that you bear no grudge for the way I pulled out on you up there above the Stinking Water. I had damn little choice at the time."

"Why, man," said Henry Edgar, "we could read that like it was bound in a book. Those Crow pony tracks were so thick around that blessed creekbank it looked as though they'd spent the winter there. We thought for sure they had put you under."

"They did their best, you may be sure."

"Well," said Bill, "your luck's turned now."

"Yes it has. I keep thinking it can't get any worse, but it does."

"How's that?" asked Edgar, frowning curiously.

"I'm on my way out to Lewiston. I've been given twenty-four hours to get long shut of Bannack."

"By whom, pray tell?"

"The new sheriff, who else?"

"That scoundrel, Henry Plummer? Well, you'll have no worry from him where you're going."

"That's right. And by your leave I'll be getting there. It's been good to see you, boys." I stuck out my hand but neither of them moved to take it and, instead, both looked at one another and Bill burst out, "By Gawd! he don't know!"

To which Henry Edgar said, "Yes, and I reckon it's about time somebody told him and I nominate you."

Bill Fairweather nodded, his bright eyes twinkling.

"McCandles, lad, do you see that sign? What does it say?"

"Varnia," I answered a little edgily. "What does it say to you?"

"Alder Gulch," he said, quick as the flick of a fox's ear. "That's what I named it and, by Gawd, far as I'm concerned that's still what I call it!"

"You mean *our* Alder Gulch?" I asked unbelievingly.

"That's right, man," corroborated Henry Edgar. "Varnia and Alder Gulch are one and the same place. Matter of fact they've even got a brand-new name for our diggings. Calling our strike Virginia City mostly, nowadays. Started out being named Alder Gulch by old Bill. Then some of us began calling it Varnia after Jeff Davis's wife. But the Union crowd wouldn't have that and everybody struck on Virginia City as a sort of a compromise."

"But I'll tell you, boy," said Fairweather, "we don't none of the three of us need to worry about penny-ante details like names!"

"Not ever, by thunder!" chimed in Edgar. "Now, either you shoot that roan brute of yours through the head, or tie him on back of the stage. Our driver won't wait all day, not even for his honor, the head of the Fairweather Mining District!"

"What in the hell," I pleaded desperately, "are you two old mountain goats blatting about?"

"Just this," said Bill Fairweather. "You and the little squaw get down off that red-speckled camel and hustle your backsides onto this here stage. She's Alder-bound and so are you."

"The hell we are!"

"The hell you aren't. When I said 'we're rich,' I wasn't talking about just us. I meant you, too, lad. We cut you in for Simmons' share. That'd be Number Seven above discovery. The boys wouldn't have it any other way."

I sat there stunned. Number Seven above discovery on a strike reported big enough to beat Bannack inside its first thirty days alone? A diggings already proved deep enough in less than one month to rate a full-fledged stage line ninety miles long? And panning color enough to the pound of sand to let the rough-cut likes of Bill Fairweather, Henry Edgar, Tom Cover, Hank Rogers, Irish Barney Hughes and Big Mike Sweeney be wearing plugged hats and clawhammer coats and paying somebody else to work their claims while they rode around the country in spanking-new, yellow-wheeled stage-coaches?

Mister, I wasn't rich; I was retired.

18

It was the twenty-fifth day of June, 1863, when I first saw Virginia City, Montana; the mountain mining camp destined to become the chief settlement of the fabulous Alder Gulch strike.

We had come as far the night previous as Daly's Ranch, a villanious-looking roadhouse some fifteen miles outside the Virginia City limits. We had frozen a front wheelhub to keep us there overnight; otherwise the nearly 100-mile Bannack-Virginia City stage run was a breakneck, straight-through affair; the record at the time being one spectacular daylight dash of eleven hours, fifty-five minutes—6 A.M. to 5:55 P.M.

Our trip had been a good one up to Daly's, over a road which surprised me by being acceptable at worst, and truly excellent a good part of the way. I had kept careful note of its routing and its relay stations, having better than an average intuition that I might soon have use for such "traveling" information.

The main points for passenger refreshment and team changes were Bunton's at Rattlesnake Creek down near the Bannack end of the road, Dempsey's about midway between Bannack and Virginia City, and the aforementioned Daly's Ranch up near the Alder Gulch end of the run. Other intermediate stations I memorized—and reading from Bannack—were Stone's, Copeland's, Baker's at Stinking Water, Cold Springs and Upper Valley just below Daly's on Ramshorn Creek. My purpose in taking this precaution was simply to know the road by heart, in case I had to use it some dark night, and in an urgent hurry, to get out of the rough camp into which it was leading me.

The detail may seem tedious but I never had cause to regret studying it in favor, let us say, of listening to Henry Edgar and old Bill F. trying to learn the Crow language from Lisa, or instructing the other passengers about how skill and superior intellect had been the guiding factors in their selection of Alder Creek as a prospect. Better-hearted men never lived, nor bigger liars.

From Daly's, which stood at the mouth of Ramshorn Creek where it broke into the Stinking Water's little valley, the road went in between walls and stayed there as far as the new town of Nevada (in Montana, that is—not California), the first camp on Alder Creek, where that stream in turn came into the Stinking Water. From Nevada, upstream, the gulch of the Alder widened out and from there the new camps ran like beads on a string (Central, Junction, Summit, etc.) up to the "Big City," Virginia itself.

A short way outside the latter camp was a huge rough pine billboard, so new the sap was still running off it like raindrops. I caught the heading *Fairweather District* and made the mistake of saying to Bill F. that he was certainly getting up in the world since he knocked off horse-doctoring for a living, and that I supposed the sign was some of his handiwork and contained the ten commandments of mining conduct for Virginia and all points up and down Alder Gulch, as brought down off the mountain by William Moses Fairweather.

He said, "Well, yes, by Gawd! That's so," and before I could stop him, or jump out the window to escape what was coming, he set sail to recite same for my benefit.

". . . The officers of this district shall be President, Recorder, Judge and Sheriff. The center of the stream shall be the line. Every person may hold, by preëmption or purchase, two creek, bar hill, and lode claims, and no more, but no person can preëmpt more than one kind. Creek claims shall be fifty feet on the creek, extending across the creek from base to base, including all old beds of stream. Gulch claims shall be 100 feet in length, on the gulch, and extend one foot over on each side. Lode claims shall be 100 feet on the lode and twenty-five feet each side . . ."

"Stop!" I yelled. "I take everything back, and you are the King of the Mountain."

Bill laughed and said, "All right, I was done anyway," and went back to teaching Lisa how to say "Go to hell," when anyone said "Good morning" or "How do you do" to her on the streets of sweet Virginia.

But the list of officers in the Fairweather District had caught my ear. I knew who the honorary president was, didn't care who the judge and recorder might be. It was that one other office holder I was interested in.

"Partner," I said to Edgar, "did I hear our friend rattle off the name of a law officer in vain just now, or am I suffering from the altitude?"

He looked at me rather oddly, I thought, and answered, "Yes and no."

"Now what does that mean?" I demanded.

"Yes, you heard him, and no, you're not mountain-sick."

"But I'm about to be, is that it?"

He nodded.

"Who," I said deliberately, "is the *sheriff* of the Fairweather Mining District?"

"We couldn't help it," he countered defensively before answering. "Bill and me fought it, but the damned Miners' Committee fell for it. I tell you that man Plummer is a perfect rascal. When he came up here offering to take the job on for no pay and just adding it to his regular work down at Bannack and promising the best of deputies, and all, you'd have thought bear grease couldn't shine for slickness alongside his line. He smiles and looks you in the eye and you don't know whether you're just arriving or have already been there and got back. I don't know. Sometimes I wonder myself if he's as bad as they say."

"He's not," I told him abruptly. "He's worse."

But I didn't go on with it. It was no use. I knew Henry Plummer. To make his dearest enemy believe he was guilty of anything more sinister than soft smiles and steady looks, you would have to catch him red-handed clean up to his elbows. And then you would have to run a chemical test to prove it was blood and not just barn paint.

I settled back and scowled out the window. Yonder, up the gulch, was Virginia. Journey's goal, rainbow's end, my personal pot of gold. Who the hell cared if she had a convicted murderer for a sheriff?

All new camps are basic in their likeness, the one to the other. This one sat in a dry dimple of yellow dirt, surrounded by a welter of eroded hill-wrinkles, the whole enfolded in an ugly face of brown rock, scraggly pine and dusty brush. It had neither enough of water, grass, timber, law, love, religion, sobriety, hours of sunlight or good level ground. It was filthy, noisy, tough, exciting, sickeningly expensive.

You paid twenty-five cents for six dried prunes or a withered fresh apple; fifty cents for three pounds of flour or a loaf of moldy bread; seventy-five cents for a half-pound of coffee and a dollar for anything, from salt fish to strawberry conserve, which came in a tin can or a glass jar. Eggs were six dollars a dozen; chickens a day's pay digging gravel; turkeys from Salt Lake City fifty dollars and up.

There were practically no women except the working girls up from Bannack, and far too few of them, even at their ruinous ten-dollar an hour rates.

Of whiskey there was an endless variety, all from the same green barrel, and selling by the shot from fifty cents to five dollars, depending on how new you were in town, or how far above discovery lay your claim.

Add to this 4,000 frontier toughs from every state in the Union and sixteen foreign lands, including China and the Solomon Islands; shake well with equal parts of gold dust, greed and gunpowder; pour out along a five-mile stretch of small Montana stream and stand by with a lighted match: there was your Virginia City up in Alder Gulch the early summer of 1863.

I still couldn't believe it. But it was real enough, all right. I learned that well before the gunsmoke of my first twenty-four hours in Bill Fairweather's new mining district had drifted past.

19

I stood on the corner of Wallace and Van Buren, inhaling my after-supper cigar and enjoying the view down the main stem.

From my vantage I could count four hotel, three freight office, two livery stable, one stage-line, two doctor, three lawyer and six assay office shingles; no churches, no schools, no lodge halls; three obvious brothels, some eight hurdy-gurdy houses, eleven open-front saloons.

The fact that this teeming compost was built up of box tops, barrel staves, alder poles and shipping-crate slats, mortised together with mud-wattle and packmule manure, and throw-covered with canvas wagon tarps, in no way detracted from its noisy charms.

I had taken several good pulls at the tiger's tail both before and after my five-dollar feast of boiled cabbage and antelope chops. I had bathed, shaved my beard and had my hair chopped off at the collar. To finish the cleanup I had bought a whole new outfit of sharply cut store clothes off a young California dude, flat-broke and already on his way back to the less rigorous clime. (This lad had thought he was a professional gambler until the gray-eyed Texas and Missouri inside-straight sharks had ripped his amateur belly open.) Further, I had my shapely little red baggage safely stowed away in my room at the Seneca, with orders not to answer the door or stick her head out of it for any reason. And, finally, I had met that afternoon with Esau Lazarus, the camp moneylender, arranging for his capital to take over development of my Number Seven claim on the creek; the consideration a tidy $40,000 in cash plus 50 per cent of all future profits guaranteed to me and my assigns, *"ad extremum, ad vitam aut culpam";* lawyer talk for *"a hell of a lot longer than I would be around to care about."* At least that is my memory of attorney Ben Gregg's gruff translation.

As I lingered in contemplation of time's marvelous, immutable march in Virginia—thirty days ago this gulch had held a total population of three indigent lizards, a molting mountain jay and a pair of coyotes about to quit from pure lonesomeness—my little instant of imagined security fell apart and passed away.

Down the street, a slender, pleasant-faced horseman was reining his lathered claybank through the crowd in my direction. It was Henry Plummer.

He was looking for somebody and, from the looks of the lit-up smile with which he was bearing down on me, he had just found him.

"Now," I said, when he drew up, "I am not in the mood for any fancy talk." I had on my gun, and indeed I was growing a trifle weary of Henry's war of nerves. I let drop my right hand, so that the fingers were poised at the part of my unbuttoned coat. "Whatever it is that you have to say, say it and go on. I want none of you, my friend. I know you for what you are, and for what you hope to be. Let that knowledge be your guide."

"Why, Cul," his surprise was wonderful, "whatever in the world are you talking about?"

"About you setting me up for a shooting scrape, I imagine," I told him. "If you think you're going to start anything that will let your deputies pot me the way you did Jack Cleveland, think again."

"Deputies?"

"Todd and Dillingham."

"You're off the reservation. They're not my men. Todd's in charge up here. Dillingham works for him."

"I know better."

He gave me a good long look.

"All right, let's start over again."

"Yes, let's."

"You were told to get out of Bannack."

"I was."

"And you got."

"Yes," I replied, "and here I am."

"When I rode up here an hour ago, I had it in mind to kill you. Of course you know why. I had supposed that fool Ives would have attended to it long ago, but he's crazy as a June bug butting into a tent net. So this forenoon, when I heard you'd come up here, I set out to get the job done right."

"That is to say by yourself."

"Correct. But my mind has been changed."

"Oh."

"Yes, by $40,000 in dust."

Where or how he had heard it, I never did find out. It should have been my first warning on the efficiency of his spy system, but it was not. In my eagerness to learn what he
104

thought he was going to do to get my dust, I stumbled right on over the preliminary details of the espionage.

"You know, Plummer, I never did think too much of your professional ability."

"Surely you can't mean that, Cul. What does it take to convince you? I thought Elly would be proof enough to break your back for good."

I let him have his little smile out, then dropped it on him like acid, a smoking bead at a time.

"I meant your armed assault and highway robbery record, not your pimping. At that you're the envy of every rapist, small-town window peeper and molester of little girls in the Territory."

Now he wasn't smiling. But he wasn't giving me any break to pull on him, either. Not Henry Plummer. Why gamble when he already held the deck, had the cards marked and could call the deal any way he wanted, any time he wanted?

Yet my shot got to him.

"I'll remember that," he said softly, *"After* we weigh out your dust."

"And when do you think that will be?"

"When you try to leave town with it."

"Thanks. I'll remember *that."*

I was quite smug with it. All of a sudden I felt safe. Knowing Henry, I was assured he would not harm me while I had a scad that size in my possession. All I had to do was sit tight and leave it in Esau Lazarus' safe.

"Yes," said Henry quietly, the smile back in urbane place, "I believe you will remember it. That is, unless your memory is shorter than twenty-four hours."

His upper lip was lifting a little too much now. It was uncovering his white eye-teeth to the gum.

"Twenty-four hours?" I said.

"That's the time," he answered, "you've got left in Virginia City." He took out his pocket watch and held it to the oil light flaring from the Seneca's doorless entrance.

"You will be gone," he said, *"with or without the dust,* by eight P.M. tomorrow."

My quarters at the Seneca were rough. You can imagine what kind of a hotel could be put up by unskilled labor with the crudest of materials in a little over three weeks. The Seneca, no matter, was Virginia's newest, biggest and finest.

It was laid out like a livery stable. Built at right angles to the street, it was perhaps forty feet wide, a hundred long. The windows were unglazed as yet, temporarily covered with red and white calico nailed tight down, all around. The rooms gave off a common hall in the exact manner of a center-aisle

105

horse barn, and they were as narrow and dark and richly odored as any single stall, as well. The doors were slab pine, saggingly hung on leather, sans any kind of latch or lock and only a two-inch auger hole bored through the wood to serve as doorknob, inside and out. One outdoor privy and two guttering oil lamps accommodated all twenty rooms and eighty feet of drafty hallway.

In this frontier palace I now paced the puncheon floor of room eighteen trying to decide what to do about Lisa Red Bear, Henry Plummer and William Cullah McCandles.

The pretty, completely unconcerned party of the first part sat on one of the lower bunks—these came four to a cubicle, nailed two high on opposing walls, just like a prison cell—combing out her glossy black hair and humming some sort of a Crow happy song. The moment I had come in she had started to take off her clothes. She had been quick and bright about it, exactly as though there could be no question of what came next, and as though she were highly in favor of that fact. It was all I could do to persuade her to remain clad, at least until I had had a chance to think. This had not disturbed her, as she patiently interpreted it as no worse than a slight delay.

At this point it must be made clear that, subsequent to our initial meeting at the alder pool, we had not been together. This was accounted for by no prudery of mine, nor hesitation of hers. It was a matter of human nature. When one is first running, then fighting, then fleeing for his life, the weary, frightened body makes precious few demonstrations of the mating urge.

Now I was set either to fight or run again, and the last, far thought in my mind was for physical love.

Still, Lisa was my first concern. It was presently impossible to carry out my Bannack plan for turning her over to Black Blanket and his Beaverhead tribe. I knew she would not move without me, and should I try to get down to the other camp with her now, Henry would have me knocked off my horse before I got around the second creek bend outside Junction. No, I had to think of a new place to leave her. A better, quicker, above all a closer place. The necessity had no sooner jumped into view than the solution came chasing after it.

Esau Lazarus, of course! I had known the little money-lender but six short hours. Yet, before taking me to him, Bill Fairweather had told me enough about him to make the appearance of his name in my mind seem entirely logical. To begin with he was the patriarch of the Gulch. At an apparent age of about sixty, the eldest of the camp's handful of elders, he stood out as a wise and quiet old man in an ignorant and noisy community of brawlers whose average years would lie closer to twenty-five than thirty. (As an example: Henry Plummer was at this time some months shy of his twenty-seventh birthday.)

Lazarus was a long-time widower, a devout Jew, a Mason, an honorary member of the Miners' Council, or Committee, as it was variously known, and the silent grubstaker of half the biggest fortunes being made on Alder Creek. A man assumed to be enormously wealthy, he lived not only alone, but was indeed very lonely, according to Bill. I could not imagine, knowing this, that he would not welcome into his silent house the sound of my little Indian ward's delightful laughter.

At any rate, he was certainly the safest man in Virginia with whom to entrust a child of Lisa's obvious charms. There was the main statement of my case.

Twenty minutes later I stood with Lisa in Esau Lazarus' tiny shack on the hill above Wallace Street.

My luck with the kindly old Jew was all good. He proved not only happy to have Lisa stay with him, but most anxious to probe into and be of any possible further assistance in whatever trouble it was which had brought me to lodge the Indian girl with him. Making one of my rarely correct spot decisions, I told him exactly what my situation was. I began with the first day I ever saw Henry Plummer and ended with the last.

Brought up to within a few hours of all I knew about the Bannack sheriff, Lazarus had a shrewd answer for my immediate dilemma. It was one of which I had already been apprised by James Stuart, but of which I would never have thought again, without the reminder.

"My son," said the old man, "you have your passport on your ring finger, and I will tell you how to use it." He made it quick.

In April last a lodge had been organized at Bannack by Nathaniel P. Langford, one of the first three Master Masons in Montana. Langford was a thoroughly trustworthy man of superior education, if somewhat pompous expression. He was a man who saw great things ahead for the territory and was determined to leave a record of his vision for Montana posterity; he was, in brief, determined to be a historian, said Lazarus, but at the moment the most important thing about him was his mastership of the Masonic fraternity in Bannack.

My shrewd-eyed instructor studied me a minute to make sure I was paying strict attention, then went swiftly on. Henry Plummer, elected sheriff on May 24, married June 20, had made application on June 23 (the day before my return to Bannack) for membership in Langford's lodge. The immediate prospects were that he would be admitted, as he had acquired a very strong, if limited popularity in Bannack. A meeting was scheduled for the following night, June 26, and among the business, Lazarus now informed me, would be a vote on Plummer's application.

As a Mason, he went on quickly, I would be free and welcome to attend that meeting myself. As an interested party to the success or failure of Henry Plummer in gaining admission to the Bannack Lodge, I should at once make plans to do so.

The old Jew's reasoning was as sharp and two-edged as a skinning knife. And it placed Plummer in an impossible position: that of wanting more than ever to kill me, but of having his hands figuratively tied behind his back by the very situation which would increase his murderous desires in my direction. That situation was his yearning to belong to the Masons and my power either to promote or prevent that ambition. All I had to do was make a public announcement of my intention of going down to the Bannack Lodge meeting to say a few words in behalf of candidate Henry Plummer. It would follow, the wise-eyed old moneylender promised, that the latter would not then dare to touch me.

The reason for this immunity would lie in Henry's cold-eyed and correct assaying of the social and political advantages of freemasonry membership in Montana. As a Mason he would be practically beyond reach, or at least as far beyond reach as a man could possibly put himself, of moral question or social reproach. And lodge membership was the *only* protection with which he had not so far supplied himself, and which he knew to be his last necessary and vital shield. The deadly simple truth was that he was already the top law officer in the locality and had married a Montana girl of good family and fine reputation. If he could now add the magic advantage of Masonic brotherhood to that powerful beginning, he would be as hard to tie down to organized crime in either Bannack or Alder Gulch as a Mormon bishop to sin in Salt Lake City.

Running the risk of losing this ultimate opportunity for local intrenchment by carrying out his threat to put me under, providing I *was right* about his master plan, would be a very bad gamble even for $40,000.

My little poke would be peanuts to what Henry Plummer stood to take out of Alder Gulch if he could put a Masonic ring like mine on his own crooked finger.

But the gamble, good or bad, *was still a gamble*.

I could be wrong about the Bannack sheriff. If I was, and

Henry was indeed but a random murderer intent only on stalking my Claim Seven scad, and with no "big plan" at all, such as I imagined him to have, for a wholesale gutting of Alder Gulch, then I might very well get myself killed somewhere between the new camp and the old. *That,* Lazarus concluded, was *my* gamble. However, he added softly, it was a good one.

Of the respective choices, Henry's was clearly the more difficult. He had to decide between a $40,000 bird in hand and an untold fortune in the bush. I had only to make up my mind as to when and where I wished to call his hand: tonight on the streets of Virginia City or tomorrow night in the lodge hall at Bannack; my bet in either event being the same—my life.

I took a good five minutes to study the matter after the gentle-voiced old man had laid it out for me. At the end of that time I stood up and put on my hat. "All right," I said, "let's go."

20

The night of June 26 the lodge met in Bannack and moved not to approve Henry Plummer. The precise opinion of Nathaniel Langford was that he was "neither a fit nor a proper person to be received within the circle." The main reason he was so deemed was my own testimony.

Plummer had been smart enough, just as he had been with John Bozeman, to admit his "early errors" to Bannack's leading electoral lights. And, like Bozeman, his listeners had given him the benefit of the doubt and a generous second chance.

However, his earlier confession hardly matched my subsequent testimony in legal detail. In his version such an item as the Josef Vedder affair became an ill-advised but "boyish rashness," into which he was led by a worldly woman. By my description it was a brutal, cold-blooded murder; the seduced mate of the victim a barely twenty-year-old girl of previous good repute.

There were other variances. I read same into the lodge record, quoting chapter and verse from my leather-bound casebook on the smiling nominee. A resolution was passed awarding me a vote of thanks and pledging those present not to divulge the relationship of my information to the ruling on Henry Plummer's application. At the same time it was duly and fairly noted that my report did not constitute proof of any present crime, or intent to commit same, against the applicant. It was accepted simply as a bad character reference, all that was needed, in so strongly moral an organization as that of the Freemasons, to guarantee denial of membership.

The lodge never did, to my knowledge, violate its oath. But details of his refusal were not necessary to Henry. He knew that same night that he had been turned down, and that was all he needed to know. He had lost his gamble. He did not need any eyewitness to tell him who had lost it for him. Yet when I met him an hour later in front of the Bannack House, he did not turn a hair.

"Well, Cul," he shrugged pleasantly, "I hear it went against me. Too bad."

"That all you hear?" I watched him narrowly.

"That's all."

"You know I was there, of course."

"Of course." His smile was still good, but his eyes were not. "I imagine you made a fine talk, too."

"Effective would be the better word."

"Yes. Well, we all guess wrong sometime."

"This was your time," I said.

"Hmmmm," he let it trail off, looking at his cigar ash with measured care, before tapping it into the gutter.

"Is that all?" I asked curiously.

He nodded affably.

"What?" I persisted, pressing my imagined advantage. "No more threats? No more time limits? No more blue tickets?"

"No," he said, "nothing."

I couldn't believe it, and chided him in that direction. He measured me like the cigar ash, before tapping me into the gutter.

"Cul, I may not be as smart as I think I am, but I'm not quite as slow as you figure me, either. You know very damned well that if I touch you after tonight I will have the whole Scottish rite down on my neck. No thank you. That doesn't fit my schedule. I still mean to make good here"—he had deliberately raised his voice, so that at the last several bystanders heard him clearly—"and I do not intend to let you ruin me in Bannack, as you did in California."

He put out his hand with a big, forgiving smile.

"But what say we let bygones be bygones and pull together instead of opposite ways? Here's my hand on it, and my heart too, if you will have them!"

I would have dearly loved giving him my hand just then, balled into a good hard fist and swung from the boardwalk. Instead, I dropped my voice and said, "You go to hell, you mealy-mouthed son of a bitch!" and brushed past him to go into the lobby of my hotel.

He didn't alter his grin by a tooth, as he stepped after me. But he did drop his own voice out of range of our idle witnesses.

"Oh, by the way, Cul . . ."

I came around, clenching my jaw.

". . . what I said about you being a bit out of reach just now?"

"Yes."

"It doesn't go for your little Indian friend."

"What!" I blazed, going white and stepping in on him. *"She isn't a Mason,"* said Henry Plummer, and turned and smiled his way off through the street crowd, before I could think to shoot or strangle him.

I had come down to Bannack by stage, with two other Alder Gulch men bound for the same meeting. Esau Lazarus had made the arrangements for me to do so (in a loud, clear voice in front of Plummer in the Orphir Saloon) the previous night in Virginia, and I had felt reasonably safe under the circumstances.

Next morning, however, when I came to depart for Virginia again, the cases had been altered.

My two friends and quondam bodyguards, Wash Stapleton and R. I. Dodge, were waiting for me in front of the A. J. Oliver & Company's Express office, just down Main from the Bannack House. With them was a man I had seen in Virginia the night before. And seen him in company I did not like nearly so well as the present. That would be with Mr. Henry Plummer in the Orphir.

I was thus not greatly surprised, upon coming up to my traveling companions, to hear this third party introduced as Deputy Sheriff Dillingham, Plummer's man in the Gulch district.

What I was greatly surprised at was what I heard after the introduction.

Dodge led him off.

"Dillingham here tells us we've been marked for an unscheduled stop on the way back up. Seems the local roughs have gotten the idea we're carrying a load of dust. I'm quitting cold. There have been just too damned many of these 'stops' lately."

I didn't say anything, waiting for Wash.

"Likely R. I.'s right," he told me. "But I can't believe it. I'm going on back up. If the rascals pick me they'll find a mighty poor chicken. I'm carrying a hundred in paper bills and that's it. No man is going to murder me for that."

"I know a man," I said, watching Dillingham, "who will do it for ten."

The deputy returned my look, nodding soberly. "Could be I know him too. Local boy?"

"Very local," I said.

Again, the quick, friendly nod. "I wouldn't have believed it yesterday morning. Even though I got my first noseful of it the night before."

Now he was watching me and I had to decide whether or not Henry had been lying when he told me this man was "one of his." What I decided to do was to find out. Then and there.

"In the Orphir?" I asked.

"Yes," said Dillingham.

I turned to Dodge and Stapleton and asked them if they minded if I had a word in private with the sheriff, as there was a personal matter here I wanted to clear up. They indicated this was all right, and the deputy and I moved off three steps.

"Go on," I said, low-voiced.

"He told me you might be taking out $40,000 in dust, and proposed I arrange to relieve you of it between Daly's Ranch and Rattlesnake Creek. With his official blessing, of course, and being very careful to see you did not get shot, as he wanted no trouble from Langford and the lodge. You could have brushed me down with a turkey duster. I'd heard he had a bad record over in California, but he had seemed straight as a stretched string while here. You just never know, I guess."

"You guess right. That why you came down here?"

"Yes, I trailed the stage all the way."

"Well, many thanks. Anytime I can return the favor, let me know."

"How about right now?"

"How's that?"

"Ride the stage with Wash and I will tail you and we will see what happens." He paused, glancing down at my side. "I like the way you wear that," he said, "and I believe that you can use it."

"In a bad pinch. What's this about the roughs laying for Wash and R. I.?"

"Buck Stinson, Haze Lyons and Charley Forbes are the ones. I didn't let on to Plummer the other night that I was surprised when he told me to go after you. I let him think I was trailing you here, as he had suggested, and he evidently believed that I was on the level with him. Last night he came and told me about this new setup for taking care of these other boys on the way back up to Virginia today. He then gave me the names of the three, just mentioned, as the ones who would do the job. He had the gall to give me the devil,

112

as well, for letting you get down here with the dust yesterday."

"But he told you," I guessed, "that all would be forgiven and you could come back home a hero, if you got it on the way back up today, eh?"

"Providing you didn't leave it with Oliver this morning, yes."

The express offices were the banks in those days, but I had by now decided that Dillingham was telling the truth and so assured him I had no dust to leave and that I would be glad to ride the stage that morning and to back him in any serious trouble we might run into up the line. We left it that way and went back to the others.

Dillingham, after cautioning all of us not to talk about our discussion of the roughs, turned to me and said, "The most likely place for a try will be Bill Bunton's at Rattlesnake. Bill's a hard lot, and I have seen Stinson and the other two at his place many times. If you get past there, things will be easier. But keep your hand under your coat at all times."

I told him I would do that and he added, "When we get back up to Virginia we will call a Miners' Council meeting and pin down Mr. P. before he gets any better organized. We can make a good start with taking Stinson, Forbes and Haze Lyons."

Wash and I thanked him, shook hands with Dodge and climbed on the 6:05 for Alder Gulch, just then rolling up in front of the Oliver office.

It always took me about five minutes to settle down to the seasick motion of those cursed Concords, rocking back and forth on their leather thorough braces like a cattle barge bucking short swells across the bay. But by two miles out I had found sea legs enough to dig out my notebook and enter the following badly joggled thought for June 27, 1863:

"... It looks as though P. is about cornered at last. He has made the fatal error of trusting an honest man, and if Deputy Dillingham will go before the Miners' Meeting with his evidence, I will back him to the hilt. Between us, we should be able to put Mr. P. in his place, beneath the sod. He has had his six feet staked out for a long time. God willing, we will put him in it this time. Actually, we may do no better than getting him voted a blue ticket—unless his boys get careless and hurt poor Wash (on this stage) or Dodge back in Bannack—but even getting him run out of Montana on a blue ticket is at least better than a poke in the eye with a sharp stick...."

I put the diary away, satisfied that indeed Plummer's unbelievable luck was due to run out. Also, I was sure his threat against Lisa had been rendered harmless by Dillingham's discovery. When the good citizens of Virginia learned that the head of the ruffians who had lately begun to waylay anybody carrying more than a dollar's worth of dust, was none other than Bannack's law chief and self-elected "Sheriff of Alder Gulch," there would be hell to pay and Henry Plummer stuck with the account for collection.

However, Dillingham and I were still some miles from home. At Bunton's, ten miles or so out on Rattlesnake Creek, I got my first hint of this.

As we were about to leave the station, a very rough-looking fellow lounged up to the coach window and poked his head in for a talk with Mr. Washington Stapleton.

"Wash," he said, "where's Dillingham? I tailed him out from town, but lost him about two miles back. You seen him?"

Wash took his oath that he had not, in his strained reply identifying our accoster as Haze Lyons.

Haze looked at him, scowling hard.

"Now, don't put off on me, you hear? Your friend Dodge went to talking back yonder in Bannack, and Buck and Charley and me understand that damned Dillingham said we tried to get him to come in with us on robbing you boys."

"I will swear," said Wash, "that I don't know anything about that. I've got just $100 in greenbacks and you are welcome to them and my pants to go with them, if you wish."

"I don't want your damned money!" snapped the heavy-bearded Haze. "What do you think I am, a cussed road agent?"

Wash wisely did not make known his thoughts on that subject and the swarthy outlaw growled on. "It's that mealy-mouth little deputy I want. I mean to kill him for the wrong he's done me and the boys, but I fear he has heard of it and left the country."

"Well," said Wash candidly, "I will tell you, Haze, that I have been considerably more comfortable asleep in church than I am with your face in that window. Now if you don't want our money, we would surely appreciate it if you . . ."

Haze cut him off by producing a Colt and warning him to shut up.

"It's all a damned lie about me and Buck and Charley. You just remember that when you get back up to Virginia and you needn't worry about nothing else. We never wanted your son-of-a-bitching poke nor your damned pants in the first place!"

With the oath, he strode off into the timber. Shortly, we heard a horse take off, going back down the road toward Bannack. Our driver gathered his lines, kicked off the brake, had a word for his wheelers and a cut of the leather for his leaders and we were on the way again.

This time we got only about a mile, when Dillingham rode out of a clump of trailside brush and waved the driver off the road. I was out of the stage before the wheels stopped turning. I had learned by now that the rocks had ears and the canyon walls listening horns in this queer country, and I wanted my report to be taken in by the little deputy alone.

When I had told him of the threat against his life, he thanked me for the warning but minimized the actual danger.

"Haze is a talker. I don't mind his kind. The man that means to fight seldom makes speeches about doing it. But I'll look out, nonetheless. Forbes is a crazy devil, and Buck's a quiet one. Might be some trouble there."

He climbed back on his horse.

"We'll have to move a bit livelier now that Dodge has tipped them to me. I'll see if I can get a meeting tonight. Tomorrow at the latest. Take care, McCandles."

He touched his hat brim and rode off.

I watched him go. He was a friendly little man, with steady brown eyes and a crinkly smile. His was the sober, thoughtful kind that took some time to grow on you.

In my case he wasn't meant to get that time.

For some reason Dillingham did not get his meeting called that night, but did get it set for the next day, the twenty-eighth. Then, at the last minute, he had to go chasing out of town after some stolen horses and the meeting was put off until the following night.

The following morning I was standing outside a brush wickiup on the edge of town, listening with a score of other loafers to a bar-claim dispute being heard by Dr. Steele, the district judge. The heated-up disputants (Frank Ray and Doughton Jones) were miners I knew from Bannack and I was so absorbed in their antics inside the makeshift, mud-daubed courthouse that I did not see Dillingham walk up.

Presently, however, he caught my eye and I went over to him.

"Got to see the judge, soon as he gets done here," he told me. "Can't wait for the meeting tonight. Something's come up."

Looking past him, down the street, I saw three men coming toward us. "You mean our friends, yonder?" I asked.

He didn't look around but said, "Haze and the boys?"

"Yes," I replied.

"Well, that's part of it, yes." He moved away from me. "Now, stay clear and don't mix in. I can handle them."

"The hell," I said. "I'm right behind you."

For truth, though, I was not. At the last minute and as he started away, I was blocked off from him by a passing rig with two dance-hall girls in it. I saw and heard every bit of what followed but could not fire for fear of hitting the girls.

"Dillingham!" yelled Haze. "We want to see you!"

The three were facing the deputy in a bad way, Stinson in front a step, Forbes off one flank, Haze the other, both spread by about ten feet. They had the little law officer enfiladed.

"Bring him along! Make him come on a little!" directed Stinson nervously, motioning for the others to flank their victim even more tightly. As they obeyed, Haze shouted loud enough to have been heard in Bannack, "All right, Dillingham! Damn you, you take back those lies!" and before the latter could so much as open his mouth, all three of his false accusers cut down on him.

Dillingham never got his own gun free of its holster. And I never learned what it was that had "come up." Haze Lyons' ball took him in the thigh. He spun half around, crying aloud with the pain of the shattered bone and clapping his hand to the gaping hole. The movement sent Buck Stinson's bullet harmlessly over his head, but as he staggered upright again, Charley Forbes' shot smashed him in the chest. He collapsed to his knees like an empty sack, and without another sound. Carried inside the wickiup, he was dead almost before his bearers could put him down.

While he was still lying in the dirt, I got around the blocking rig. My Colt was out and I was meaning to use it on the murderers without further call or question, but I was too late.

Jack Gallagher, who was, with Buck Stinson, Ned Ray, George Ives and the dead man himself, one of Plummer's several deputies, had by this time run out of the Golden Gravel across the street and put the killers under his pistol.

I knew, as well as I was standing there enraged, that the whole thing, including Gallagher's opportune appearance, had been staged. *Ordered* would have been the more accurate word. And ordered by no one else than Henry Clay Plummer.

If I needed any further proof of my instant suspicion, I got it in the next moment when Gallagher told Forbes to hand over his gun. Instead of keeping the fired weapon for evidence against its owner, Plummer's deputy calmly ejected the empty casing of the bullet which had killed Dillingham, replacing it with a fresh shell and returning the now fully loaded, hence ostensibly innocent, weapon to Forbes. No less than ten witnesses saw this brazen act, which was accompanied by Stinson and Haze Lyons as coolly reloading their own revolvers.

Thus, while we all stood there and watched, the three assassins were allowed to "get rid of their empties," this to the end that none of the witnesses could subsequently swear as to which one of them had actually fired the fatal shot.

But there was precious little doubt about who had ordered the killing, regardless of any confusion as to who had carried it out. It was a clear-cut case of Henry Plummer's paid hirelings shooting down in broad daylight a man who was generally known to have proof of the Bannack sheriff's leadership of the Alder Gulch killer-pack, and who was rumored about to expose publicly the smiling lawman for the cold-blooded organizer of extortion, armed assault and commercial murder that, in deadly fact, he was.

Poor Dillingham had paid with his life for having the courage to denounce Henry Plummer, and the bad judgment to *announce* his intention to do so beforehand.

If I never performed another public service in my career, I was presently determined that the plucky little deputy should not have died in vain.

Jack Gallagher, meanwhile, was watching me. He seemed to read my resolution in the way I stepped toward him. "Stand back and keep clear!" he warned me sharply. "These men are under arrest!"

I put my Colt away and shook my head.

"They're not only under arrest, Jack," I said, "they're under indictment."

"For what? On whose charge?" he countered frowningly.

"For murder and on my charge," I answered. "And with you as accessory after the fact. Do you think any of us are taken in by this act of yours and theirs?"

"Don't talk crazy, McCandles," he cried. "It wasn't nothing but a gunfight. Here, help me with these men. And keep the crowd back, will you? We've got to see these boys get a fair trial."

I nodded grimly. "They would already have had their fair trial," I rasped, "if you hadn't of horned in when you did." I tapped my gun butt to make certain he understood I had meant to sit on their case with Judge Colt, and he drew away from me in crudely feigned dismay.

"One shooting doesn't solve another, McCandles!" he claimed piously aloud for the rapidly swelling crowd's benefit. "Due process of legal law is what I'm paid to stand up for and I aim to stand up for it all the way. These men must be given a fair trial and full right of society's protection!"

"Hurrah!" shouted someone in the crowd. "By God, boys, pull up the wagon and let's give 'em a dose of both right here and now!"

There were immediate, raucous sentiments expressed in

117

favor of this direct course of justice. The crowd was by now 95 percent composed of people who had not seen the shooting but had run up after they heard the guns go off. They seemed to me, by and large, to reflect the image of Gallagher's loudly planted lie that the affair had been an honest shooting scrape, and for a bad moment it seemed the discharge of the murderers would take no longer than ten or fifteen minutes. But there was, fortunately a hard core of eyewitnesses who, like myself, not only knew that murder had been committed but realized both *why* and *by whom* it had been ordered; and who accordingly saw in the trial of Forbes, Stinson and Lyons a legitimate opportunity to tar Plummer with the brush of association with his three hired killers, thus pinning on the Bannack sheriff this brutal crime which was so patently a product of his vicious, hidden rule.

This little group stood like a rock against the rising popular tide of acceptance for Gallagher's "fair gunfight" fabrication, and in the end were able to bring some semblance of legal order and public responsibility to the scene.

A detail of miners took charge of the prisoners, while a "captain of the guard" took charge of the miners. The entire "amalgamated" group repaired to a stout log saloon across from the Golden Gravel, and set out to get good and whiskied while the "law" part of the court was being "put together" outside.

Here there was a bit of trouble. Some shouted for a twelve-man jury, some for a "people's trial." A vote was called for and taken by counting the two factions through a narrow chute formed by parking two wagons side by side. Popular justice won by a mile. A third wagon was drawn up and the three lambs marched out of the saloon and stood up in it to face the fury of the vox populi.

"Doc" Steele was shouted down as magistrate and in his place Judge G. G. Bissell appointed. The latter was the elected first president of the Fairweather District (Bill F. holding but the "honorary" title), and hence the logical man for the historic job coming up. Bissell, a courageous man but no yearner after the dead hero's toga, wisely insisted on two associate "judges" being appointed to share the blame of any finding which might irritate the "sheriff's office." The voice of the people quickly swore in Dr. Steele and Dr. Ruter for this unwanted distinction, and the mills of Virginia's little gods began to grind away at the grist of the Gulch's first formal murder trial.

I had seen these miners', or people's, courts in session before, and could describe this one with my eyes shut, not missing a single ludicrous detail of the entire travesty. And do it before ever Judge Bissell banged his gavel for order, or the first witness opened his mouth to put his booted foot in it. But I am going to let another qualified observer do it for me.

"It was," says Tom Dimsdale, Virginia's first schoolmaster and the best of all late eyewitness writers on the vigilante theme, "a trial by the people en masse. For our own part, knowing as we do the utter impossibility of all voters hearing half the testimony; seeing also that the good and the bad are mingled, and that a thief's vote will kill the well-considered verdict of the best citizen, in such localities and under such circumstances verdicts are as uncertain as the direction of the wind on next Tibb's Eve. We often hear of the justice of the masses—'in the long run'; but a man may get hung 'in the short run'—or may escape the rope he has so remorselessly earned, which is, by a thousand chances to one, the more likely result of a mass trial. The chances of a just verdict being rendered is almost a nullity. Prejudices, or selfish fear of consequences, and not reason, rule the illiterate, the lawless and the uncivilized. These latter are in large number in such places, and if they do right it is by mistake. The favors of the dangerous classes are bestowed, not upon the worthy, but on the popular, who are their uncommissioned leaders. Such favors are distributed like sailors' prize money, which is nautically supposed to be sifted through a ladder. What goes through is for the officers; what sticks on the rounds is for the men. . . ."

The justice sifted down in the trial of Haze Lyons, Buck Stinson and "Handsome Charley" Forbes for the vicious murder of Deputy Sheriff Dillingham fell to earth exactly in the manner of Dimsdale's nautical ladder.

The taking of testimony went on all that day. Court was adjourned at dark, the prisoners placed under armed guard. A motion was made to chain them but Charley Forbes took violent oath that he "would suffer death first." All too anxious to accommodate him, the captain of the guard lowered his shotgun in line with the complainer's navel and Charley added meekly, "Chain me."

There was no further incident until midnight when one of the guards came to my blankets and said Haze Lyons wanted to see me.

When I confronted the rascal, demanding to know what he could possibly want of me, he said, "Why, I just want you to let these other men off. I am the man that killed Dillingham. You know that and you know that I came over here to do it, and you know that these men are innocent. You know who sent me, too. Dillingham told you who it was. And you all know him for one of the best men in Bannack."

When pressed for expansion of this peculiar remark, the

119

prisoner, to everyone's complete surprise, admitted, "Henry Plummer told me to shoot Dillingham."

The next dawn, after three rounds of whiskey and a hearty breakfast, the trial resumed. Haze's startling confession was read into evidence and the question of "guilty or not guilty" at once submitted to the 600-man miners' jury.

"Guilty!" rang out with a hoarse-throated roar heard halfway to Daly's Ranch. The court formally confirmed the verdict by rapping its gavel on the wagon's tailgate and issuing the terse order, *"Hang them."* With the animal growls of the crowd still echoing, details were told off to erect the gallows and dig deep the graves of the condemned men.

With impressive speed and stern justice, the voice of the people had been heard. There was but one small complication. The voice was still talking.

At once, a movement arose to spare Forbes, who was only a boy and a veritable young demigod in looks and catlike grace of physique. This motion, sparked by a knot of dewy-eyed women, spread like dry-grass fire. Judge H. P. A. Smith, the youth's attorney, at once leaped on the wagon and called for a voice vote. There was a roar of "By God, turn him loose!" and Forbes jumped down off the wagon a free man.

While I was still standing there, stunned by this, somebody jumped on the empty wagon, seized the reins of the team and yelled, "Well, say! we've still got two to hang! Let's get on with what's left of the party!"

At once the crowd broke happily for the log saloon. Here the wagon was backed up to the door and the "less handsome" Haze and Stinson loaded into it for the short trip up the street to the new gallows.

At this point my eye caught Henry Plummer and Jack Gallagher moving in on the flanks of the mob. I saw them stop and talk quickly, then saw Henry hand something to his deputy. The latter at once shoved his way through to the wagon, jumped into it and shook hands warmly with Haze Lyons, managing in the emotion of the moment to pass along the mysterious article to the scowling murderer.

He had no sooner done so than he turned to the crowd and announced that Haze had a letter of farewell which he had written to his dear mother, and that he had requested permission to read aloud to his friends.

Instantly the shout arose, "Read the letter! Read the letter!"

Haze, who had never read the note himself, now proceeded to do so for his "friends."

It was a masterpiece.

I had heard nothing like it since the item in the *Portland Oregonian* anent the quiet and seemly courage with which

Henry Plummer had met death upon the scaffold in Walla Walla, Washington.

To my editorial ear there was no mistaking the authorship of this maudlin jewel. I was as familiar with the clear-eyed style, as with my own, far muddier, less inspired prose.

It was an outcry of undying love for the aging parent and, indeed, for all mothers of wayward sons, the wide earth over; a wondrous prayer for the salvation of sinning boys and the heavenly blessing and benediction of their sainted dams in this and the following world. It ended with a stirring vow to "be in the next world, Mother dear, all that you dreamed I might be in this," and with a passionate promise that should Providence, by any miracle, spare him this time, the remainder of his mortal days would be spent by the redeemed prisoner in atoning for his past life of "accidental" small crimes and youthful misdeeds.

The reading was punctuated by a series of sobbing commas from the crowd and a final period supplied by a woman's agonized cry, *"Oh, my God, spare the poor young boys' lives!"* That did it. Someone shouted, "Give him a horse!" and a second voice added, "Yes, let him go to his mother! Where's that horse?"

By this time Haze and Buck were looking for their own horse. They spotted an Indian pinto, standing saddled in front of the Golden Gravel, and with Attorney Smith pushing them over the tailgate with loud shouts of "Praise God, they're cleared, they're cleared," they legged it across the road, piled on the cayuse and made off. Charley Forbes had long since melted away in the crowd and was seen no more in Virginia City. No pursuit was made of Haze or Stinson, no apparent adverse question called on "Judge" Smith's extra-legal ruling in their behalf.

All that remained was the burying of the forgotten victim, now lying stiff and chill upon a gambling table in the Golden Gravel. There were no more than twenty souls in the little group who lingered for that unwelcome chore, but those who did (I remember J. X. Beidler, Neil Howie, the Lott brothers, Colonel Sanders, Jim Williams, Paris Pfouts, Brookie, Nye and some others) were a hard and dry-eyed lot.

When, half an hour later, we stood atop Cemetery Hill lowering the packing-crate coffin into the first grave opened in Virginia City's new burial plot, things had turned off pretty grim.

Now there were but eleven of us, and Jim Williams said, "Who do we have that will say the service?"

Neil Howie stepped forward with Judge Smith by the arm. "The very one who ought," said Howie softly.

The attorney for the defense was feeling unwell. He was

drunk. And beginning to be frightened. He mumbled a wan remonstrance. Neil Howie said, "Judge, you have been doing plenty of talking, you had better do some praying."

Minutes after that it was over, and we were going back down the hill. Not another word was said, nor had to be. The war with Henry Plummer was on.

21

Dillingham died the twenty-ninth of June. His murderers were set free July 1. Within forty-eight hours the reign of terror began in earnest.

The trial had been a test of strength—the sheriff's office against the people. From the day they wept and shouted, "Give him a horse! Let the poor boy go to his mother!" the good citizens of Virginia didn't have a chance. Nor, in my opinion, did they deserve one.

But insofar as my fate (and my $40,000!) was bound up with the common weal of Alder Gulch, I had to ignore Tom Dimsdale's agreeing cynicism on "justice in the short run," and pitch in for self-defense.

For, indeed, after the abortive release of Dillingham's murderers, the shape and form of Henry Plummer's monstrous plan began to emerge with fearful speed.

Between July and September 1, thirty-five travelers died or disappeared on the stage road between Bannack and the Gulch. That was just the one road, mind you. How many other poor souls got their quietus along the lonely hill trails out of Virginia for other points than Bannack and the main Salt Lake route, God alone would know. It is a safe assumption that in those opening sixty days of highly co-ordinated road agentry, at least fifty men were murdered for their gold in and around Alder Gulch.

And murder stood out as the operating method of the many robberies, exactly as Henry Plummer had predicted. The entire pattern of the outbreak of armed assault was so precisely the terrible one described to me by Henry that there could exist no doubt whatever as to his authorship of the atrocities.

But suspicion and proof—absolute, noncircumstantial evidence—were as odd a team of horses in the mountains of Montana as any place else in the world of English jurisprudence.

I could "suspect" until my beard got as long as Rip Van Winkle's. Henry would continue on his homicidal way, unhampered. What had to be gotten somehow was proof positive of (1) Henry's leadership of the gang and (2) a list of his principal assassins.

We—and by "we" I mean the little nucleus of outraged men who had stood over Dillingham's grave on Cemetery Hill—we, I say, already had Haze Lyons' midnight admission of Plummer's guiding hand in the little deputy's killing. But connecting that nebulous clue with his suspected leadership of the road agents who were completely disrupting the peace and debauching the security of some 7,000 Bannack and Virginia citizens, might be, we well knew, a legal impossibility.

There was always, of course, the hooded mask and flaming pine-knot of the night rider. But here, too, Henry had been before us.

In those same sixty days of disorder which saw three dozen travelers vanished from the public highway, another series of disappearances were occurring inside the corporate limits of the camp itself. Seven men were murdered or met with foul play from "party or parties unknown," between July 3 and August 27, right on the streets of Virginia. The victims were of varied callings and were not killed for their money. In fact, it was not until the last of them had been mysteriously dealt with that the common denominator of their deaths was made apparent. Each had just previously testified before one or the other of the camp's various "law and order" groups (Miners' Council, Citizens Committee, etc.) to his certain personal knowledge of a situation which might serve to indict the Bannack sheriff, or one of his prominent underlings.

These calculated killings of witnesses proved the final straw. It became impossible, after August, to get any sort of public or private testimony against Henry Plummer. It was clear that his agents had infiltrated into every legitimate organization in the Gulch, and that to speak against the master or his men was tantamount to signing one's own execution order.

Although at this time I may have been the only one with certain knowledge of Henry Plummer's guilt, these opinions as to the nature of his methods and their terrorizing effect upon the community were no private property of mine. Several influential citizens were "beginning to smell a wolf in the wind."

Prominent among these was Colonel Wilbur Fisk Sanders, a fearless, public-spirited Bannackian destined for a leading role in the coming swift hour of vigilante vengeance in Montana.

"Late in the summer of 1861," Colonel Sanders confirms

123

my contentions, "it began to dawn upon the Virginia City citizens that these highway robbers were plying their vocation with great industry, but as they dominated the executive offices of the volunteer tribunals the mouths of the suspicious were sealed."

Still, some kind of a resolution *was* forming among a quiet minority of determined men. Again, Sanders was among the first to sense it.

"With increasing certainty and ever-widening scope, this open secret, at first a suspicion, grew into an absolute certainty, told in whispers; and strangers in the country, who had gained each other's confidences, began to consult as to the protection of their enterprises and themselves, and even dared to speak confidentially the names of the guilty parties.

"Plummer's prudent reticence delayed suspicion of him longer than some of the others, and quite a number of the robbers were known before Plummer was suspected. He was a candidate for United States Marshal of the new territory, with respectable but limited support. He was able to render his subordinates good service by misleading public opinion and misdirecting this suspicion, but by the autumn of 1863, public fame, informed by a multitude of circumstances, pointed her unerring finger at as bloody a company of bandits as ever rode the plains."

Among the most important of Colonel Sanders' "strangers in the country," were three I will mention now, for when their parts in the final drama begin, there will not be time.

First was James Williams, a medium-sized, level-eyed young man newly arrived from the Colorado diggings and hence thoroughly familiar with the grim short cuts of justice served up by committees of vigilance.

The second was John X. Beidler. Beidler was a very short, rotund man of German extraction. Stolid in temperament, he still had a certain quick humor about him.

Neil Howie, the third "stranger," was that rarity of the day and place, the trained gunman with previous law enforcement experience. Having been lately in the California camps, he knew as well as Williams the dread workings and effectiveness of the Vigilance Committee. And so he was a double-edged weapon. He had, for a third qualification, the toughest look to him of any man in the Gulch. Yet this latter attribute was no thing of gnarled feature or ferocious expression. Howie, like Jim Williams, was a calm-faced, good-looking chap. His menace came from within—like Henry Plummer's.

Williams, Beidler, Neil Howie. Add to their names that of W. C. McCandles, and remember all four. Then move silently ahead to a date destined to supply the "d" in Plummer's downfall—September 2, 1863. The time, eleven P.M. The place, Virginia City, Montana. The ageless theme, *murder will out.*

22

It was a raw night. A cold north wind was cutting down the Gulch. A light rain, coming with the wind, was beginning to spit a little snow. I was glad enough to be inside, even my chilly cell at the Seneca seeming cozy in such weather. Accordingly, the knock at my door was not a pleasant surprise.

Answering, I found young Nicky Tiebalt with a message from Esau Lazarus.

Asking the lad in, I got down my wolf coat and began tugging on my winter boots.

I was fond of the young Dutchman. Going down the hall, we talked freely, our speculation centering on what the old man might possibly want of me this time of night. Tiebalt could offer no help. He had come into town to see Lazarus on some banking business for his employers, the ranching partnership of Butschy & Clark. The weather turning foul, he had gladly accepted the moneylender's invitation to stay over.

The boy, actually a young man of about twenty but rather slow of mind, was an orphan. His emigrant parents had gone under in a Sioux raid on the North Platte. Harry Clark had adopted him and, after Harry, the entire Gulch. He certainly would have been welcome to stay the night in any home in Virginia but had surrendered to the old Jew's hospitality, I rather suspect, because of the other young house guest presently sharing same.

As we bucked the wind up Wallace Street I inquired after that other guest with some belated guilt. I had not seen Lisa for a fortnight. This was due partly to my stern desire to wean her away from the idea of looking upon herself as "my woman," partly to the recently developed necessity for playing mighty careful mouse to Henry Plummer's cat.

The Bannack sheriff had moved George Ives up to Virginia as his sub rosa deputy. The latter, with friendly leers, walleyed claps on the back, et al, had been stalking me for the past ten days. It made for a nice balance of duties to keep an eye on him in my own behalf, and one on Henry in regard to his threat against Lisa.

Now, as I asked young Nick about the Indian girl, he blushed and stammered most unhappily. Taking pity on him, I directed the discussion toward the weather. Here, we both agreed it was very early for a real norther, such as this one

125

gave promise of becoming before morning. But we felt, too, it might be a good thing to have some hard cold just now. It would bring the deer and elk herds down from the high country and that would be a most welcome result, the way fresh meat was getting to be such a problem with the Gulch peopling up so mortal fast like it was.

This weighty matter lasted us to the little cabin on the hill, where Lazarus himself let us in.

When I asked about Lisa, the old man said she was fine but had already gone to bed. He said it as though he had more important business to hand, and he had.

Nicky Tiebalt took the hint, excused himself and retired to his loft room in the rear of the house. Lazarus let him go, then motioned me toward the side parlor. This was a curtained alcove opening off the front room, which he used as an office at home. He held the velvet portiers for me, and I went through ahead of him.

There was a fire inside, and no other light. It took me a moment to adjust my eyes. She was standing as I had seen her that first night, before the fire, at Sun River. And now, as then, she was waiting for me. In the rose glow of the cedar flames, graceful body poised, curving lips parted expectantly, she was still the most exciting woman I had ever known.

Within the first caught breath, I was going under all over again.

"Hello, Cullah." She used that voice whose thrill would haunt me forever. "I hoped you'd come." She glanced nervously past me, to Lazarus, and he nodded understandingly.

"Wait a minute!" I said, as he started out. But he dismissed me with a wave. "We have already talked, Mrs. Plummer and I. When you, too, have heard her story, come to the other room. I shall be there."

I turned back to Elly, and we stood looking at one another. Perhaps fifteen seconds passed before she talked.

Somehow she had found out all about Plummer. She told it in the hushed monotones of deep emotion. It was a story whose sordid whole I already knew but whose ghastly new detail was well-nigh past belief.

Sometime that past summer Lloyd Magruder, the popular Lewiston merchant, had driven into Virginia a most welcome mule-train load of the latest frills and fripperies of West Coast civilization, as well as all the core necessities of mining life. So large was his supply of merchandise he had put up a log store, which still stands on Wallace Street, to hold it. Now, his goods sold and his panniers bulging with $14,000 in gold dust, he was contemplating an early return to the Snake River town.

While remaining yet another few days in Virginia, he was engaged in soliciting the suffrage of the locals in support of his proposed candidacy for Congress. In view of his low prices, fine stocks and excellent services, he was virtually assured of the high office. Magruder was, in every meaning of the word, a Christian gentleman. And the grisly burden of Elly Bryan's report was that Henry Plummer was going to murder him for his summer's profits.

This was incredible, and I told her so. Not even Plummer would dare touch a man like Lloyd Magruder. However, to make certain he did not, I promised her I would help Lazarus spread the warning through the camps. With the dark plot thus given the light of wide publicity, Plummer's hands would be tied and she, Elly, could return to her bloody mate satisfied she had done her duty by society, if not the vows of sacred matrimony.

I could not keep the abrasive edge of sarcasm from showing in my reply to her confession. It was impossible for me to believe, despite her opening claim of innocence, that any woman could share the nights of such a monster and not know something of his daytime trade.

But if I expected Elly to return my forthright ire with a flare of defensive guilt, which I almost certainly did, I was gratefully surprised.

"Cullah," she murmured, glance downcast, "I ask only that you believe me now, as I believed you long ago. Until last night, when I heard those men at the rear door, I knew nothing of all this."

She then told me that, upon getting up about midnight to take a headache powder, she had noticed Plummer was still up and moving about in the kitchen. About to join him, she had heard voices raised on the back stoop. Hesitating, as was only natural, she had heard the heavy scrape of entering boots, and the subdued tones of her husband's cultured voice outlining swiftly for the visitors the details of the Magruder murder plan.

I looked at her soft beauty, made softer still by the charity of the firelight, and was lost.

"And now that you know?" I said. "What then?"

"I am going away. Back home to Iowa. Cedar Rapids."

"When?"

"Tomorrow morning."

"By way of Salt Lake?"

"Yes."

"Elly . . . !" I blurted it out, starting toward her with absolutely no idea what I meant to do beyond some vague impulse to seize her and hold back a dawn I suddenly felt I could not face.

"Cul! Oh, Cullah!"

There was no premeditation, no false awkwardness, no thinking or feeling whatsoever beyond the broken pleading of my appeal and the low throatiness of her reply.

One minute we were two tragic lives apart. The next, we were crushing the breath out of each other with our wild embrace. And the third minute we were torn apart by the stab of the sharp cry behind us.

I wheeled in time to see Lisa standing just inside the parted alcove curtains. She made a pathetic picture of child-like trust, her little girl's face framed in candlelight, her slim body draped in the incongruous folds of one of Esau Lazarus' old-fashioned nightshirts. Then, as quickly as it had appeared, the picture faded. Dropping her candlestick, she turned and fled. I thought I heard a low question from Esau, a muffled sob for an answer, then painful silence on both sides of the curtain.

Elly moved past me as I stood there. I waited for her to do so. When her swift footsteps had faded and I heard the street door close behind her, I went into the outer room. "Where did Lisa go?" I demanded sharply of Esau.

He cocked his wise old head to one side. "Where would an injured child go?" he chided me gently.

"She's not been injured!" I snapped at him, in no mood for lectures. "Where did she go?"

"To her room, where else? She was hurt and she was crying."

"Oh, I know that!" I was still snapping at him. "Will you fetch her out here, please."

"Fetch her yourself, my son. It will be better that way. But do not worry, meanwhile. She will be all right."

"All women," I shook my head, "are crazy. Indian women especially, and especially this Indian woman. She might do anything. Her pride's been wounded. To an Indian that's worse than adultery or defamation of character."

The old moneylender smiled, palmed his hands. "No matter, my boy. You'll see. A kiss will make everything right." He pointed down the bedroom hallway. "Go and prove it for yourself."

I nodded and pushed past him to do as much. All at once I felt afraid. Of what, I had no least idea. But of something for very sure.

At Lisa's door I knocked quickly, impatiently. Receiving no reply, I flung open the rough panel and stepped inside.

It was a small room, furnished in Spartan style. There were no closets, screens, or other obstructions to the view. The single window stood open. Through it the wind drove the rain in a steady pelting slant, the lonesome sound of the cold drops turning me weak inside.

The room was empty.

I did not find Lisa. The following days of search and inquiry up and down the Gulch were wasted. No one had seen her, no one heard tell of her whereabouts. She had simply vanished. After a week I gave up.

The rain which had begun the night of her disappearance had turned into a forty-eight-hour ice storm. With temperatures skidding toward zero before morning, and with the wind building to hurricane force all during the next day and night, there was little reason to keep looking. Not unless all I wanted to find was her beautiful body huddled frozen and frost-black beside some mountain brush clump. There are some things it is better not to know. What had happened to Lisa Red Bear was surely one of these. One thing and one alone about her disappearance was a certainty: when the Indian girl fled the cabin of Esau Lazarus, her tiny room was not the only space left empty in Virginia City—so, suddenly, was my heart.

My sole comfort in her passing so swiftly out of my life was that her injured flight had at least taken her beyond the harmful reach of Henry Plummer. The arising of this thought put a hard set to my jaw, brought an angry narrowing to my eye. Henry Plummer. The Nevada City baker's boy. All right, let him look to himself now. I had had enough of his hounding. It was time to bring his casebook to a close.

23

Ten days after Elly Plummer took the stage for Salt Lake and the States, Lloyd Magruder left Virginia for Lewiston, by way of Elk City.

Lazarus and I had planted the warning of Plummer's intent to murder him most carefully. Magruder himself had been apprised of the situation, along with his friends, but felt, as did the latter, that any substantial threat had been dissipated by the campwide publicity given the ugly rumor. To be on the side of circumspection, however, he took with him four trusted companions; Charley Allen, the Chalmers brothers and Linton Phillips. All five men were experienced in the mountains and went heavily armed on the trail.

It was not until the day following their departure that word came to me of a singular development. The night before leaving and without consulting anyone, the good-hearted

Magruder had agreed to let four other men join his little company on the excuse of "traveling with it for safety, as far as Elk City." It was the names of the four who felt they needed chaperoning to that point, which put the chill up my spine: Jem Romaine, Doc Howard, Billy Page, Bob Lowry— Plummer men and known murderers all.

Neil Howie, John Beidler, Jim Williams, Colonel Sanders and myself set out at once along the day-old trail, but were already too late. Near the summit of the Bitter Roots, Plummer's harpies had murdered Magruder and all four of his friends. The bodies, together with the camp baggage, had been rolled in the bloodstained blankets and tumbled off the nearest cliff. The killers had fled westward, skirting Elk City to catch a California coach out of Lewiston.

It is not a part of this tale to recount the manner of Lewiston Marshal Hill Beechey's famous single-handed capture and return to justice of the killers. For our purposes the significant thing about the Bitter Root atrocity was that it marked the third of Henry Plummer's tactical blunders.

The first had been his marrying of a decent woman, Electra Lee Bryan. The second had been his trusting of an honest man, Virginia City Deputy Sheriff Dillingham. The third was the presently recounted murder of a leading Montana citizen *after* his intention to do so had been thoroughly advertised in advance. Secret killings and suspected killers were one thing. Publicly premeditated murder was another.

After the death of Lloyd Magruder no man's life was safe; and each of the Gulch's responsible residents had become uncomfortably aware of the fact. That was the change; that was the singular difference from then on. In every camp throughout the Virginia diggings decent men began to gather and to talk in guarded places. There was no longer any safety in refusal to testify, or to convict on clear evidence. A new grimness was in the crisp fall air—not yet grown to outright accusation, not yet angered to direct action—but ominously present in the silence of good men and true, who had been ridden too far, driven too fast. From Virginia to Junction, through Central to Summit to Nevada to Daly's Ranch, on down the ninety miles to Bannack's Yankee Flat and Confederate Gulch, Henry Plummer's name began to be cursed in sullen and ugly fury. The Butcher of Bannack had overreached himself at last.

October slipped past. The first real break came in late November. On a bleak afternoon some days before Thanksgiving, the Salt Lake coach left Virginia City for Bannack. Driving was A. J. Oliver's senior man, Tom Caldwell. Passengers were Leroy Southmayd, Cap Moore and a discharged Oliver employee, Billy Becksmith.

Nineteen miles out, the stage was crowded to the canyon wall by three masked men. Each of the bandits was heavily wrapped in a green and blue blanket. The first wore a stovepipe hat over a full head hood of black silk. The second was hooded with a piece of ordinary gray burlap, the third with a shag of hickory shirting. All three horses were hung, croup to forelock, with dirty canvas packing tarps.

Three professionally handled rifles swung to cover the unhappy passengers, who at once and without awaiting the customary road agent command of "Halt! Throw up your hands, you sons of bitches!" piled out of the Concord and elevated their arms.

Leroy Southmayd gave up $400 in gold, Cap Moore $100 in Federal notes, Billy Becksmith $3.75 in loose coin. It was a bad haul and the bandits lost their tempers over it. As a result they lingered so long in their cursing and reviling of their Bannack-bound victims that one of the latter recognized them all.

The gravelly voice of the top-hatted brigand began to ring familiar to the alert ears of young Leroy Southmayd. He was sure this first man was Whiskey Bill Graves. The tall figure and lisping manner of speech of the second outlaw also began to arouse accurate memories. He would take an oath this one was "Big Bob" Zachary. A fateful gust of the freezing wind whipped up the canvas blanket of the third man's mount, disclosing the spotted rump of George Ives' famous pinto racing mare and naming her rider as surely as if he had doffed his mask of hickory shirting and introduced himself deliberately.

Hours later, when the delayed stage at last rolled into Bannack, Henry Plummer met the robbery victims with his standard easy smile and a softly dangerous leading question.

"Was the stage robbed today?" he inquired soberly of Leroy Southmayd, the first man down.

Young Southmayd, a man who would box ten rounds with an untrained bear, was on the point of telling him how it damn well was robbed, and by whom, when Judge Bissell, who fortunately happened also to have met the stage, gave him a hasty handsign to step aside and say nothing. Southmayd obliged, the Judge muttering to him as he did, "Be damned careful what you tell that man!"

He meant Plummer, of course, and Southmayd understood that he did and obeyed the warning. Plummer, however, was not to be so easily put off. He knew Southmayd for a fighter and so baited him craftily.

"I think," he volunteered suddenly, "that I can tell you who it was that robbed you, Leroy."

"Who?" demanded Southmayd directly and belligerently.

"George Ives was one of them," suggested the sheriff.

"I know!" blurted the incautious Southmayd, "and the others were Whiskey Bill and Bob Zachary, and I will live to see them hanged before three weeks!"

Plummer smiled, said nothing, walked off.

Judge Bissell lost no time in advising his friend Southmayd, "Leroy, your life is not worth a cent!" But the latter, brave as he was foolish, said he was not to be disturbed by such prophecies and that he would proceed to stay three full days in Bannack to prove it, giving the sheriff and his "cowardly bunch" all the chance they needed to "get him if they had the sand for it."

Perhaps it was the sheer audacity of his defiance that saved the tough young Virginia Citian. Perhaps it was nothing but the luck of fools. Whatever the reason, the three days passed and Plummer had made no move to shut up this dangerous witness. Lulled by the apparent success of his calling of the Bannack sheriff's supposed intent to do him in, Southmayd decided the game had gone far enough and bought a stage ticket back to Virginia.

He soon enough found that he would have some interesting company for the return trip. While waiting in the Oliver office for his coach to draw up for loading, two men came in to inquire of the agent who was for Virginia. Leroy Southmayd's eyes narrowed warily. These two were Ned Ray and Buck Stinson, Plummer's chief deputies and pet murderers in Bannack. But the Virginia man's alarm was only beginning to grow. He now heard the agent tell the sheriff's men that he, Southmayd, and a sixteen-year-old boy were the only passengers for Virginia so far. Then his nerves really tightened when he heard the two roughs quietly reply, "Well, in that case, we'll go along."

When the agent could, he got Southmayd aside. "For God's sake," he pleaded with him, "don't go; I believe you will be killed!"

Leroy Southmayd did not scare. "If you will get me a double-barreled shotgun," he said calmly, "I will take my chances."

Not being able to dissuade him, the agent did the next best thing; he furnished him with the requested shotgun, securing a similar weapon, as well, for the sixteen-year-old boy.

The coach just then rolled up, veteran driver Tom Caldwell at the lines. The four passengers piled aboard; Southmayd on the driver's box with Caldwell, Stinson and Ray inside with the boy. Loaded and cocked shotguns across the knees were the traveling order of the day, both above and below decks.

For the rest of that historic journey I would like to quote Tom Dimsdale's account, later given in his famed *Vigilantes of Montana,* and which he claims to have had directly from Southmayd himself. Dimsdale's picture of the ride is admittedly sketchy and, in places, downright opaque. However, it is worth repeating here simply for that feel for the argot and actions of the road agents which he had developed so much more acutely than any of the rest of us who later wrote about the times.

"The journey was," he records, "as monotonous as a night picket, until the coach reached the crossing of the Stinking Water, where two of the three men that had previously robbed it (Bob Zachary and Bill Graves) were together in front of the station along with Aleck Carter. Buck Stinson saw them and shouted, 'Ho, you goddamn road agents!' Said Leroy Southmayd to Caldwell, 'Tom, we're gone up.' Said Caldwell, 'That's so.'

"At the Cold Spring Station, where the coach stopped for supper, the amiable trio again came up. They were of course armed with gun, pistols and knife. Two of them set down their guns at the door and came in. Aleck Carter had his gun slung at his back. Bob Zachary, feigning to be drunk, called out, 'I'd like to see the goddamn man that don't like Stone!' (the station owner). Finding that, as far as could be ascertained, everybody present had a very high opinion of Stone, he called for a treat to all hands, which having been disposed of, he bought a bottle of whiskey, and behaved miscellaneously till the coach started.

"Before leaving Cold Springs Ranch, Leroy Southmayd told Tom Caldwell he saw through it all and would leave the coach; but Tom said he would take Buck up beside him, and that surely the other fellow (the boy) could watch Ray down below. Buck did not like the arrangement, but Tom said, 'You're an old driver, and I want you up with me, by God!'

"The two passengers inside the coach sat with their shotguns across their knees, ready for any move on the part of either of the robbers.

"At Loraine's Ranch, Leroy Southmayd and Caldwell went out a little way from the place, with the stage teams' bridles in their hands, and talked about the situation. They agreed that it was pretty rough, and were debating the propriety of taking to the brush, and leaving the coach, when their peace of mind was in no way assured by seeing that Buck Stinson was close to them, and must have overheard every word they had uttered. Buck endeavored to allay their fears by

133

saying there was no danger. They told him that they were armed, and that if they were attacked they would make it a warm time for some of the robbers; at any rate they would get three or four of them. Buck replied, 'Gentlemen, I pledge you my word, my honor and my life, that you will not be attacked between this and Virginia.'

"The coach went on as soon as the horses were hitched up, and Buck commenced roaring out a song, without intermission, till at last he became tired, and then, at his request, Ned Ray took up the chorus. This was the signal to the other three robbers to keep off. Had the song ceased, an attack would have been made at once; but without going into algebra, they were able to ascertain that such a venture had more peril than profit, and so they let it alone. The driver, Southmayd and the young passenger were not sorry when they alighted safe in town. Ned Ray subsequently called on Southmayd and told him that if he knew who committed the robbery he should not tell, that death would be his portion if he did."

A matter of hours after the coach got into Virginia, I had much the same story from Southmayd myself, and thought its new details of Plummer gang complicity important enough to saddle up Cassius and ride down to report it to Colonel Sanders, then heading our secret group in Virginia, though residing at Bannack.

It was early Thanksgiving forenoon when I talked to Leroy Southmayd about the robbery. It was three hours after dark that night when I pulled the roan up in front of Colonel Sanders' house in Upper Yankee Flat, at Bannack. I was stiff and cold as an embalming board and Cassius was in no better condition. And understandably so. Even for the indestructible red brute, eighty-eight miles in eleven hours was going a distance of ground in respectable time.

The Colonel's house, when I approached it, stood dark and still. Considering the lateness of the hour, this was to be expected. Colonel Wilbur Fisk Sanders was a man of the most circumspect habits and admirable demeanor.

I went up to the door, my way well enough lit by the flood of lamplight coming from the house next door. Upon knocking, I was informed by the housekeeper—from an opened upstairs window—that the Colonel and his lady were next door attending a Thanksgiving dinner being tendered the Honorable Sidney Edgerton, Federal Chief Justice for the Territory of Idaho, at that time still including Montana, of course. I thanked the surly woman and turned my cold-numbed steps in the new direction.

I did not do so without some interesting speculation. The

neighboring dwelling was owned by a Mr. and Mrs. Vail, whose name may seem familiar. Sanders' neighbors were, in fact, the same Vails I had stayed with at Sun River. They had recently removed to Bannack for the same reason, I suppose, which brought the rest of us to the Grasshopper diggings—namely, an easier wealth than might be had through arduous toil. Since their arrival they had done well, I was led to assume, both by visible circumstance of their residence and by inter-settlement report which asserted that Mrs. Vail, a woman of decency and safe reputation whatever her other faults, had gained the friendship and respect of Bannack's best set and had, indeed, become quite the popular hostess. She had lately, however, the same report insisted, acquired a serious chink in her armor of respectability and under that circumstance I was quite surprised that such social pillars as Colonel W. F. Sanders and Chief Justice Edgerton would be sharing her board, no matter its previous popularity.

The chink in question was a tall, slender, gray-eyed one. It had a fine set of white teeth and a genius for ingratiating its oily self swiftly and solidly and securely into the higher strata of each new community to which it fled to avoid paying the price put upon its sleek head by the outraged citizens of the last.

In this instance my friend Henry Plummer had scored a center bull's-eye upon Yankee Flat society by moving into his highly regarded sister-in-law's household upon the recent occasion of Elly's deserting him to go back to Iowa.

Considering the delicacy of our past relationships, my feelings, as I approached the home of Elly Bryan's sister, may be rather easily imagined. I owed Virginia Vail nothing but ill will, beginning with her blunder in giving both my notes to Henry back at Sun River. Further, although I believed her innocent of any moral lapses with Henry—he was using her for far more sinister purposes, certainly—I could not forgive her, any more than I had been able to forgive her beautiful younger sister, for failing to take heed of her brother-in-law's obvious and repeatedly publicized rottenness.

Still, I had more serious considerations than my bad debt to Mrs. Vail to worry about at the moment. Henry might have his watchdogs on guard. Accordingly, I circled the place like a twice-trapped wolf coming in on a suspect bait. Seeing and hearing no sign of any posted sentry, I went over to the porch rail on the dark side of the house.

Coming to stand in a corner shadow which allowed me an excellent angle of view through the dining-room curtains, I made a quick check of the guests. There proved to be several beyond Sanders and Edgerton, who should have known better than to be there. But then the sheriff's blandishments were considerable. Who, actually, was going to resist imported Utah turkeys at $50 a throw? Or Salt Lake hams at $25? Not to mention California port and champagne and the finest of fancy foreign liqueurs shipped in straw skirts around the Horn? As well as every conceivable canned and glassed delicacy, from the roe of Russian sturgeon to the filet of Bristol sole, carried up the Columbia to the Dalles and thence by the Snake to Lewiston?

In their place I doubt I would have done the same, but I knew their host far better than they. As things were, I could not blame them too severely. Life in Bannack was not so captivating that sterling silver, cut-crystal and damask napery did not bid successfully to outshine everyday moral compunction upon signal occasion.

Further, my first disturbance over the mortality of fools, wherever found, was soon overridden by my fascination for the man who was so effortlessly twisting this particular set of incompetents around his trigger finger.

"Plummer was the soul of hospitality upon that occasion," Sanders recalled later. "His easy flow of conversation, his elegant manners, his gracious attention to his guests made him an ideal host. No person seated there could realize fully that this smiling gentleman was the archdemon of the trails, that the well-modulated voice which entertained with compliment and jest could thunder out the vilest blasphemy, and that the hands which served them had put to death countless victims."

But not all saw him in the same false light, regardless. "Affection," insists Bannack's faithful historian Nat Langford, who next to myself knew him most thoroughly, "fear, hate, grief, remorse, or any passion or emotion found no expression in his immovable face. One might as well have looked into the eyes of the dead for some token of a human soul as to have sought it in the light gray orbs of Plummer. Their cold, glassy stare defied inquisition. They seemed to be gazing through you at some object beyond, as though you were transparent."

How Plummer could thus affect intelligent men in such vastly different ways, I do not know. For myself, I knew him for a coin of brass from the first words I ever heard him speak to the old man on the freight wagon that long-gone afternoon when we had ridden together into the foothills of the Mother Lode. I could even remember the old driver's nailhead description—a steady eye and a double-hung tongue—and since nothing in the intervening years had altered that first opinion or changed the accuracy of the grizzled freighter's forecast of a fast rise and a short drop for his clear-eyed young passenger, there was now no reason for further delaying my report of the Leroy Southmayd story to Colonel Sanders.

In accordance, I stepped to the door, knocked, and Plummer answered. The inside lamp glare hit me full-glow when he did. His "immovable face" held faithful to Langford's overblown phrase concerning its cold, glassy, inquisition-defying stare.

"What is it?" he said, looking a hole through me, not one iota of recognition stirring his handsome features. The time had gone when Henry Plummer would light up a smile and cry out my name in feigned delight. Our war was on, its lines sharply drawn by that late November night. The only pretense remaining between us was entirely on his part and for the benefit of the innocent bystanders, present examples very much included.

"I want to see Colonel Sanders," I told him flatly.

Now the smooth voice went high with false good feeling. "Why it's you, Cullah! Of course, man. Come in, come in!"

"I'll wait here."

Shadows across the gray eyes then.

"Nonsense, Cul. Come in out of the cold, it's not . . ."

"You son of a bitch," I said. "Call the Colonel out here."

He answered me with his eyes, but was smiling when he turned back to the dining room to announce cheerfully, "Colonel, it's McCandles here to see you. He won't come in for fear of getting snow on Virginia's rugs."

Sanders, knowing I had not ridden ninety miles to worry about puddling a little snow-water in Mrs. Vail's parlor, came at once. "McCandles!" he greeted me. "What the devil are you doing here?"

"Step outside," I said. "And close the door."

I gave him Leroy Southmayd's story. When I was done he thanked me but at once complained, "I wish you hadn't come here, but had waited till morning. We don't want to alarm him."

"Don't we?" I said.

"What do you mean, sir!"

"I mean, Colonel, that it's long past time for playing 'look the other way.' "

"And what do *you* propose, sir?"

"Just this. You're an Easterner. Back in Minnesota they had laws and obeyed them. Here it's different. A few of us up in the Gulch have been talking about that."

"Which few? About what?"

"Williams. He's from the Colorado diggings. Myself and

Neil Howie from the California camps. John Beidler and some others from other camps. All with the same common gravel in our backgrounds. *Legalwise.*"

"Meaning precisely what, sir?"

"That the best witness chair is a wagon box. The most feared judge a masked man on horseback. The most honest jury a thirty-foot rope flung over the nearest tree limb."

"Vigilantes in Montana, McCandles?"

"Right now, Colonel. Tomorrow at the latest."

I saw the freeze hit his handsome features.

"No. The law is coming in due course now. We are moving well. Our petition to set up Montana east of the Bitter Root Divide as a separate territory cannot fail. We will have duly constituted Federal enforcement officers here within six months. Edgerton is going to Washington to plead the case, and has been given every inside assurance of a sympathetic hearing in the White House. No, sir, I shall not be willing party, meanwhile, to any extralegal resorts to nightriding hysteria, which might entirely wreck our careful plans and work and prayers for an autonomous Montana."

"But you will 'meanwhile,' " I mimicked him acidly, "be 'willing party' to cold-blooded murder in its place."

"Do not twist my words, McCandles!" The Colonel was uncomfortable from more than the cut of the wind across the icy porch. "Moreover, there has been no murder here, only another stage robbery. Am I not correct, sir?"

"You are not correct, sir!" I aped him again with deliberate anger. "There was no murder because brave men gambled with shotguns at six feet for their lives, and won. The intent to commit murder must be clear to you, Colonel, Thanksgiving turkey from Salt Lake or no."

He avoided the innuendo, once more demonstrating that complete coolness which at times, such as this one, struck me as being more vice than virtue. "We must still hold off for better conditions," he said evenly, "under which to apprehend and punish these criminals. And by better conditions I mean the existence here of Federal laws and law officers, which will allow us to make sure of sentence and conviction, as well as simply apprehension. We have waited too long, McCandles, and worked too hard, to spoil everything by resorting to bloody lawlessness at the last minute."

He paused thoughtfully, nodded, went on.

"Besides, man, I believe we have convinced them we mean business since the Magruder tragedy. Witness their definite pains to avoid violence in this Southmayd affair."

I looked at him unbelievingly. I could not imagine he meant such a statement seriously.

"Do you mean to say, Colonel, that it will take another

138

terrible crime like the Magruder Massacre—honest men being slaughtered like sheep, butchered in their own blood by these Bannack wolves of yours—before you will agree to act, short of the arrival of the Federal law?"

"I most certainly did not say that, sir!"

"But you implied it, nonetheless! I suppose if Southmayd had been murdered now . . ."

"But he was not, McCandles."

He put his hand on my shoulder, lowering his voice as a suggestion for me to do likewise.

"McCandles," he said, "you know these few good men with whom we have cast our lot, both here in Bannack and in Virginia. Do you really think these men will soberly vote to hang Plummer for a stage holdup in which he did not personally appear, and in which no one was so much as physically scratched? Put yourself in my position as moral leader of our group, regardless of the law, duly constituted, or masked and hooded, and give me your exact answer."

I gave him back his direct look, not buying his appeal to reason and logic.

"My exact answer remains the same; you must have yet another murder and yet another murderer before you will act."

"Very well, McCandles, if you insist."

"It is not I who will insist, Colonel Sanders, but Henry Plummer. His compliance will not come within the next six months, either, but inside of the next thirty days." I turned swiftly away. "Good night, sir, sleep well on it," I bade him, and went down the steps not waiting for his reply, nor wanting to hear another word from him.

It was a bit overdone, I will admit.

Yet I was seethingly outraged, not so much at Colonel Sanders, as at the frightening truth of his allusion to the tragic slowness of good men, even in fighting for their lives, to come down to the murderous level of bad ones. I knew and knew well that any man must be ready to commit murder in his own behalf, where the price of legal delay may be his own life. My anger in that moment of crunching across the shadowed snow between the two houses was enough to nauseate me. Yet, full of its sick fury as I was, one small sign of hope showed itself to me in the last moment of my departure.

Before I could get back to Cassius to untie him and mount up, the Sanders and Edgerton parties were both already out on Henry Plummer's front porch making their hurried excuses for leaving so abruptly.

I nodded grimly to myself, swung up into the saddle and gave Cassius his head.

My long cold ride had been premature only. It had not been without sobering point.

Cling as he might to his rightful ideals of ordered justice among civilized men, Colonel Wilbur Fisk Sanders had read my message from Virginia for what it was.

He knew from the moment he saw me standing outside Henry Plummer's door that the Thanksgiving party was over.

24

The "necessary murder," ironically, was neither Henry Plummer's direct command or doing.

Yet it came well within my thirty days of threatened grace. And it came, if not from the master, then from the next best man.

Early in December, after a long fall of rain, wind and wet snow, the weather turned off rock-bursting cold. On or about the seventh young Nicky Tiebalt went to pick up a pair of pack mules boarding at Dempsey's Ranch in the Stinking Water Valley. He had sold the animals and had with him their small purchase price in gold. When he failed to return to the Butschy & Clark Ranch, Harry Clark, his guardian, unhappily suspected he might have "gone south" with the money.

Ten days passed.

On the seventeenth, William Palmer, a citizen not concerned with Plummer's affairs, hunting birds along the frozen Stinking Water above Dempsey's, shot a snow grouse on the rise. The bird plummeted to earth. Pushing through the icy brush Palmer found his game—lodged between the frost-rimed shoulder blades of Nicky Tiebalt.

The youth's body had been there some days. Removal of the hat showed Palmer the back of the skull blown away by a large caliber bullet, which had entered the left eye. Efforts to move the body proved futile. It was frozen as stiff as a chunk of dog salmon.

Inquiring in the vicinity for help to put the corpse in his light hunting buggy, Palmer approached a brush wickiup behind Dempsey's main house. At his hail two men came out but refused the requested aid. "They kill people in Virginia every day, and there is nothing done about it," one of them growled. "We want to have nothing to do with it."

Being wise enough not to push his point, Palmer went back up the stream and somehow got the body loaded by his own effort.

He did not get to Virginia City with his sorry cargo, but

was stopped by a crowd of the morbidly curious in Nevada, the next biggest camp down the Gulch from Virginia. Once informed of young Tiebalt's identity, the mood of the people changed quickly enough. Punitive anger replaced prying curiosity. A posse was formed at once. With the men from the various camps—myself and three omnipresent friends (Beidler, Howie, Williams) included—the number totaled over two dozen. Jim Williams was elected captain and we set out.

Purposely, we rode under restraint until dark. Then we went ahead at good speed.

We did not travel the main road, but moved by the bluff trail, circling downwind of our quarry as it were and so doubling back to cross Wisconsin Creek and come up from below Dempsey's. It was 3:30 A.M.

The creek ice would not hold a horse and rider. Some mounts went under, even when hand-led. These had to be hung onto and "walked" out. By the time three more branch streams were crossed in the pitch-black, every man had at least his lower clothes soaked through and frozen fast to his skin.

It was five A.M. when we stood in the timber outside Dempsey's. But there was no light yet and our captain would not go in.

"We will wait right here until there is good daylight, and we can see the wickiup with no mistakes," said Williams.

At dawn—the most haggardly cold one I ever spent—we mounted up and went on in. At once a dog barked up by the ranch. Somebody shouted a warning and we put in our spurs to the shank. At the wickiup not a man had moved. Seven of them were bedded down in blankets under canvas tarps outside its entrance, several others we suspected were inside the crude structure.

Jim Williams leaped down from his horse and said in a tone no more strenuous than that he might employ to ask for the salt at supper, "The first man that raises up gets a quart of buckshot in him before he can say Jack Robinson."

No one raised up.

But one of the party, a petty robber named John Franck, known locally as "Long John," waved his hand for permission to do so. This being granted he sat up and whimpered, "Gentlemen, I know why you are here, and I did not commit that crime. If you will give me the chance I will clear myself."

"John," advised our leader, "you can never do it; for you knew of a man lying dead for nine days, close to your house, and never reported his murder; and you deserve hanging for that. Why didn't you come to Virginia and tell the people?"

Long John was a simple man but no moron. "I was afraid," he pleaded honestly, "and dared not do it."

"Afraid of what?" demanded Williams, though he knew full well the answer before it came.

"Afraid of the men around here, Cap'n."

"Who are they?"

"I dare not tell you who they are." The poor devil glanced toward the silent wickiup, gray with fear. Then, suddenly, he cringed to Williams' stirrup and whispered desperately. "There's one of them in there that killed poor Nick!"

Williams leaned down, pulling the wretch to his feet.

"Who is he?"

"George Ives."

"You are sure he is in the wickiup?"

"Yes."

Williams straightened and handed his reins to me. "You men wait here," he ordered. "I'll go up." Stepping from behind his mount, he started toward the brush hut. He did not get three steps on his way before a tall, curly-headed figure lounged out of it, grinning friendly as a stray dog in a strange town. "You men looking for me, Cap?" the tall robber inquired laconically.

"Are you George Ives?" Williams countered.

"Yes."

"Then I want you."

Ives shrugged off another wide grin. "Now what you want me for, Cap?"

"To go to Virginia City."

"Ah," said Big George, "I thought as much. However, I do not care to go so early in the morning. What would you say if I told you I wouldn't do it?"

Shotgun hammers clicked and rifle levers slotted mechanically in the dead stillness.

"Nothing," said Williams.

"In that case," said George, "I expect I will have to go."

He was certainly correct. After a search of the wickiup for hidden arms (recovered: seven dragoon and navy revolvers, nine shotguns, thirteen rifles and Leroy Southmayd's pistol) we set out on the return journey. In addition to George Ives we took with us Long John Franck and George Hilderman as material witnesses. Left behind at the wickiup with vast regret and some little indecision (the rope was discussed) were Whiskey Bill Graves, Aleck Carter, Bob Zachary and Johnny Cooper—villains all but unhappily innocent of direct connection with the murder charge of the moment.

We came back into Nevada at dusk of that same day, the eighteenth of December. The temper of the camp had not changed. There was no discernible sentiment for delay. Trial was set for noon of the following day.

This time there was a singular difference at once apparent to experienced senses.

You could smell it in the winter air. You could see it in the glittering dance of the frost crystals in the bright December sunshine. You could hear it in the growing, low animal rumble of the gathering crowd. It was all around you like your own skin.

There were some of the same rough jokes, some of the same heavy whiskey drinking, some of the same good-humored fraternizing with the accused, as at the Dillingham trial. But this time, somehow, it was all different. And inside, deep and sure, you knew *how* different. This time somebody was going to get hurt.

The previous night had passed without incident among the prisoners. Separated and log-chained and surrounded by a hollow square of standing shotgun guards as they had been, their meekness was guaranteed. Further, rumor had it that Plummer "and the boys" were on the way from Bannack and that a "delivery" had been secretly promised the accused. Despite the pretended calm of Ives and his fellow robbers, however, the feeling described above persisted. Plummer's promises or no, wagers on the successful escape of our prisoners could not have been placed at a hundred to one, as the morning wore ominously on.

The whole of that first day, the nineteenth, was given over to organizing the court and examining witnesses. In the latter process, since outraged accusers were suddenly coming forward—at times it seemed out of the very woodwork of the surrounding structures, the first fairly complete picture of the gang's operational procedures began to emerge. It startled even those of us who would have thought we already knew its every line.

"At one of their meeting places, a ranch occasionally used as a tavern by delayed travelers (Daly's)," ran one deposition, "targets were put up and they (the road agents) practiced assiduously to improve their marksmanship—all in full view of the road along which they intended to put into use the newly acquired skill. Their plan of operation was simple but well systematized and disciplined. A constant correspondence was maintained between Bannack and Virginia City and all trails were carefully policed by picked men whose sole job it was to report to the 'cavalry detail' any movement of paying traffic. No miner ever made a decent strike but what word of it got to 'headquarters' within the day. No appreciable quantity of dust ever left either town without the 'correspondents,' as the road-watchers were known, being aware of its departure."

Attested another witness: "Since not all of them were known to each other personally, each made use of a peculiar knot in his neckerchief to mark his membership in the organization. They carried as weapons two revolvers and a double-barreled shotgun of large bore with the barrels cut short. In addition to the firearms they usually carried daggers. They saw to it that they were mounted on the very fastest horses the region could supply, thus to insure the advantage whether pursuing or being pursued."

Added a third victim: "The horses of the travelers, the very clothing of the potential victims at times, and always the tailgates of freight wagons or the luggage boot of line coaches, were marked with a secret device known to the road agents, to designate them as fit objects for plunder. In this manner the liers in wait along the road had only to look for the 'mark of Cain,' before riding out to demand their levy, or to make their murder, without any fear of wasted energies."

Over three dozen men, members of the mining community in good standing, and late members of the road agent fraternity in present odious repute with their fellows still at large, paraded their stories before the court. All testimonies bore out the rough outline of the gang's operational plan, each witness but repeating the one before him in differing words.

Other fragments of information came through. The password of the bandits was "I am innocent," and they laughingly called themselves "The Innocents." The lethal mark placed upon mount, person or vehicle to tab same for detention along the eighty-eight mile stage road from Bannack to Virginia was variously described as "a bull's-eye target of a center dot and two outside circles," "a simple slip-knot drawn in chalk," "no more than an 'x' scrawled in haste," "the initial 'P' written as a capital letter enclosed in quotes," and at least three other definite designs or symbols, all as dissimilar as those given. To my certain knowledge it never was established what mark the gang used. Nor was the lack of that detail considered important at the time. The people's court was not interested in cryptology, but in criminal evidence. No one, to my memory, cared *how* Henry branded his victims. The single interest was that he *did* do so.

And when dusk fell on the nineteenth that fact had been established. That such attestings came in voluminous detail from men who were being asked only their qualifications to appear for or against the accused, and not yet for their formal testimony, was a chill forecast for the future—the immediate future.

The next day, the twentieth, dawned clear and warm. Court opened with the presentation of the case for the prosecution.

Here, rather than transcribe the minutes of this whole procedure, I will only state the general atmosphere and conditions surrounding the legal arguments.

In this trial Virginia residents were excluded on the grounds of palpable, past prejudices toward the captives. This suited me admirably, because I had not cared for my role of impotent witness in the Dillingham travesty.

A miners' jury of twenty-four men, twelve from the Nevada camp, twelve from the Junction camp, was impaneled to hear the evidence and to guide the "people's court"; the mob, as usual, retaining final authority to its self. Colonel Sanders, as a neutral Bannackian, was voted in to conduct the prosecution. The Honorable Harry Percival Adams Smith represented George Ives, who was to be tried before and separately from the others.

The scene, the physical scene of the trial, was striking. "A semicircle of benches from an adjacent hurdy-gurdy house," remembers Prosecuting Attorney Sanders, "had been placed around the fire for the accommodation of the twenty-four jurors; and behind that semicircle a place was reserved for a cordon of guards, who with their shotguns or rifles as the case might be, marched by the hour. Beyond them, and 'round on their flank stood a thousand or fifteen hundred miners, teamsters, mechanics, merchants, gamblers—all sorts and conditions of men, deeply interested in the proceedings."

As for the progress of cross-examination of the prosecution's witnesses by the Attorney for the Defense, the bumbling, self-important H. P. A. Smith maneuvered himself straightaway into a trap.

Smith, it will be remembered, was the same maudlin hypocrite who wept over Deputy Sheriff Dillingham's grave, after doing his best to free that brave officer's murderers in his role, then as now, of "attorney for the defense." A more odious and unpopular rascal would be hard to find in any of the Alder Gulch camps, and the Nevada crowd was entirely happy to stand by and hear him draw out Sanders' witnesses to the clumsy point where their testimony shortly drove his own defense witnesses to begin disappearing before they could be called to add to the damage being done their reputation by their own counselor.

His opponent, Colonel Sanders, put it this way: "As the

questioning of the Attorney for the Defense proceeded to trace the whereabouts of Ives for the summer and fall just past, the circumstances of robbery and murder only thickened around his client. Shortly, the names of Ives' companions on these forays were blurted out by my witnesses with a brutal frankness, and the testimony began to assume a wider and more sinister scope than the mere proof of connecting Ives with the killing of Tiebalt.

"As Smith stubbornly persisted in this line, the names of these accessories to Ives' crimes were constantly repeated and circumstances set forth to show their positive association with the accused.

"And as their names were thus imprudently bandied by their own attorney, the men concerned (many of them actually defense witnesses) began to discreetly withdraw from the case.

"Showing an admirable regard for their own safety and none at all for that of their friend, Ives, they retired quickly to the rear of the crowd. Here they became rapidly less prominent and, indeed, long before Smith had finished orating as to their impeccable reputations, had disappeared completely from the jurisdiction of the court."

Put in a less scholarly, less gentle-humored way than that of Colonel Sanders, Defense Attorney Smith succeeded in getting the prosecution witnesses to indict at least fifteen or twenty of Plummer's gang who weren't even on trial but who were present only to perjure themselves in George Ives' interest and on Plummer's orders.

On this note of hastily departing friends and rapidly disappearing friendship for the accused man, the first day's official testimony and examination of witnesses drew to a close.

But before nightfall a very interesting "unofficial" deposition had been added to the evidence. It was reported by one of our own scouts that a road agent courier, Clubfoot George Lane, had ridden to Bannack on a dead gallop the night of the eighteenth—two days ago. Our man also was able to inform us of the content of the message Lane had carried to that town from Defense Counselor H. P. A. Smith: that Henry Plummer must come at once to Nevada City, demanding the prisoners be released to him as the duly constituted legal authority in the land, and to come prepared with a writ of habeas corpus properly drawn in Bannack by Chief Justice Sidney Edgerton.

This information, of the type once so well calculated to intimidate the weak and frustrate the strong, now failed to arouse any wide concern for the outcome of the proceedings. And with grim reason. In the thawing mud of Main Street, waiting with a silence which grew more ominous by the hour, stood those 1500 bearded men, determined to the last, tough soul, that the day of first reckoning with the road agents would be dated December 21, 1863.

It is a fact, though denied by many, that Plummer himself was in the Nevada camp during the trial of his principal henchman. The reason he was not generally recognized, was simple: he was not generally seen.

He came to the camp after dark on the nineteenth, took immediate and sensitive note of the strange new ugly mood of the people and retired at once to a favored and partisan-owned saloon. From a barricaded back room of this retreat he henceforth conducted his lieutenant's defense entirely "by ear" and from a reasonably safe distance.

As for proof of his presence in the Gulch camps, I saw him myself in an alley behind the Orphir in neighboring Virginia, the night of the twentieth. And I was informed by Beidler and Williams, who were trailing him, that he was still "hanging on the outskirts" early on the morning of the twenty-first. Of course, common sense would indicate he had to be there. He knew, certainly, that the day of threatening was done, that his last remaining chance was to "buy off" the witnesses who were tying the noose for George Ives in Nevada.

We understood he came well prepared. Various reports were furnished but it remained a sound and conservative estimate that the Bannack sheriff came up to Alder Gulch on the nineteenth with no less than $10,000 in dust for the express purpose of paying witnesses to perjure themselves.

The danger for Plummer, naturally, lay not in letting Ives die, but in permitting the incidental evidence of his—Plummer's—behind-scenes connection with the road agent ring to be further brought out in the continuing testimony designed primarily to hang his chief subordinate.

When this fact is understood, it is academic to argue that Henry could have stayed in Bannack. Not when all his past experience had shown him that the word of most men could be twisted with a sufficient sum of gold, and not when his bloody band's treasury must have been bulging with enough of the necessary yellow dust to buy off half the honest men in Montana.

But Henry was behind the times, and the times had changed. Alder Gulch had gone off the outlaw gold standard.

With nightfall of the twentieth, and the close of legal argument for the day, the case for the people stood unshaken.

Nothing remained but to present the remaining witnesses for both sides and the trial of George Ives would be done.

147

The final day began ominously. Having failed to bribe the witnesses, Plummer ordered a last minute and desperate campaign of brute intimidation. It was a touch-and-go time in those gray morning hours of first daylight. The cold had returned during the night and, with it, the fear.

"The crowd which gathered around that fire in front of the court is vividly before our eyes," says Tom Dimsdale, that always salty chronicler of the vigilante days in Montana. "We see the wagon containing the Judge, and an advocate pleading with all his earnestness and eloquence for the dauntless robber, on whose unmoved features no shade of despondency can be traced by the fitful glare of the blazing wood, which lights up, at the same time, the stern and impassive features of the guard, who, in every kind of habiliments, stand in various attitudes, in a circle surrounding the scene of justice. The attentive faces and compressed lips of the jurors show their sense of the vast responsibility that rests upon them, and their firm resolve to do their duty. Ever and anon a brighter flash than ordinary reveals the expectant crowd of miners, thoughtfully and steadily gazing on the scene, and listening intently to the trial. Beyond this close phalanx, fretting and shifting around its outer edge, sways with quick and uncertain motion the wavering line of desperadoes and sympathizers with the criminal; their haggard, wild and alarmed countenances showing too plainly that they tremble at the issue which is, when decided, to drive them in exile from Montana, or to proclaim them as associate criminals, whose fate could neither be delayed nor dubious. A sight like this will ne'er be seen again in Montana. It was the crisis of the fate of the Territory. Nor was the position of prosecutor, guard, jury or judge, one that any but a brave and law-abiding citizen would choose, or even accept. Marked for slaughter by desperadoes, these men staked their lives for the welfare of society. The hero of that last hour of trial was avowedly W. F. Sanders. Not a desperado present but would have felt honored by becoming his murderer, and yet, fearless as a lion, he stood there confronting and defying the malice of his armed adversaries. The citizens of Montana must ever recollect his actions with gratitude and deep feeling."

Dimsdale was right on all counts. But it was the miners, not Colonel Sanders, who supplied the chill clincher to the ambitions of the muttering bandit fringe.

When the taking of the testimony for the people began to falter that early morning of the twenty-first, a delegation from the street stood forth to inform both sides that "all evidence must be in and the trial closed at three P.M."

So ordered, so done. The outlaw rebellion died silently

aborning. The prosecution closed its case; the defense took over and presented its feeble best in behalf of its still confident client.

On the stroke of three the jury of twenty-four went out. At twenty-one minutes past three, they were back. The verdict was guilty; it was in writing and signed by twenty-three of the twenty-four jurors, the last man declining the honor for "reasons concerning the safety of his person."

There flowered then two hours of motions of appeal by the defense, all shouted down by the voice of the people.

Then, although it was already dark and most of the miners moving away under the assumption that sentence would be announced and carried out next day, Colonel Sanders once more demonstrated the quality of the granite in his craw.

Stepping up on the wagon he made a short hard résumé of the findings against the prisoner and concluded, "I move that George Ives be forthwith taken and hung by the neck until he is dead."

This was sudden. The opposition was caught off-guard. George himself was stunned. Bob Hereford, Deputy Sheriff of Nevada, and Adriel Davis, his like number from Junction, were ordered to proceed with the sentence.

Upon hearing this, the prisoner seemed to realize for the first time what had happened. Leaping from his chair in front of the wagon, he came running around the bonfire to Sanders' side. Seizing the latter's hand with great emotion he struck a dramatic pose and cried, "Colonel, I am a gentleman and I believe you are, and I want to ask a favor which you alone can grant!"

There must be no mistake here. Ives was not groveling for his life; he was pleading for it on a calculated gamble of half-legal, half-emotional appeal. He was the toughest man ever observed under those circumstances, and no witness to the excitement of that minute has ever claimed him to be less. He was simply demanding, for public effect, what he mistakenly assumed to be a right, and he was intending to play it for all it might be worth dramatically. Nor was the move without previous successful pattern. He had, after all, seen precisely the same emotional gambit carry in the earlier case of "Handsome Charley" Forbes, Haze Lyons and Buck Stinson, in the Dillingham Trial.

Sanders, ever too fair a man for his own safety, agreed that Ives might now say what he had to, but warned him it could not avail him of ought at this late hour.

Regardless, George did his best. "Colonel," he vowed fervently, "if our places were changed I know I would grant this favor to you, and I believe you will to me. I have been pretty wild away from home, but I have a mother and dear

149

sisters in the States, and I want time to write them a letter, and to make my will, and I want you to get this execution put off till tomorrow morning."

"George," said the Colonel, "there is not a chance."

Ives threw up his right hand, oathwise.

"Colonel, I will give you my word of honor as a gentleman that I will not undertake to escape, nor permit my friends to try to change this matter!"

Sanders again started to deny him, but before he could do so barrel-chested little John Beidler moved out of the crowd.

"Colonel!" shouted the stocky immigrant. "Ask him how long a time he gave the Dutchman!"

He of course meant Nicky Tiebalt, the popular German boy murdered out at Dempsey's Ranch by George Ives for the miserable price of two pack mules, and the blunt question about the harmless lad's brutal death entirely destroyed whatever mood of misplaced sympathy might have been growing in the listening crowd for the prisoner's request of a delay.

George saw this final change in the crowd's temper all too clearly, and knew what it presaged for him. He did not need to wait for his answer from Wilbur Fisk Sanders. He could read it in the stony faces and frightening silence of the huge pack of people who had heard John Beidler's angry cry, and who knew as well as did George Ives that there was only one reply to it.

Nevertheless, Ives remained the indestructible outlaw, the classic badman, to the end.

As calmly and quietly as though he were asking him for a smoke on the trail, he turned to Sanders and said, "Colonel, it is all over with me, and I want you to get on with it."

Then, seeing me close at hand, he came over and asked for my hand.

"Red," he grinned, "we have been there and back together and there is no doubt but what we saw the dodo bird. I will put in a good word for you down below."

Our grips met and parted quickly, and he winked at me and smiled his crooked smile once more as Hereford and Davis came up to take him away. He went quietly, making no show of last-minute bravado, nor saying another word against his fate.

So died Plummer's main, and most likeable, lieutenant. Without weeping, remorse, futile struggles or other signs of human terror or ordinary mortal weakness, George Ives walked unassisted to the gallows which waited for him not ten yards from the firelit scene of his last hour upon this earth. He got a good drop and did not kick much.

25

Plummer now felt the cold breath. It came to him that the chill winter sun which had just gone down had not set for George Ives alone.

The day of the road agent in Montana had of a sudden grown fearfully short. The evidence brought forward in the Ives trial proved the existence and inhuman methods of Plummer's organization, and all tolerance of him and it vanished from the scene.

The complexion of these proofs, moreover, was ugly enough to remove forever from the Gulch the absolute last of such previous mutton-headed sentiments as "Let him read the letter!" "Give him a horse!" and "For God's sake, spare the poor boy's life!"

For a hard fact, the hanging of George Ives should have served Henry Plummer as a twenty-four-hour notice to get out of Montana. A blind man could, by that late time, have seen the shadow of the noose darkening the trail ahead. But Henry saw it not. Or, if he did see it, refused to believe that the rope which cast that shadow waited for him.

Having failed in his purpose to intimidate the people and disrupt the courts of Alder Gulch, Henry left Virginia's sister camp of Nevada as he had come into it—furtively, by a back trail, and in great haste.

The story persists that he never left Bannack—that Club-foot Lane's message from lawyer Smith to rush himself and a writ of habeas corpus to Ives' assistance, fell on deaf ears, and that Henry was at once more interested in preserving his own hide than that of his loyal employee's.

This last, of course, was true. And it is precisely why he *did* come up to Alder Gulch. And precisely why, once having arrived, he went back even faster than he had gotten there.

On his precipitous return to Bannack the sheriff put into execution a bold plan which, for all its desperate improvisation, could have worked. Coupling his, Ned Ray's and Buck Stinson's names with those of several of Bannack's most respected citizens, he circulated the wild rumor that an armed posse of vigilantes was on its way from Virginia to provide the Bannackians, clean and soiled alike, the same coarse hempen judgment they had just afforded "poor innocent George."

This crafty tactic was initially effective, as indeed its

principal ingredient of "guilt by association" has always been.

The completely innocent men included in Plummer's false list began to panic. *They* knew they were guiltless of any part of Henry's crimes, but did the Virginia vigilantes know it? The very best of them had been social supporters of the sheriff. Who was to say, or who would stop long enough to ask, in this aroused hour of public vengeance, whether or not that support stopped at the social level? Confirmation of the manner of Ives' death soon came from other sources, and the contagion of fear spread like smallpox.

I knew two of these blacklisted unfortunates personally and well—George Chrisman and A. M. MacDonald, community pillars both—yet each man freely admitted attending more than one meeting called after Henry's return with the serious intent of organizing armed resistance against the invasion of the "lawless Virginians."

While this uproar was going on down on the Grasshopper, a far more deadly development was taking place in grim silence along the creeks of Alder Gulch.

Henry Plummer's false prophecy was being implemented in true fact.

The Masons were on the move.

The words of Bannack's own lodgemaster best describe the quite opposite end-meaning of this ostensibly benign statement, to the remaining road agents.

"It is a remarkable fact," claims Nat Langford, quietly and with entire truth, "that the roughs were restrained by their fear of the Masonic fraternity. Of the reported 102 persons murdered by Henry Plummer's gang not one was a Mason. It is worthy of comment that every Mason in these trying hours adhered steadfastly to his principles. Neither poverty, persuasion, temptation, nor opportunity had the effect to shake a single faith founded on Masonic principle; and it is the crowning glory of our order that not one of all that band of desperadoes who expiated a life of crime upon the scaffold, had ever crossed the threshhold of a lodge room. The irregularities of their lives, their love of crime, and their recklessness of law, originated in the evil association and corrupt influences of a society over which neither Masonry nor religion had ever exercised the least control. The retribution which finally overtook them had its origin in principles traceable to that stalwart morality which is ever the offspring of Masonic and religious institutions. All true men then lived upon the square, and in a condition of mutual dependence."

The physical proof of Langford's testimonial came forward

before George Ives' body was cut down and pried into the frozen ground.

On the twenty-third of December twenty-four men, including myself, met in the Lott Brothers' store in Nevada. Of the twenty-four, twenty-three (James Williams excepted) were Masons.

The summons had been circulated on the twenty-second by Paris Pfouts, Master of the Virginia Lodge; a man recently from the California camps and, before that, from the San Francisco waterfront—important and significant background in this fateful moment. Preceding Pfouts' call, five men, all Masons, had been brought together by Colonel Sanders within the hour of Ives' hanging on the night of the twenty-first, the basic proposal of the present meeting having been there outlined.

The legal content of that proposal was nicely phrased in the so-called "California Oath," administered us by John S. Lott, which closed the Nevada session and which bore the signatures of all in attendance. This copy of that document, complete with the misspellings of the original rough draft, is the one I made for inclusion in my casebook on Henry Plummer.

> "We the undersigned uniting ourselves in a party for the laudible purpos of arresting thieves & murderers & recovering stollen property do pledge ourselves upon our sacred honor each to all others & solemnly swear that we will reveal no secrets violate no laws of right & not desert each other or our standerd of justice so help us God as witness our hand & seal this 23 of December A D 1863 . . ."

In immediate sequence, in Fox's Blue House in Virginia, a third meeting took place. Twelve men were there sworn to, and affixed their signatures to, the same oath. Before nightfall of the twenty-third, fourteen more recruits raised their hands and put their names to the pact. There were then some fifty men of the utmost reliability ready and willing to ride out on the "business of the committee" of the Virginia City vigilantes.

The "committee" referred to in this case was the Executive Committee, headed by James Williams, with Neil Howie, John X. Beidler and W. C. McCandles as Assistant Executives—"executive" being a vigilante euphemism for "executioner."

At eight o'clock the night of December 23, 1863, a field posse of twenty-four members left Virginia on a scout toward Deer Lodge. Object of the expedition: apprehension of Ned Ray and Buck Stinson, the principal murderers implicated in the Ives testimony. Intent of same: the rope. The night of the strangler had begun.

We went by way of the Stinking Water to the Big Hole River. Crossing the latter, we put our horses over the Divide in the main range and thus down onto Deer Lodge.

The weather was pure hell all the way. Ice and snow caked every mount during the day and locked each miserable rider in his thin blanket at night. It was viciously, unbelievably cold. Nor did we dare light any fire to alleviate the terrible night frost, for fear of alarming our wary birds. Our trail time suffered accordingly.

At the hideout near Deer Lodge, where we had hoped to take the outlaws, we found their campfire coals still smoldering, their plates of food set down untouched. Local inquiry revealed that a letter had arrived from Virginia City only hours ahead of us warning the robbers to "get up and dust, and lie low for black ducks."

The message had been prepared by a man named Charley Brown and brought over the Divide by one "Red" Yeager, who had killed two horses to beat us to Stinson and Ray. Both Brown and Yeager were among those labeled "brother" by the detailed confession of Long John Franck in the Ives testimony. This hind knowledge we found of slight comfort, but determined, all the same, to keep the two loyal "roadsters" in mind for a compliment should we come up to them in the future.

Bitterly dispirited, we started on, determined now that we were out, to run the scout on down toward Bannack in the forlorn hope of stumbling across some sign of Ray and Stinson short of that town. If we could, we might still take them. Once they got into Bannack and pinned back on their deputy sheriff badges, we could, for the purposes of this trip, forget them.

At Stone's Ranch we requisitioned a change of horses from the A. J. Oliver stage-line stock boarded there. The fresh mounts helped some, but nothing could ease the ache of exhaustion for our posse men. And the cold! There was simply no believing it. It raled your lungs, burned your throat, glued your nostril together. There was no standing it. Our search would have to be called off. We had nearly reached our objective, only to be defeated, in the end, by the merciless Montana weather.

But the quality of despair, like the price of scarce goods, is subject to change without notice.

It was twenty marrow-freezing miles to Rattlesnake

Creek, last scheduled stop before Bannack. It seemed like eighty. We were all of us like to die from prolonged exposure when, coming into Bill Bunton's place under cover of a black snow squall, we got a warm and rewarding welcome.

The friendly, smiling ruffian who opened the ranch-house door to Jim Williams' demanding knock was Red Yeager, the man who had ridden to warn Stinson and Ray that we were coming for them and who, in so doing, had placed his own neck in the same jeopardy as theirs.

Williams, confronting him, did not vary a hair. He simply nodded to Red and said to him, "You're one of the men I'm seeking; come along with me." For his part, Red made no serious objection.

We put our horses in the barn and advised the proprietor, Bunton, not to leave the ranch under pain of accompanying us back to Virginia himself. Since the rascal understood that the invitation was issued with an implied "as a guest of the Executive Committee," his protests were as perfunctory as Red's.

Next morning, knowing there was no chance remaining of apprehending Ray and Stinson, we turned for home. The weather let up after a bit, and we reached Dempsey's Halfway House that night. Here, a second welcoming surprise awaited us.

Dempsey had on the day previous hired a new man-of-all-work. At the moment of our arrival, this new man was busy tending bar in the main roadhouse, up front. He greeted us all very pleasantly, receiving salutations as neighborly in return. All hands then joined in a hearty toast of Dempsey's best. After a second carbolic peg, all around, we put down our empty shot glasses and placed the genial barkeep under arrest. His name was Charley Brown. It was he who had sent Red Yeager to warn Stinson and Ray, thus qualifying himself for the noose as surely as had Red before him.

With daylight, we rode on to Smith's Ranch. The time was taken up with detailed discussion of the fate of the prisoners. The weather continued to improve.

At the old wagon bridge just short of the ranch, we got a signal from our captain to "whoa up." We swung our horses off the road and dismounted.

"Now, boys," said Williams, "you have heard all about this matter, and I want your vote according to your conscience. If you think they ought to suffer punishment, say so. If you think they ought to go free, vote for it."

He paused, eyeing us, the eager and the shrinking, alike.

"All those in favor of hanging these two men step to the

right side of the road and those who are for letting them go, stand to the left."

Painful silence. Guilty exchange of sidelong looks. Scuffing of boot-toes in the snow. Setting of bearded jaws. More uncertain looks.

"Well?" said Jim Williams.

The tread of booted feet crunched briefly across the wagon ruts. The left side of the road was occupied only by the whistle of the wind.

The outlaws had been aware of this vote and were standing by, watching it. Seeing how it had gone, Brown at once raised a great cry, thinking we meant to execute sentence then and there. He called weepingly for the usual time to write mother and sisters dear. He fell on his knees and made all the other unmanly displays common to ordinary murderers facing the fate they have in the past so callously meted out to their helpless victims.

By remarkable contrast, Yeager bore himself faultlessly. A little man only five feet five, with fiery red whiskers and the unlikely proper name of Erastus, Red never lost his good humor, his genuine friendliness, nor his amazing self-control. From the moment of his capture he conducted himself in a manner well calculated to make the most dedicated vigilante think seriously about the validity of his deadly franchise.

We now assured Brown that he and Yeager would be taken on to Virginia for formal review of their case. At the same time Williams warned both men that our vote, just taken, was the likely end for them.

Williams then selected me to take an escort posse of seven men on the best horses and proceed with the prisoners at all speed ahead of the main party. This I did, arriving at Loraine's Ranch in mid-afternoon. But here we were held up by Brown's horse having thrown two shoes (with its rider's sub rosa assistance supplied at some careless rest halt along the way) and before we could get another pair set on the brute, Williams and the main bunch came up with us.

Since it was by then nearing dark, we voted to stay at Loraine's overnight.

Grateful for the respite from special guard duty, I relinquished the prisoners to our captain to get some sleep. It was the first, incidentally, most of us had had under decent shelter in five days, the other undercover halts having been spent either in the shaken-down hay of a stage-line horse barn, or upon the drafty puncheon or packed dirt floor of a roadhouse taproom.

The luxury was short-lived. About ten o'clock Neil Howie

and John Beidler awakened me and said, "Come on along, Cul. There has been a change in the vote and you will want to see the way it went."

There had indeed been a change. Fearful that the Plummer gang might attempt an armed delivery due to our long delay on the road, the majority had proposed an immediate carrying-out of sentence. There was, too, another factor at work in this belated reversal. We did not yet fully trust the people's justice. Despite the Ives' trial, or perhaps because of it, our members felt hesitant about submitting the futures of our prisoners to the mercy of the Gulch. George Ives, after all, had been a main and monstrously guilty fish in the outlaw pond. Red and Charley were minnows. The big-meshed seine of public opinion was all too likely to let such little shad slip through.

There being nothing I could do by way of demurer at this hour, I asked if the prisoners had been informed and when told they had not, requested I be allowed to apprise Yeager.

Permission forthcoming, I went with John Beidler to carry out the odious duty.

Red and I had struck up a "riding acquaintance" along the trail, perhaps drawn to touch stirrups by the similar hues of our long hair. I had found him a delightful murderer, if there can be such a thing. He had all of George Ives' villainy, but entirely without the latter's vicious streak. "Little Red" was of the poetic mold of highwaymen best typified by California's crown prince of illegal pistoleers, "Black Bart" of Wells Fargo fame. I have never been able to picture him as one of Plummer's executioners and of all the road agents I personally had a hand in helping upward, I regret most my part in the swinging of the little red-haired man with the lion's heart and laconic philosophy.

When I had conveyed the bad news to Red, he told me not to worry about it and said, "I want to thank you boys in some way for your good treatment of me, and so I am going to tell you something you will find useful in your work."

With that, he calmly announced, "It is pretty rough, gentlemen, but indeed I merited this years ago. What I want to say is that I know all about the gang, and there are men in it that deserve this more than I do; but I should die happy if I could see them hanged, or know that it would be done. I don't say this to get off. I don't want to get off. Now, you had better send up a man with a pencil and paper to take this down."

What his statement might prove to be we had no idea, but

thought we had better tell our captain, to be safe. Informed, Williams had an idea Red might be correct, and that it would be wise to follow the little outlaw's advice.

Accordingly, one of our number got out pad and pencil and we gathered around the good-natured penitent. We dropped our jaws in amazement at what followed.

"To start off," said Yeager, "Plummer is the chief and that's a fact. Bill Bunton is his second in command on the road, now that George has gone up, and is the main stool pigeon of the band. His brother Sam Bunton is a roadster, but has been sent out of the country by Plummer because of drinking. Cyrus Skinner is a roadster, fence and spy.

"Up in Virginia the usual outfit was George Ives, Steve Marshland, Dutch John Wagner, Aleck Carter and Whiskey Bill, all roadsters. George Shears is a roadster and horse-thief specialist. Johnny Cooper, Mexican Frank, Bob Zachary are all roadsters. Frank Parrish is a roadster and horse supplier. Buck Stinson is head roadster, and Ned Ray the same, with Ned being the council-room keeper at Bannack.

"Clubfoot George and Boone Helm are roadsters; the same for Haze Lyons and Bill Hunter, who are also telegraph men. Other ordinary roadsters are George Lowry, Jem Romaine, Billy Page, Doc Howard, Billy Terwilliger and Gad Moore. Charley Brown, yonder, was sort of a secretary, like you know, and me, I mostly rode the messages up and down the line.

"The key password was 'I am innocent,' and the company sign was that kerchief tied in a sailor's knot, the same as John Franck brung out in the trial. We all went shaved down to mustache and close chin whiskers for further sign. Now I am one of the gang, as you know, but I never committed murder and you must believe that, too."

Red waved his hand at this point, and stepped forward as though to say that was it and he was ready.

We set ourselves and got on with it. Two low stools were brought from Loraine's kitchen. We took axes and went across the creek into the timber. Spare limbs were lopped off two trees which stood just so to suit our purpose.

Brown went first and went very bad. The men were too quick to kick his stool out, and it made your hair crawl to listen to him choke and moan.

Little Red Yeager was ice water to the end. His last words were, "Good-bye, boys. God bless you! You are on a good undertaking."

Elkanah Morse and Dutch Charley jerked the stool.

The bodies were left hanging for six days. On the back of each man's coat was pinned a crudely scrawled sign:

We got back to our horses and rode out of there. No one cared to look back. No one talked. It was a bad feeling.

Back in the Gulch we expected trouble of a kind, and were not disappointed.

George Ives had had a people's trial performed under, and presumably purified by, God's sunshine. Yeager and Brown had died in the dark of night by the hands of men who did not want their faces seen in daylight.

The uncomfortable word "stranglers" began to be used in the muttered undertones by honest men along the mud borders of Wallace Street in Virginia and on down the line of Alder Gulch's six lesser camps.

The Executive Committee heard the mutter and understood its implications. Our time was being circumscribed but our grim intent must not waver.

We had still another sign to write:

PLUMMER! PAST PRESIDENT

26

The crucial ride was not long in forming up. The road agents were now leaving the country. The least of them we let go as good riddance. The worst we persuaded to stay.

"Dutch John" Wagner was one of these latter. Prominent upon Red Yeager's list, he was a depraved criminal and not, as some of the other boys truly were, merely an ordinary "hell-raiser." His behavior, to say the least, had been something more sinister than felonious assault and second-degree murder.

It fell Neil Howie's lot to go after him.

The Executive Committee was made up of twenty-four men; six under each of the four executive officers, or captains, who were Williams, Beidler, Howie and myself, with Williams as Chief Executive.

There was some dissension among Howie's men in this case (Dutch John's scowl alone would have intimidated a tiger), and their captain, in quiet anger, told them to wait up a bit where they were (Fox's Blue House) and he would return shortly with the solution.

What he meant, of course, was that he regarded Dutch John as the solution, and that he would go and get him without their assistance.

Beidler and I at once desired to set out after him, for no man, not even Neil Howie, should approach Wagner alone. Williams vetoed this. Howie was an experienced law officer and would pick up help along the way, as was the common practice in that day of quick and easy deputizations. Moreover, he, Williams, expected momentary word from Bannack of such a nature as would require the immediate attention of his "remaining administrative assistants," meaning nobody but Beidler and me, naturally.

His information was accurate. But slow in coming. It was the last day of December when Howie set out, posing as a merchant with a small train of mules bound for Salt Lake, where our report said Dutch John was headed. Days went by with no word. The New Year became a week old. The Executive Committee met three times. Had Williams been right to let Howie go it alone? Was he right in not having sent him subsequent aid before this? Was he right in continuing to insist, even now, that we wait for positive word either from our Bannack man or from Neil Howie?

No one knew the answers, but our senior captain held firm. If Neil Howie was our fire, Jim Williams was our steel. You could not shake him, or back him down. He would not yield the road to anything less than death, nor would he bow save to beauty, old age, or the word of God. We would wait for a definite word.

This decision was not altogether a matter of Jim's quartz-hard core. It was imperative that we let—in fact, that we make sure—Bannack's be the honor of initiating any move to take Henry Plummer. He was their sheriff. They had pinned the star upon him and must be allowed to unpin it from him. Rival gold-camp jealousies being what they were, there was no other wise course. In this, Paris Pfouts, the Lott Brothers, Brookie, Nye and the other leaders of the Virginia vigilance committee, agreed with Williams. Word from down below was hopeful, if not hurried. Our cynical report was that they were busy organizing a "Yankee Flat chapter of our night-riding fraternity," and would move within the coming week to "settle up the sheriff's account in a way satisfactory to all, with the possible exception of himself."

Forty-eight hours later, on the night of January 9, Beidler and I were in the Orphir. Our business there was the taking aboard of a last fifty-cents' worth of Montana Tanglefoot before marching up to the lodge hall to announce to Jim Williams our departure for Bannack within the hour, with or without the blessings of the brethren. We were just raising our glasses (was it the fourth or fifth time?) to this bold proposal, when our man stalked in.

"There is a light in the Blue House," said Jim Williams, and we put down our whiskey, untasted, and went with him.

There were upward of thirty hard-eyed men waiting for us. The news was not good. Our courier had just come up from Bannack. The movement down there was wavering. Plummer's deputies were prowling Main Street around the clock. Every secret meeting saw one or the other of his murderous minions in watchful attendance. Nothing was getting done. With the likes of Ned Ray and Buck Stinson watching and listening to his every word, no honest citizen dared open his mouth. The Bannack branch of the Virginia City vigilantes was, as of that moment, completely intimidated. Its very existence was at stake. A few more hours of indecision could well mean its dissolvement and a serious, if not crippling setback to our plans for taking Henry Plummer.

Something must be done to prevent the threatened breakdown of the Bannack chapter. Here was work expressly cut out for the Executive Committee of the Alder Gulch mother group.

An order was at once drawn up in writing, signed by all present and given over to Captain James Williams for personal delivery to the head of the faltering law-and-order movement in Bannack. Neil Howie being absent, Colonel Sanders, who was in the Gulch on business, announced himself determined to ride with us in his place. Ten minutes after the meeting in the Blue House broke up, the four of us were in the saddle.

The order in Jim Williams' pocket was terse. It did not spare feelings, nor mince facts. It was, simply, a letter of instruction from the Virginia City vigilantes to their weaker sisters in Bannack for the immediate taking and summary execution of Henry Plummer, Buck Stinson and Ned Ray; the four bearers of said authority to carry out sentence upon arrival, with or without the aid of the Bannack organization.

We made Bill Bunton's, at Rattlesnake, by one A.M. By two, we had rounded up the key man in the Bannack movement and were reading him our letter of instruction. He was considerably cheered by our explicit orders and our clear intention to carry them out, and said he had something of importance to add to them which he considered equally exciting.

His news was indeed dramatic. Neil Howie was here in Bannack. He and John Featherstun were right now sitting shotgun guard over an empty cabin on Yankee Flat. Only the cabin wasn't empty any longer. It had a singular and much-sought-after tenant. His name was Dutch John Wagner.

We could scarcely believe it, yet it was true. Howie, in

one of the greatest of single-handed hunt-downs of a dangerous criminal, had trailed and taken Dutch John without resistance. Featherstun had met them on the trail back to the Gulch and had helped Neil bring the prisoner on in. Nor was that all. The two of them had subsequently succeeded in getting Dutch John to admit his crimes and write down their grim list, together with a full list of the names of his accomplices in their commission. This formal confession was at the very moment in the hands of the Bannack leader to whom we were talking. It was, furthermore, a completely damning document. It confirmed every road agent named on Red Yeager's previous list, named Plummer in exact turn as the robber chief, with Stinson and Ray his right and left gunhands.

That was the good news. There was bad immediately following. That same evening, only hours before our arrival, a public meeting had been called in Peabody & Caldwell's Express Office to announce publicly the contents of the Dutch John Wagner confession in certain expectation that the incriminating details it contained would prove the so-far-lacking spark for local vigilante action against the sheriff and his dangerous brace of chief deputies.

But it was not to be. At the last minute, and just before our Bannack informant himself (his name is not given, nor will it be, out of respect to his honesty in professing his own lack of courage) began to read Dutch John's confession—with its full indictment of Henry Plummer, deputies Stinson and Ray stalked into the meeting hall and, with a show of deliberate threat, closed the doors tightly after them.

Under the cold eyes of the killer pair, whose names he had been about to read off with the others of the road agent guilty listed in the Dutch John document, our Bannack leader readily admitted to us that his nerve had given out.

"I was convinced," he told us, "that one more word would have earned me a bullet between the eyes, then and there, or one between the shoulderblades later on."

He then added candidly. "This bald intrusion, with its clear purpose to pick out for immediate or subsequent murder the ringleaders of our Bannack movement against Plummer, was simply too much for me. I folded up both Dutch John's confession and the meeting called to read it, and got out of there just as quick as I knew how. And so, too, did the rest of the boys.

"We were certain," he concluded, "that a better time for taking back the sheriff's star would surely present itself than that which saw his two favorite deputies barring the doors to the hall and blocking our way out into Main Street, as well as the cowpath beyond it which led to Henry Plummer's quiet little house on Yankee Flat."

We nodded grimly when he had finished. We understood, if we did not admire, his heart failure.

He was grateful for the small courtesy and sought to make direct amends for his abrupt closing of that night's earlier meeting by now calling another in its place. The effort was somewhat late, or rather early, in the day.

It was three o'clock in the morning before he had managed to summon a scant handful of the faithful to a deserted livery barn on the outskirts of Yankee Flat.

The men were at first not so much afraid as unsure. Only four of them were ready to ride with us then and there. The others shied off badly, but finally agreed to accept our written authority and to grant us the jurisdiction of the Virginia City vigilantes over the entire area, which that authority implied. However, they hastily deferred naming a definite time of action. Instead they decided that the upcoming day could best be spent in enlisting more Bannack members, to the end that any final move against Plummer and his men would be insured the fullest measure of local support possible to attain.

Without other choice, we agreed to this. Shortly after doing so, we lay down to sleep under the friendly guard of the four Bannackians who had just shown their gutty willingness to go out with us at once after the sinister sheriff and his deadly flankers.

The agreed-to additional recruiting went on all the next day. Yet by sundown we had achieved a total of but sixteen sure men. I believe I would have quit at this point. But Beidler and Williams were bulldogs.

"We will go and get them," said the latter, "if we have to do it by ourselves."

"Yes," Beidler backed him. "There are only three of them and there are three of us."

Since that "of us" included me, I could do nothing but gulp and add my brave nod to the majority opinion. After that, the atmosphere began to change. Courage is not as contagious as fear, but it is catching all the same. In the next hour and a half we had ten more men gathered in the abandoned barn.

It was then dark. Williams began issuing his instructions (none of this group had used the rope) for handling the prisoners and withstanding the pressures of the mob whose sympathies invariably were incited on the part of the condemned once the hemp was actually shaken out.

Suddenly there was a challenge at the door and Neil Howie came in under the countersign. He had left Dutch

John with Featherstun, to bring us important information. Going out for a breath of air but minutes before, he had seen Clubfoot Lane leading three horses across the flat toward Plummer's house. The distance was considerable, the twilight quite heavy, but he had seen those horses before: Plummer's claybank, Stinson's rangy bay, Ned Ray's line-back dun.

Williams said, "All right, men, let's go."

We split into three bands, one to pick up each of the marked men, all of whom had been under day-long surveillance and were now known to be in separate places.

I asked for and was given command of the group tolled off to take Plummer. It would nominally have been Sanders' honor but he declined it on the grounds of respect for the sheriff's "fine sister-in-law," who was, of course, "Mrs. Sanders' very good and dear friend."

Beidler was given the Ned Ray patrol. Williams himself took the Buck Stinson command, the latter being acceded the "entire worst" of the lot by public and private acknowledgment. The night was intensely cold. There was on the ground an iron-hard pack of old snow, thawed and refrozen a dozen times in the past fortnight. The least footfall squeaked, crunched, echoed eerily.

Beyond Sanders' house I ordered my men off their horses. The Colonel's place was without lights of any kind, yet I knew his young wife and their two small children were within. I could well imagine the terror of the well-bred girl crouched there in the dark, knowing as she must the deadly business of the muffled figures passing stealthily across the pale snow toward her neighbor's dwelling, and knowing at the same time the deadly nature of the man those figures sought.

At Plummer's cabin there was absolute stillness, and darkness.

As it was relatively early and we knew that our man had not left the house, we had to conclude he was awake and waiting for us.

I am satisfied each of my men felt this a little in the pit of his stomach. Henry Plummer was not the revolver fighter you came up on in the dark with any great sense of security.

Despite the fact his right, and natural, pistol arm had been badly withered by a shot-wound taken in a duel with Hank Crawford while I had been away with the James Stuart party, Henry had subsequently developed enough skill with his unaccustomed left hand to give most men a count of two and still beat them by the necessary count of one. This wound, unknown to me until brought out in the Ives trial evidence, solved the puzzle of why the Bannack sheriff had sent Deputy Ives agunning for me, instead of coming on the assignment himself. It as certainly accounted for the hitherto baffling restraint he had shown on the occasions of our face-to-face meetings both in Bannack and Virginia. For, while such a handicap may be acceptable against ordinary guns, you do not come at a fellow professional with your second-best pistol hand.

But pitch-darkness, like the point-blank cover of a Colt muzzle, is a perfect equalizer. Crippled or not, Henry Plummer in an unlit house was about as good a nerve-shrinker as the average citizen would want or need. I knew this and did not dare keep my men idle.

"Force the door," I told them, "and stand aside."

As the shattered planks swung inward, a light showed feebly in the room beyond the parlor. I was at its open door in an instant. I crouched there, my hand dropped to the butt of my revolver, the dark hall behind me crowded with the always vocal clicks and snaps of cocking shotguns and rifles.

Plummer was waiting for us—in bed.

I stepped into the room; came to stand beside my enemy while his shaking hand was still holding the black curl of the match with which he had lit the lamp.

"I've got a delayed message for you," I said. "It got delivered to the wrong addressee some time ago."

Reaching inside my wolfskin coat, I brought out the worn and linted note which Elly had given me that unhappy June day outside the Jackhammer Saloon.

Henry took it, his expression not at first comprehending what it was. His lips moved as he read it.

> "The fool that far is sent,
> Some wisdom to attain,
> Returns an idiot, as he went,
> And brings the fool again."

Behind me, my men shifted positions. One coughed. Another blew on his hands. A third kicked the packed snow from his boot arches.

The note fell from Plummer's hand. It fluttered to the floor. His face was still blank, and so, suddenly, was mine.

"Get up," I said.

He was lying in bed, fully clothed. On the bedpost were his cross-belted revolvers. On a bedside chair lay his cocked rifle and a double shotgun, both hand-carved hammers of the latter curled backward and up. On the back of the chair hung his heavy fur coat. Beside it, on the floor, was a flour sack loaded with cold food and other provisions for an impending journey by horseback.

I picked up the shotgun, kicked the chair and the rifle into the nearest corner, tossed his two Navy Colts after them. Plummer moved like a man in a dream. I had to pick up his coat and give it to him, or he would have gone out into the winter night in his shirtsleeves. He armed into it without any idea that he had done so.

We marched swiftly to the rendezvous, a small cabin owned by Negroes, near the very gallows Henry himself had erected some months before for the hanging of a petty criminal who had made the mistake of connecting the sheriff's name (out loud) with organized road agentry in the Gulch.

The other two groups of our number, sent to bring in Ray and Stinson, respectively, were at the meeting place ahead of us, each having gotten its man without trouble. Ned Ray had been taken while asleep, fully clothed, on a back-room billiard table of a Wallace Street saloon. Buck Stinson had been arrested in the same relaxed posture, all ready to travel but getting a last forty winks of refreshment, in the loft of a friend's crosstown cabin.

We did not stay long at the rendezvous. It was a scene to send any sensitive man quickly away: the cursings and pleadings of the doomed men, the icy silence of their captors, who knew each of them so well and yet who, in this final hour, would neither look at nor speak to them; it was a tableau to test the resolution of the most righteous hangman.

Our captain, knowing this from unpleasant experience, ordered the march at once resumed. We came shortly to the gallows—two small pines lopped free of lower branches, topped, and raftered-over by the trimmed trunk of a third—and here tensely selected the order of the goings: Ned Ray, Stinson, Henry Plummer.

Now there was an excruciating delay. Someone had mislaid the ropes. A small Negro who had followed us to the grim scene from the cabin, was sent to fetch three substitute strands from Peabody & Caldwell's livery barn. During the unbearable interval of waiting his return, Plummer recognized, in the flare of a pipe-lighting match, the face and figure of Colonel W. F. Sanders. Breaking from his guard, he ran up to his erstwhile neighbor and set upon him with the most piteous and shameless pleas for his life.

Sanders at first turned away entirely from the painful scene, then swung manfully around to face it.

"It is useless for you to beg for your life," he told Plummer quietly. "That affair is settled and cannot be altered.

166

You are to be hanged. You cannot feel harder about it than I do; but I cannot help it if I would."

Ned Ray began to fight his guards when he heard this calm refusal, but was persuaded to wait less obstreperously with no great trouble.

Stinson, the many times avowed "curly wolf from Pike County, Missouri," who had, by his own repeated assertion, "hair on his brisket clear down to his knees," stood still enough and did not struggle, but fouled the night air around him with the most obscene tide of filth any man of us had heard from the lips of a fellow human.

Then our messenger was back and one of the new ropes passed quickly forward from the rear ranks to Jim Williams standing beneath the gallows frame. He threw it over the beam on the first toss.

"Bring up Ned Ray," he said.

The knot was adjusted behind the ear, and Ray was swung.

He was not well tied and managed to get his fingers beneath the rope at his neck and prolong his life for what seemed an eternity. Seeing his fellow suffocating in such terrible agony of slowness, even the brutish Stinson broke down. "There goes poor Ned!" he blubbered. "May God bless his soul!"

It is doubtful if deity heard or was interested in such addresses. Nor was time taken to wonder. Stinson was put up immediately and by a second curse of carelessness was also given an improper sendoff. His noose, hurried by its nervous tiers, was badly rove. Its knot slipped from behind his ear on the drop, failing to snap his neck. Thus he, like his comrade before him, had to wait for death.

He was still moving when Jim Williams ordered, "Bring up Plummer."

Now the smiling murderer was in his last minute on earth, and, as I had known from the day of his first crime that he must, he made the bellies of honest men crawl with his high-pitched cries for mercy.

He wheeled crazily from one to the other of us, selecting those he knew in more than passing degree for his loudest appeals, and saving Sanders and myself for the most nerve-sickening demonstrations of all. He sobbed brokenly for us to chain him down like a wild beast in the meanest and most filthy hovel. He begged us to banish him from the Territory for life, to flog him raw, to give him a jury trial, time to see his sister-in-law and to compose to her sister, his own absent and beloved wife, Elly, a letter of confession and apology. He groveled. He got down on all fours. He fought like a pawing dog for Sanders' hand. And, finally, out

167

of sheer, awed curiosity, he was granted his terminal, agonized request—the privilege of at last furnishing the names, dates and places of his capital offense crimes, so that his soul, as he put it, could at least "go before its Maker cleansed by confession."

The admission of past murders which then vomited out of him would have nauseated a carrion-hunting jackal. Not even the monumentally calm Sanders could stand it. He had to step back from him and order the proceedings concluded "in all justice and mercy."

At this, the prisoner actually fell to the ground, crying out, "For God's sake, I implore you! Give a man time to pray!"

"Come along," said soft-voiced Jim Williams, stepping over to where the third noose swung emptily in the winter wind. "We'll let you pray up here."

Plummer's last words were in the sorry tradition of the physical craven: calling piteously upon his Creator to witness his innocence of the crimes he had confessed but the moment before; imploring his stony-faced destroyers to give him a quick and Christian drop.

Contrary to the struggles of Stinson and Ray, Henry Plummer went quietly. Even the wind fell still for his departure. As I turned away, his limp body hung without motion from the gallows, and the only sound on the winter air was the retreating crunch of booted feet going quickly away from that dark and lonesome place. It was 9:15 P.M., Sunday, January 10, 1864.

27

The time of the night rider had only begun. The hard and cruel work of the Vigilance Committee went on relentlessly. By day and by dark the icy roads up and down the Gulch creeks and along the Stinking Water and the Big Hole and the Jefferson, to Bannack and back, rang to the dread, steel-shod gallop of the hanging posse's lathered mounts.

Like frightened birds the roughs now made belated, wild thrusts at the closing net. A few—the smaller ones—got through. The others—thirteen of them in sixteen days—did not. Caught in the implacable web woven of their own wrongs, they "went up" where they were taken, their bodies left to swing and stiffen in the January frost, awaiting the slow charity of relatives or friends or, if cut down by strangers, the surer services of prowling wolf and coyote.

George Ives, Red Yeager, Brown, Stinson, Ray, Plummer, Clubfoot Lane, Frank Parrish, Haze Lyons, Boone Helm,

Jack Gallagher, Marshland, Bunton, Skinner, Aleck Carter, Shears, Zachary, Dutch John and Whiskey Bill Graves—the list was to run to a full two dozen of The Innocents before that winter of 1864 was out—but for me the story was done and the trail turned at last homeward that chill night Henry Plummer died a coward's death near Yankee Flat at Bannack town, Montana Territory.

There was, beyond that last reckoning, nothing left for me in Alder Gulch.

So long as it took Cassius and me to journey back up to Virginia, say good-bye to Esau Lazarus and arrange for him to invest my money and administer my shares of Claim Seven until we met again, that long did it take me to start once more north for Fort Benton and my interrupted homing to the scenes of my Missouri boyhood.

I took with me but three things of value: my homely red roan horse; my closed notebook on the aims and ambitions of Nevada City's dead baker's boy; my poignant memories of Lisa Red Bear, the sweet and sensitive child-squaw of the Crazy Mountain Absaroka.

I intended to travel by the river, via Three Forks, Sun River and Great Falls. But there was a small detour across the Madison, which I must make en route.

I was late on this sentimental side-trail, due to heavy snows in the Tobacco Root passes. So it was that I came to that remembered tower of rock above the canyon of the Madison, at sunset. I had meant only to visit this granite bastion, where Lisa and I had sat in the darkness of that last night before coming up with the Edgar-Fairweather party in Alder Gulch, in a brief manner. Perhaps I thought to spend an emotional hour there in tribute to my last happy camp with the Indian girl. Perhaps it would be no more than a five-minute gesture of curiosity, when the scene was finally reached. Actually, I was not clear either on my motive or intent in coming here. I merely felt impelled in some strange way to do it, and do not to this day understand why.

The wise man does not seek to question the ways of Providence. Not, at least, when its ends are so wondrously wrought in his favor.

I was no more than half a minute's climb from the top of the tower trail, when there fell upon my ear the cheery notes of the sweetest bird song in the mountains of Montana. But a moment more and I had gained the summit of the rough track and was running forward, old Cassius lumbering on, completely forgotten in my wake.

They saw me in the same instant—and straightened uncertainly above their supper fire to peer in proper amazement at the mad white man bearing down upon them, long arms aflap and hoarse voice crowing like some demented and dismounted Ichabod Crane pursued by all the imps of outer darkness.

Then they knew me, and the tears and the shouts and the happy laughs and cries and glad bird whistles which burst around that little fire would have opened the heart of a glacial rock.

How they had found each other was not important. Nor, indeed, how I found them. We were there, and we were Lisa Red Bear and Singing Bird and William Cullah McCandles, and we were simply grateful to our separate gods that this was so.

When the fire had grown low that night and long after the little mother-in-law had sought her nest of blankets, the willowy daughter and the tall red-haired son still sat beneath the common buffalo robe before the cozy wickiup and watched the coals wink out.

When the last of them had done this, we lay down upon the warm earth, pulling the furry cover close. There we fell asleep in one another's arms, like children, quickly and deep, and with no thoughts of the day past but only of the one coming.

Fort Benton was very far away. Three Forks and Sun River were but forgotten names. Great Falls was no more than a place where the bed of the Missouri River dropped sharply enough to make a roar of water audible for seven miles on a clear day.

I cared for nothing in all the world save the slim red child breathing so quietly against my breast.